F L I G H T
EXPLORER

V O L U M E O N E

Villard • New York

2008 Villard Books Trade Paperback Edition

Published in the United States by Villard Books, an imprint of The Random House Publishing Group, a division of Random House, Inc., New York.

VILLARD and "V" CIRCLED Design are registered trademarks of Random House, Inc.

ISBN 978-0-345-50313-8

Printed in China

www.villardbooks.com

1 3 5 7 9 8 6 4 2

Illustration on pages 2–3 by Kazu Kibuishi

Editor/Art Director: Kazu Kibuishi
Assistant Editors: Kean Soo and Phil Craven

Contents

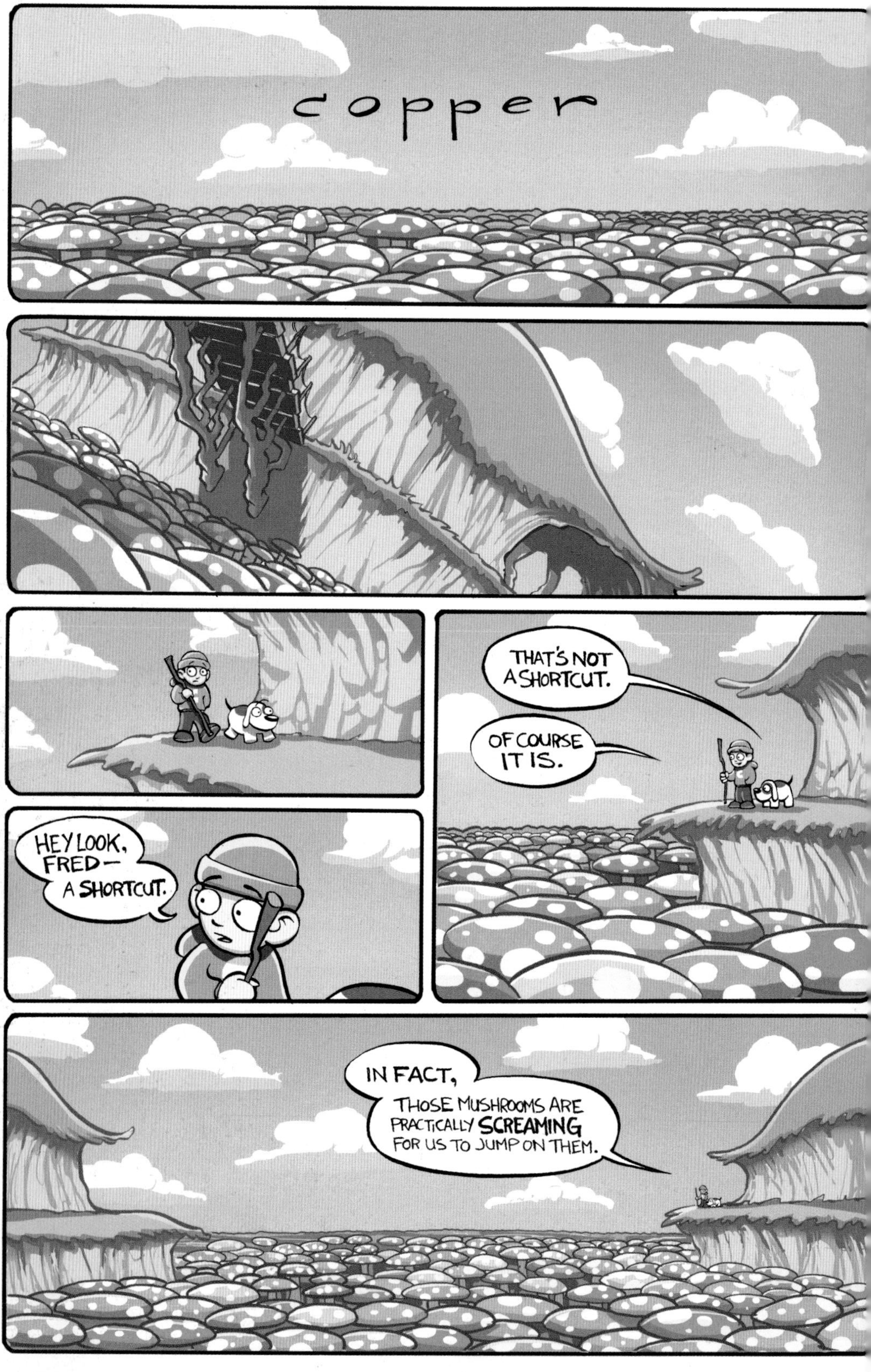
copper
HEY LOOK, FRED— A SHORTCUT.
THAT'S NOT A SHORTCUT.
OF COURSE IT IS.
IN FACT, THOSE MUSHROOMS ARE PRACTICALLY SCREAMING FOR US TO JUMP ON THEM.

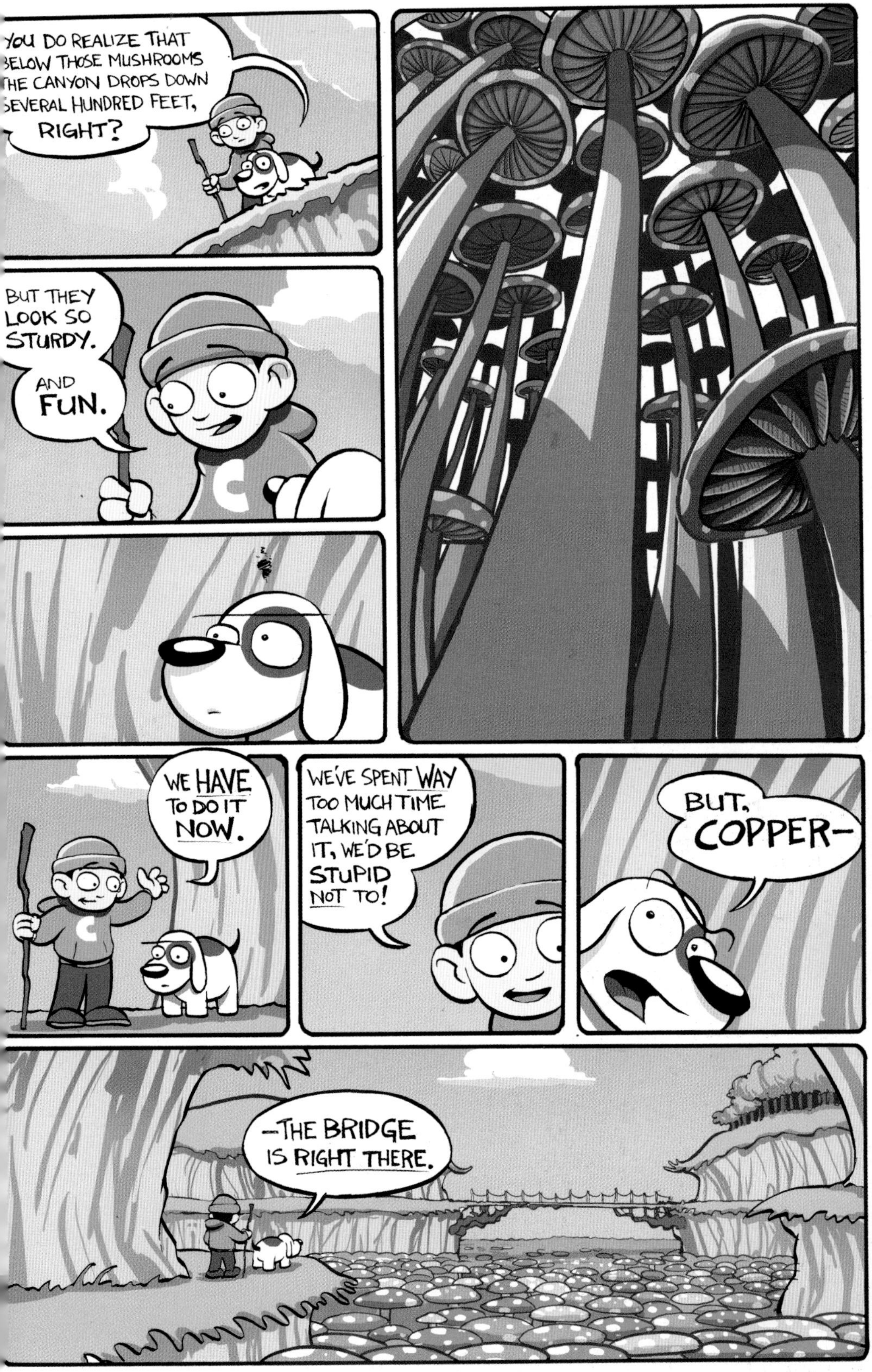
YOU DO REALIZE THAT BELOW THOSE MUSHROOMS THE CANYON DROPS DOWN SEVERAL HUNDRED FEET, RIGHT?
BUT THEY LOOK SO STURDY.
AND FUN.
WE HAVE TO DO IT NOW.
WE'VE SPENT WAY TOO MUCH TIME TALKING ABOUT IT, WE'D BE STUPID NOT TO!
BUT, COPPER–
–THE BRIDGE IS RIGHT THERE.

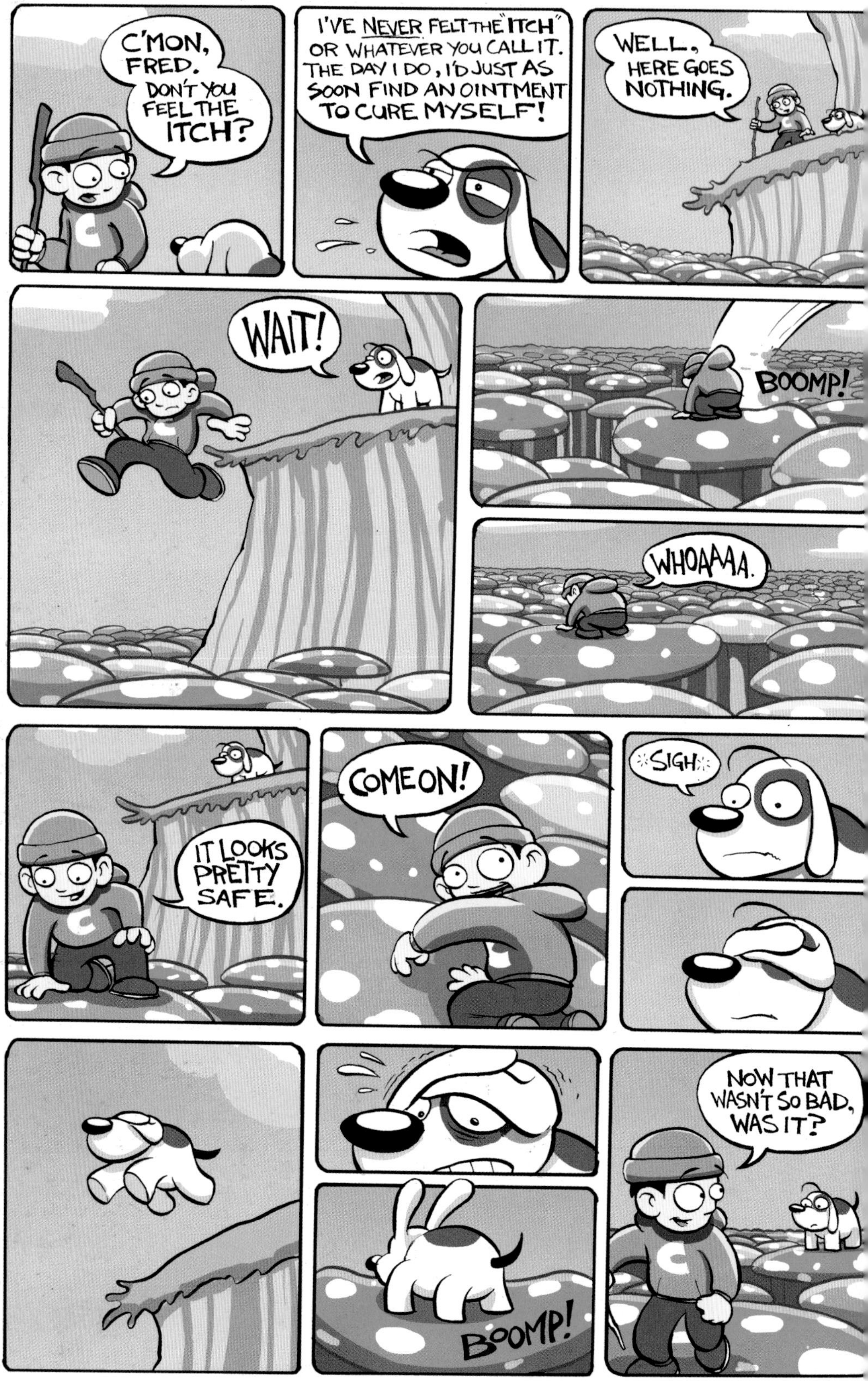
C'MON, FRED. DON'T YOU FEEL THE ITCH?
I'VE NEVER FELT THE "ITCH" OR WHATEVER YOU CALL IT. THE DAY I DO, I'D JUST AS SOON FIND AN OINTMENT TO CURE MYSELF!
WELL, HERE GOES NOTHING.
WAIT!
BOOMP!
WHOAAAA.
IT LOOKS PRETTY SAFE.
COME ON!
SIGH
BOOMP!
NOW THAT WASN'T SO BAD, WAS IT?

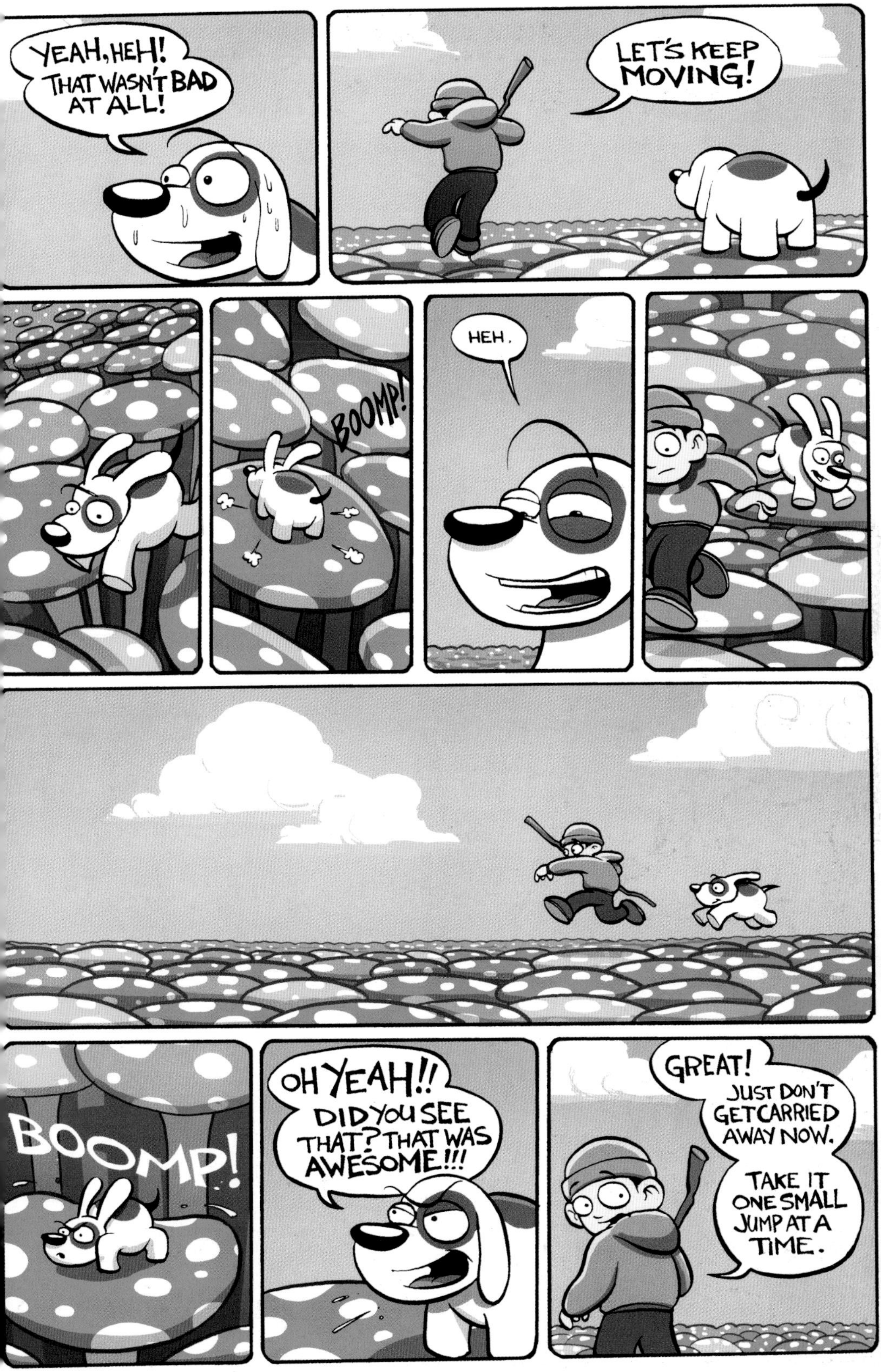
YEAH, HEH! THAT WASN'T BAD AT ALL!
LET'S KEEP MOVING!
BOOMP!
HEH.
OH YEAH!! DID YOU SEE THAT? THAT WAS AWESOME!!!
BOOMP!
GREAT!
JUST DON'T GET CARRIED AWAY NOW.
TAKE IT ONE SMALL JUMP AT A TIME.

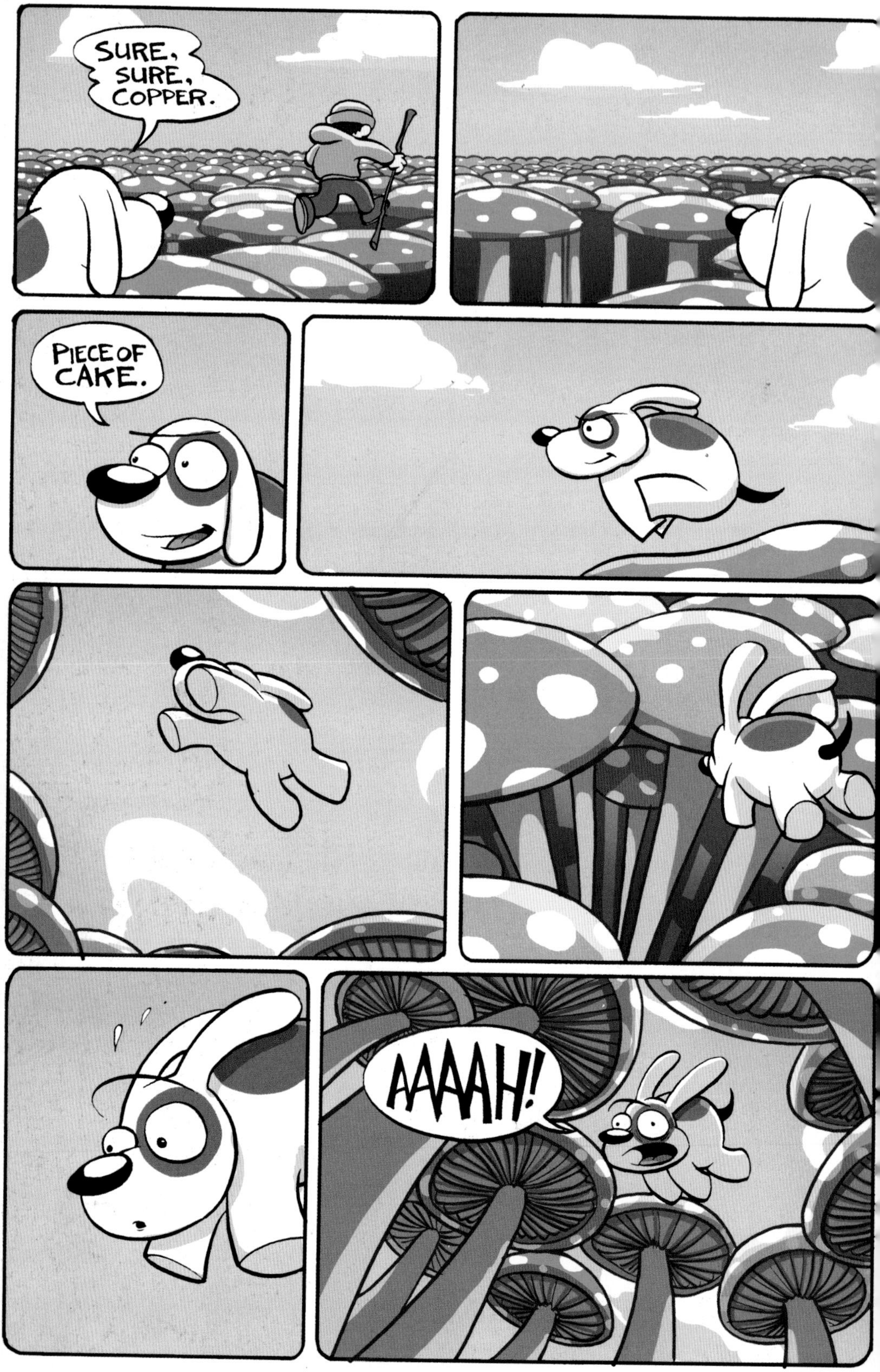
SURE, SURE, COPPER.
PIECE OF CAKE.
AAAAH!

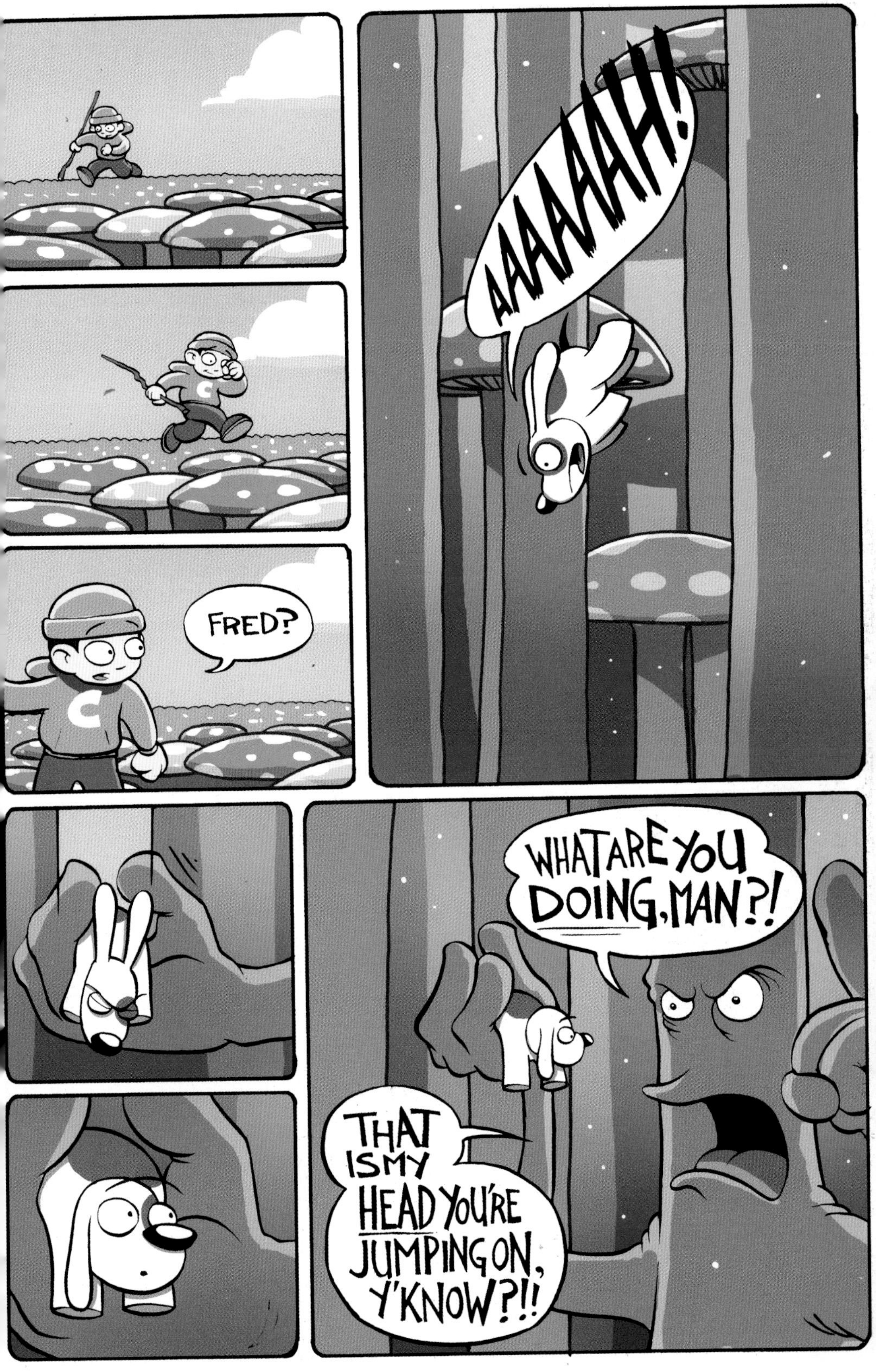
FRED?
AAAAAAH!
WHAT ARE YOU DOING, MAN?!
THAT IS MY HEAD YOU'RE JUMPING ON, Y'KNOW?!!

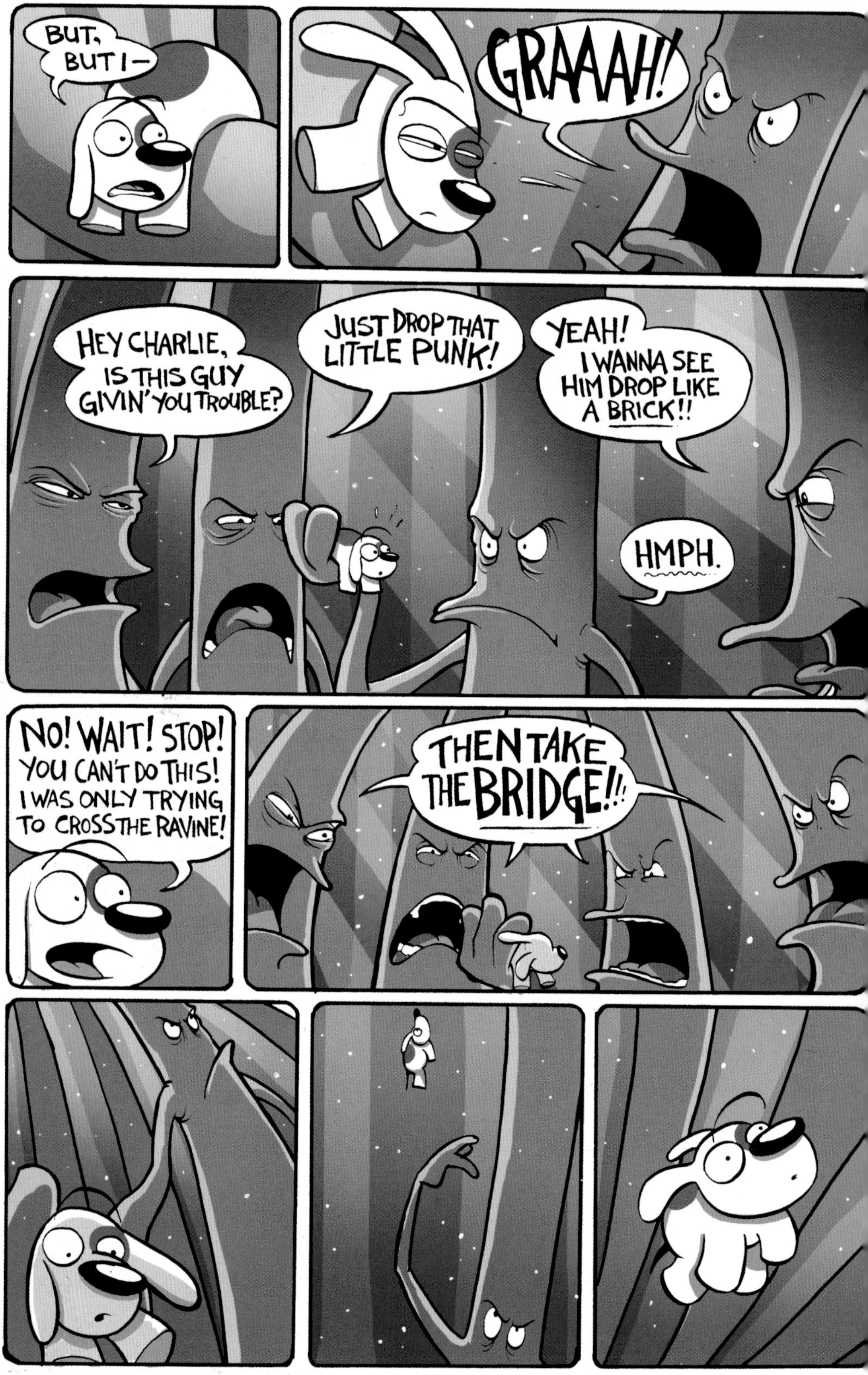
BUT, BUT I—
GRAAAH!
HEY CHARLIE, IS THIS GUY GIVIN' YOU TROUBLE?
JUST DROP THAT LITTLE PUNK!
YEAH! I WANNA SEE HIM DROP LIKE A BRICK!!
HMPH.
NO! WAIT! STOP! YOU CAN'T DO THIS! I WAS ONLY TRYING TO CROSS THE RAVINE!
THEN TAKE THE BRIDGE!!!

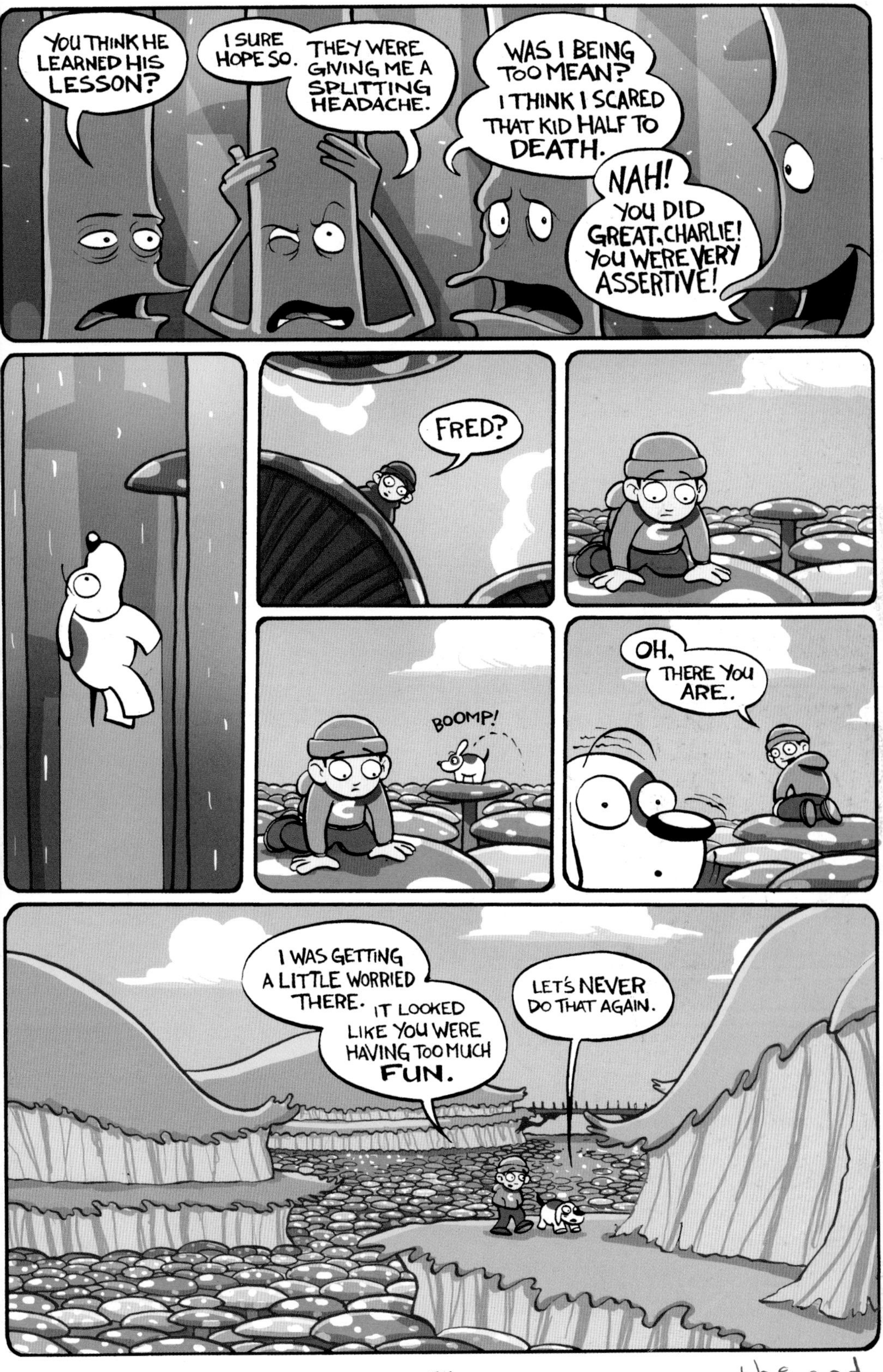
YOU THINK HE LEARNED HIS LESSON?
I SURE HOPE SO.
THEY WERE GIVING ME A SPLITTING HEADACHE.
WAS I BEING TOO MEAN?
I THINK I SCARED THAT KID HALF TO DEATH.
NAH! YOU DID GREAT, CHARLIE! YOU WERE VERY ASSERTIVE!
FRED?
BOOMP!
OH, THERE YOU ARE.
I WAS GETTING A LITTLE WORRIED THERE.
IT LOOKED LIKE YOU WERE HAVING TOO MUCH FUN.
LET'S NEVER DO THAT AGAIN.

the end.

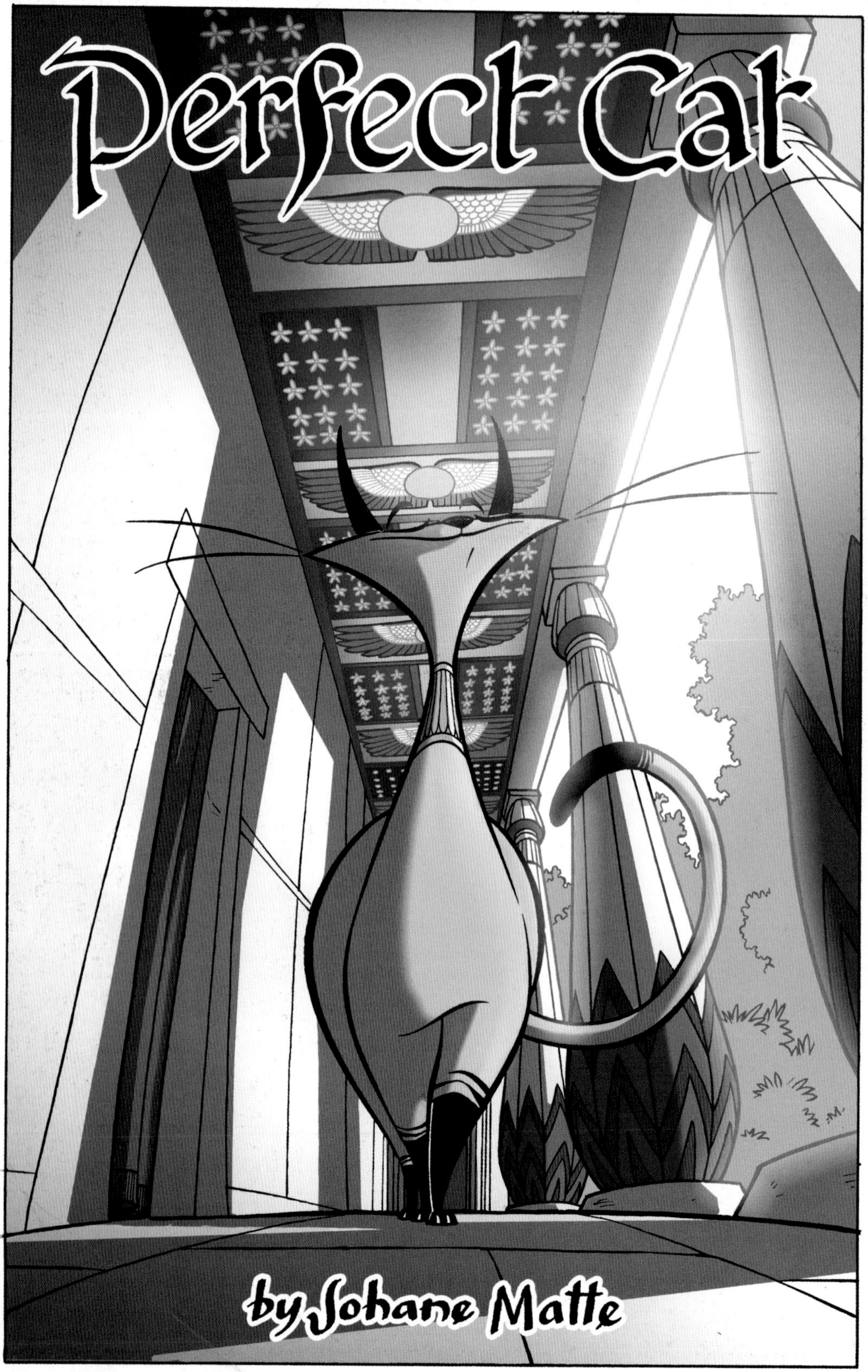
Perfect Cat
by Johane Matte

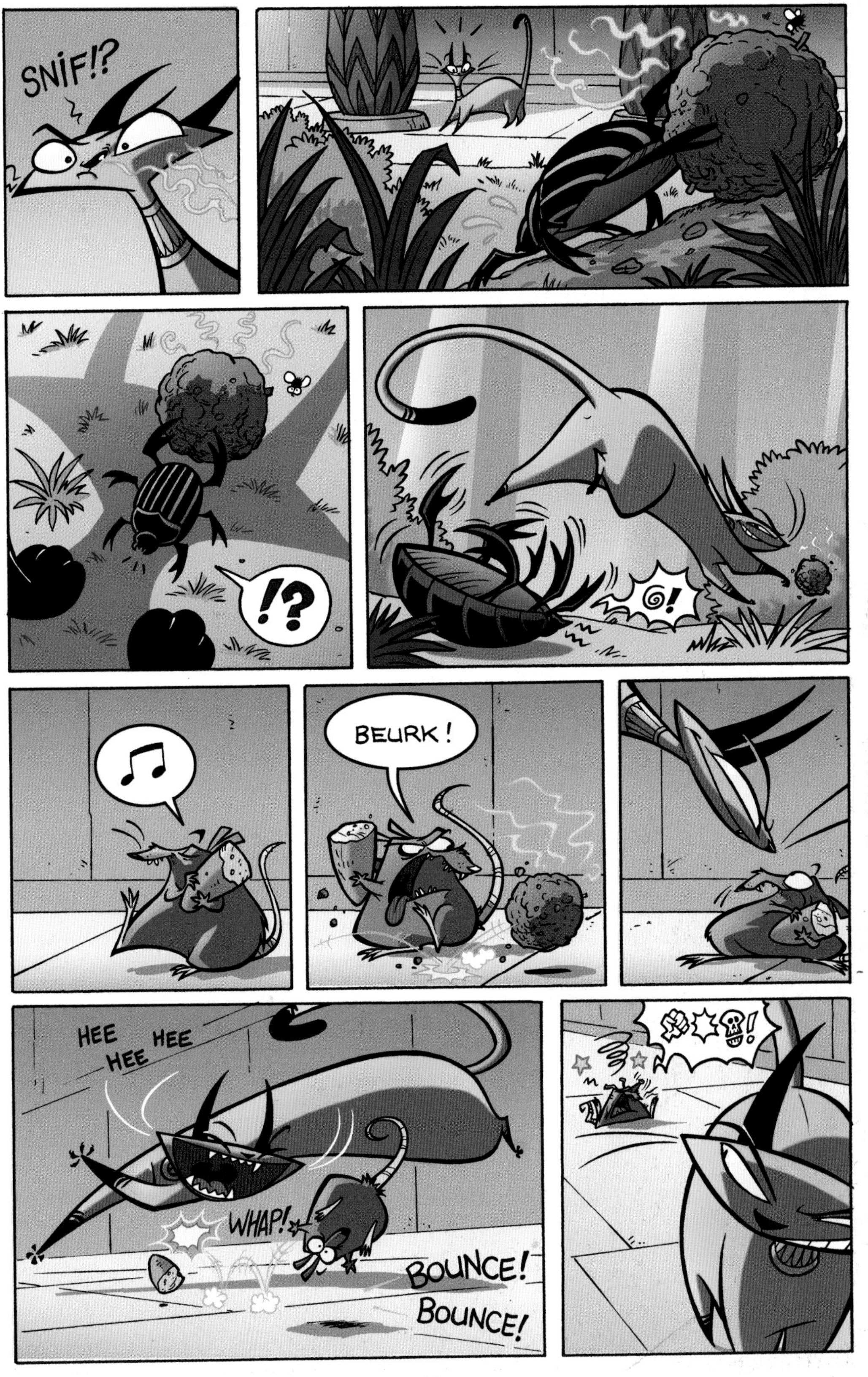
SNIF!?
!?
6!
♫
BEURK!
HEE
HEE HEE
WHAP!
BOUNCE!
BOUNCE!
!

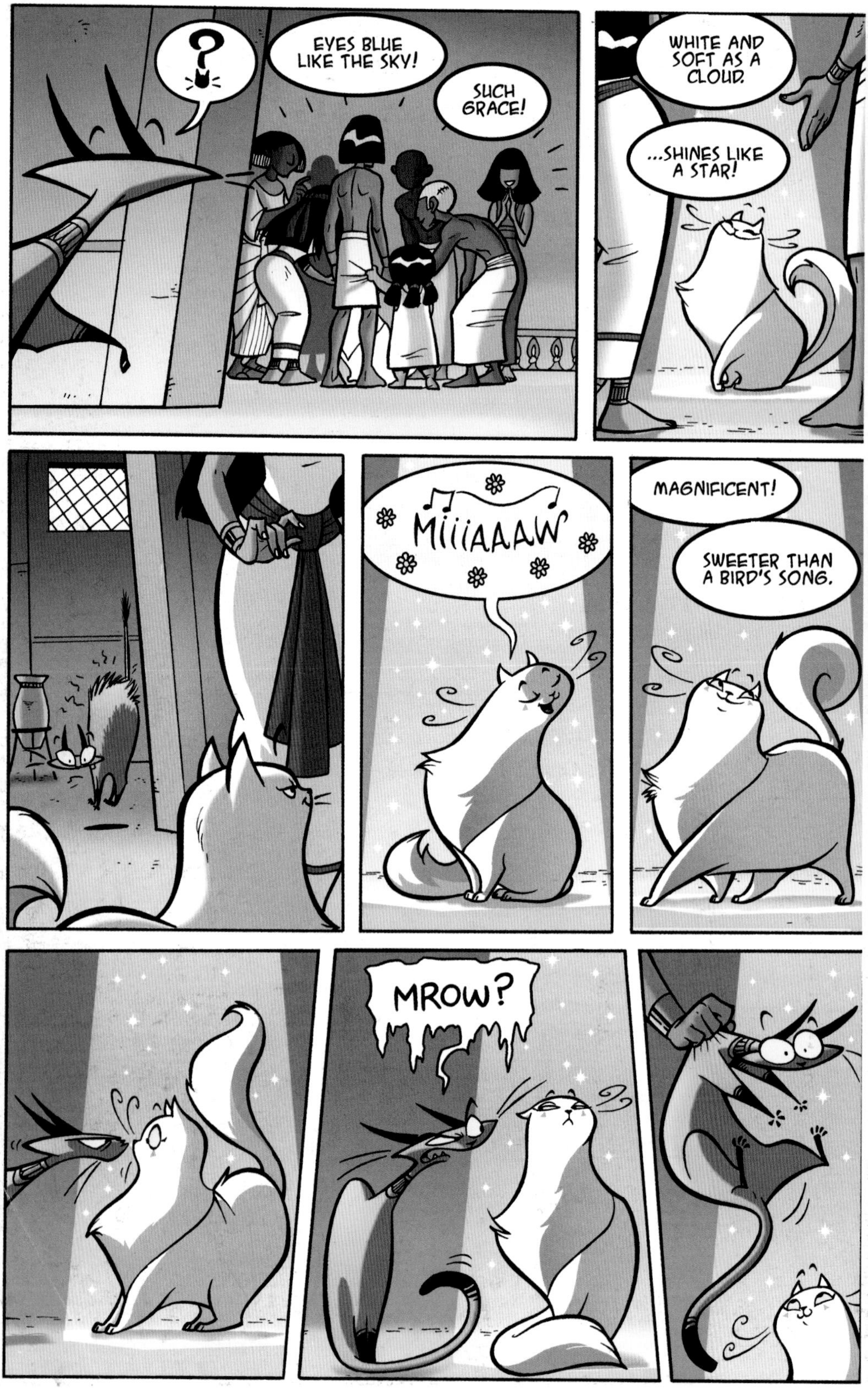
?
EYES BLUE LIKE THE SKY!
SUCH GRACE!
WHITE AND SOFT AS A CLOUD.
...SHINES LIKE A STAR!
MiiiAAAW
MAGNIFICENT!
SWEETER THAN A BIRD'S SONG.
MROW?

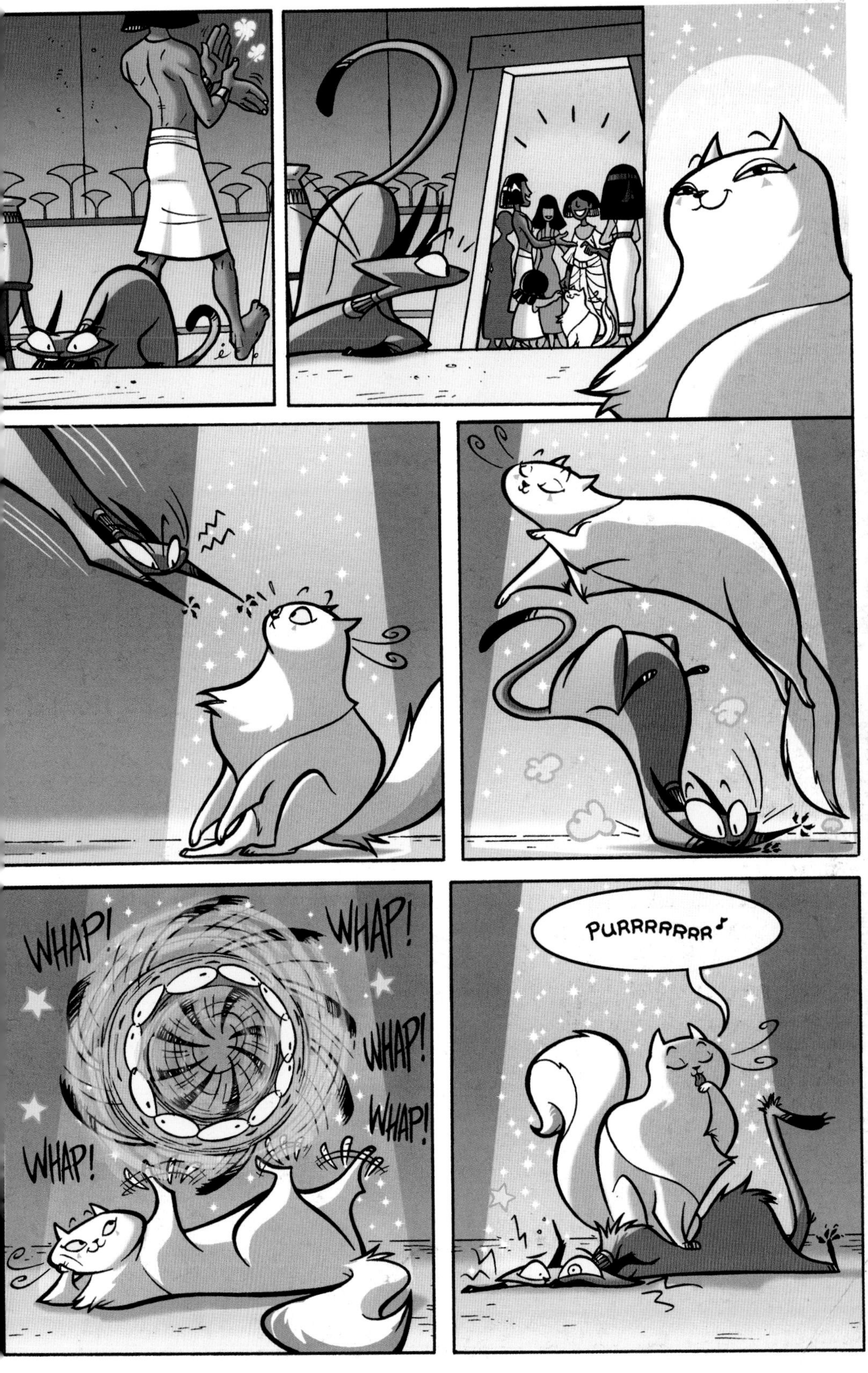
WHAP!
WHAP!
WHAP!
WHAP!
WHAP!
PURRRRRRR

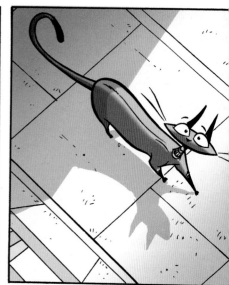

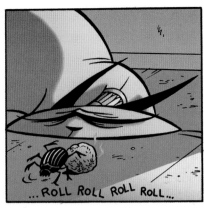

...ROLL ROLL ROLL ROLL...

WIPE!
WIPE!

...ROLL ROLL ROLL...

SNIF!

PAF!

* SIGH *

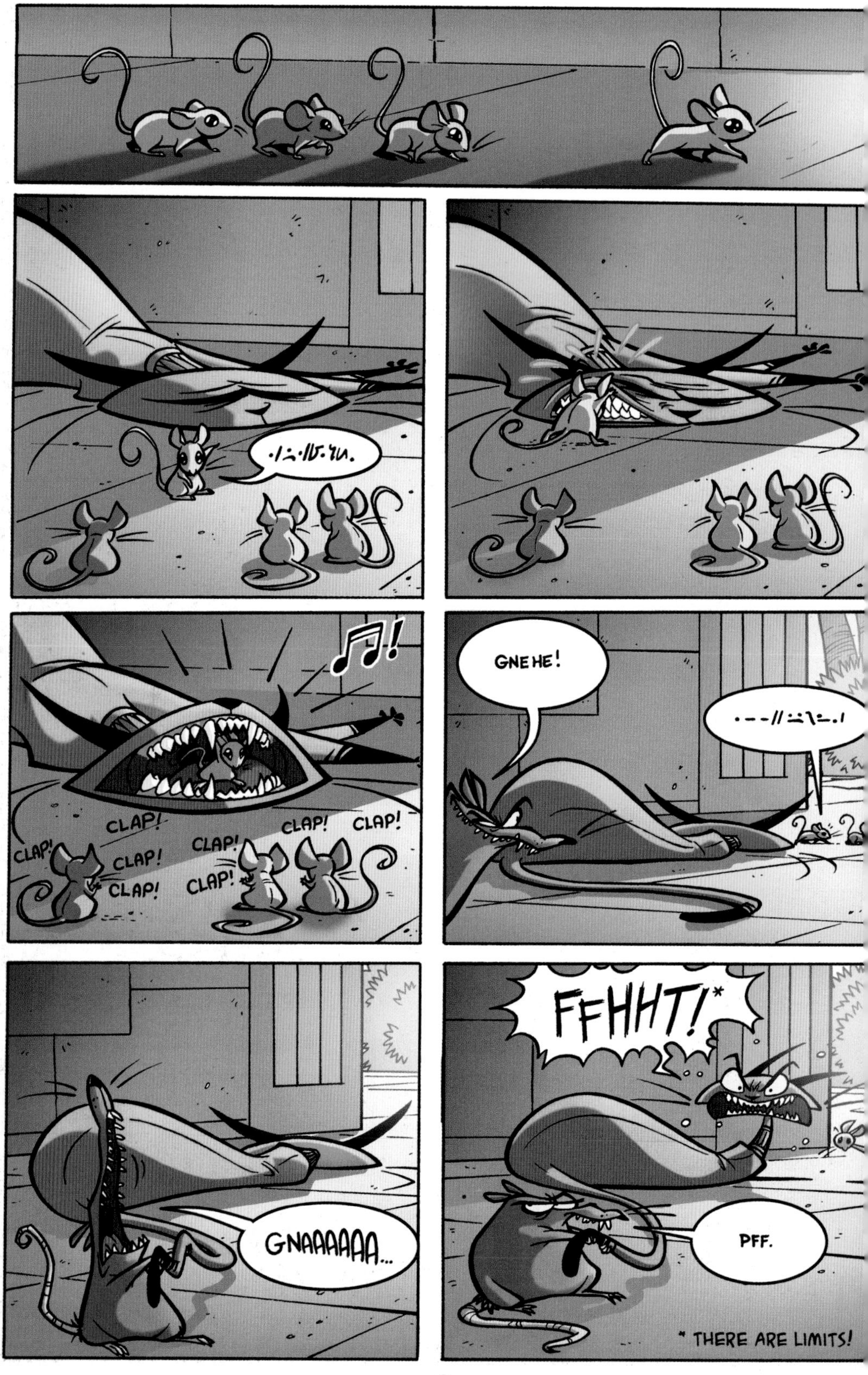
GNEHE!
CLAP!
CLAP!
CLAP!
CLAP!
CLAP!
CLAP!
CLAP!
GNAAAAAA...
FFHHT!*
PFF.
* THERE ARE LIMITS!

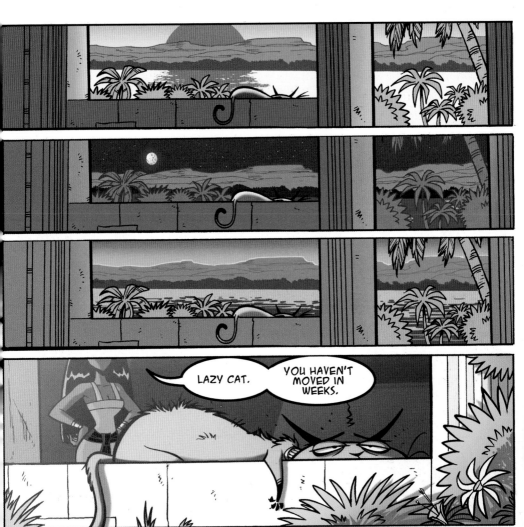

LAZY CAT.

YOU HAVEN'T MOVED IN WEEKS.

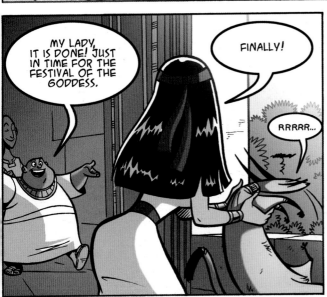

MY LADY, IT IS DONE! JUST IN TIME FOR THE FESTIVAL OF THE GODDESS.

FINALLY!

RRRRR...

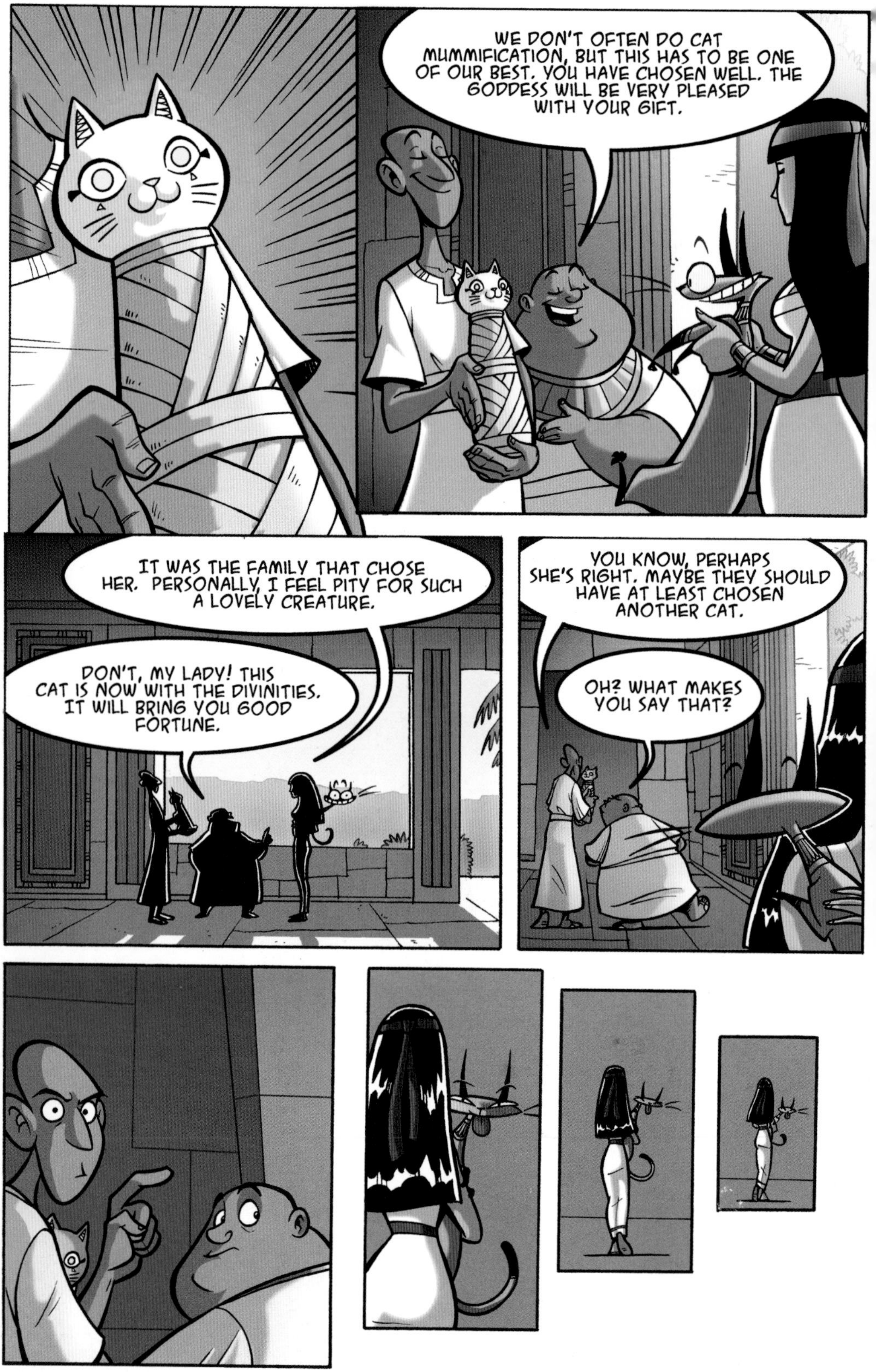
WE DON'T OFTEN DO CAT MUMMIFICATION, BUT THIS HAS TO BE ONE OF OUR BEST. YOU HAVE CHOSEN WELL. THE GODDESS WILL BE VERY PLEASED WITH YOUR GIFT.
IT WAS THE FAMILY THAT CHOSE HER. PERSONALLY, I FEEL PITY FOR SUCH A LOVELY CREATURE.
DON'T, MY LADY! THIS CAT IS NOW WITH THE DIVINITIES. IT WILL BRING YOU GOOD FORTUNE.
YOU KNOW, PERHAPS SHE'S RIGHT. MAYBE THEY SHOULD HAVE AT LEAST CHOSEN ANOTHER CAT.
OH? WHAT MAKES YOU SAY THAT?

·the end·

JELLABY

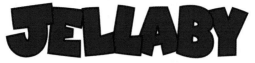

FIRST SNOW

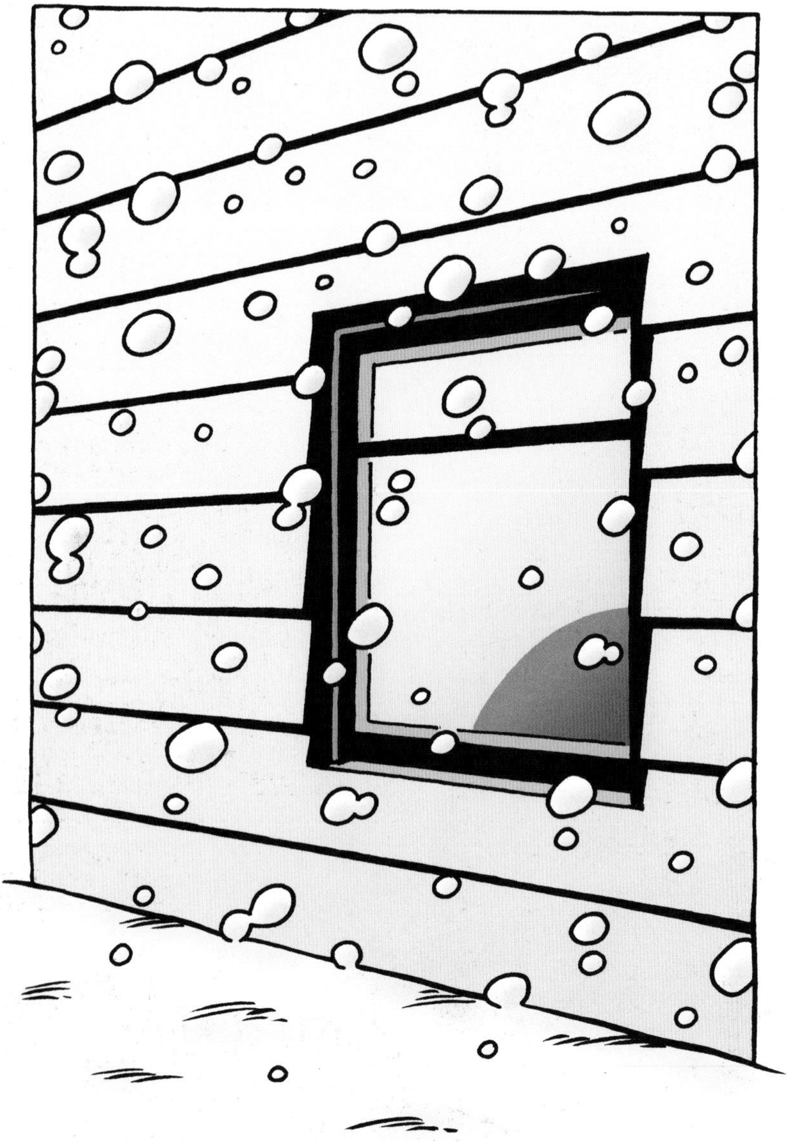

KEAN SOO

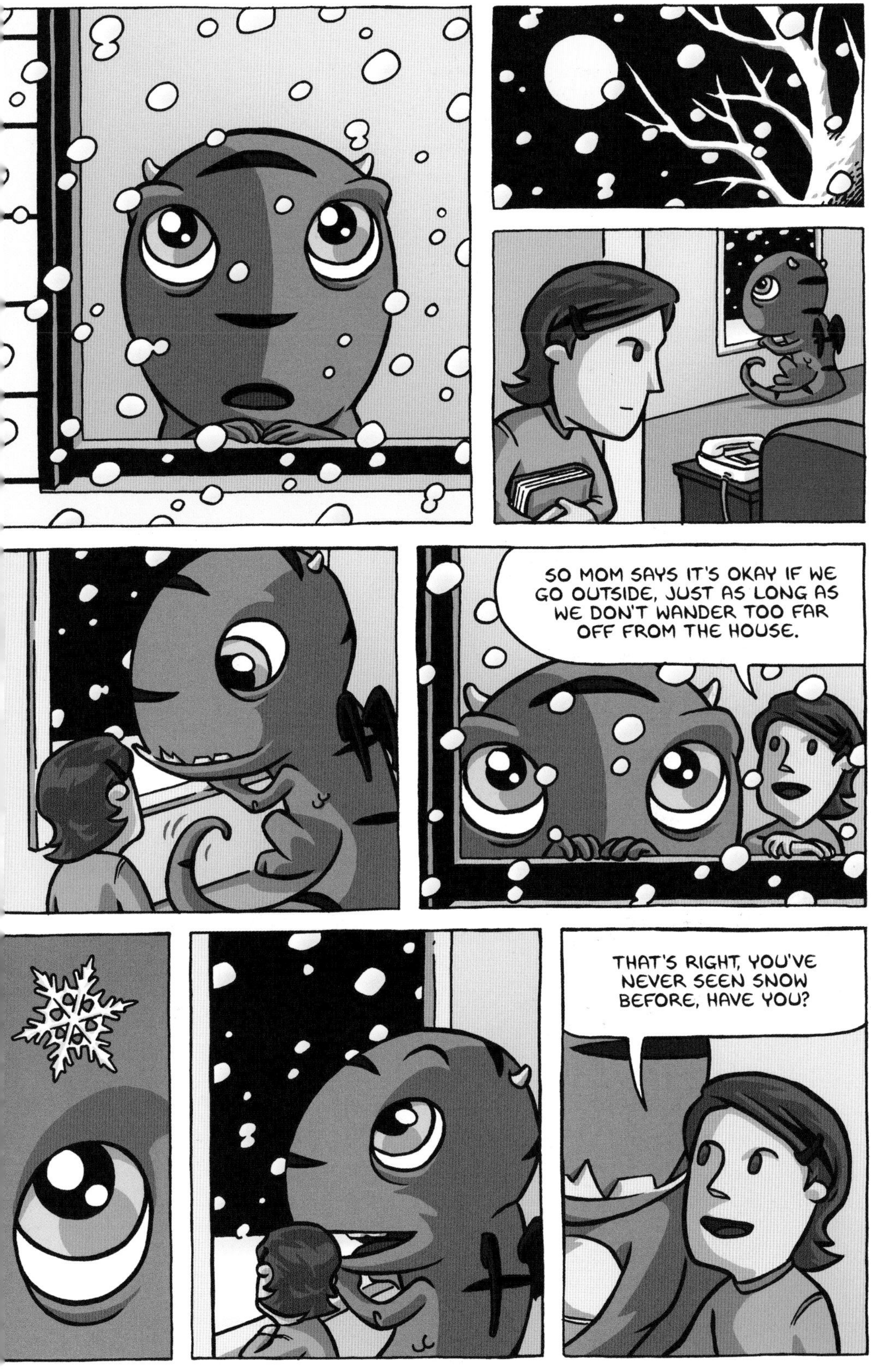
SO MOM SAYS IT'S OKAY IF WE GO OUTSIDE, JUST AS LONG AS WE DON'T WANDER TOO FAR OFF FROM THE HOUSE.
THAT'S RIGHT, YOU'VE NEVER SEEN SNOW BEFORE, HAVE YOU?

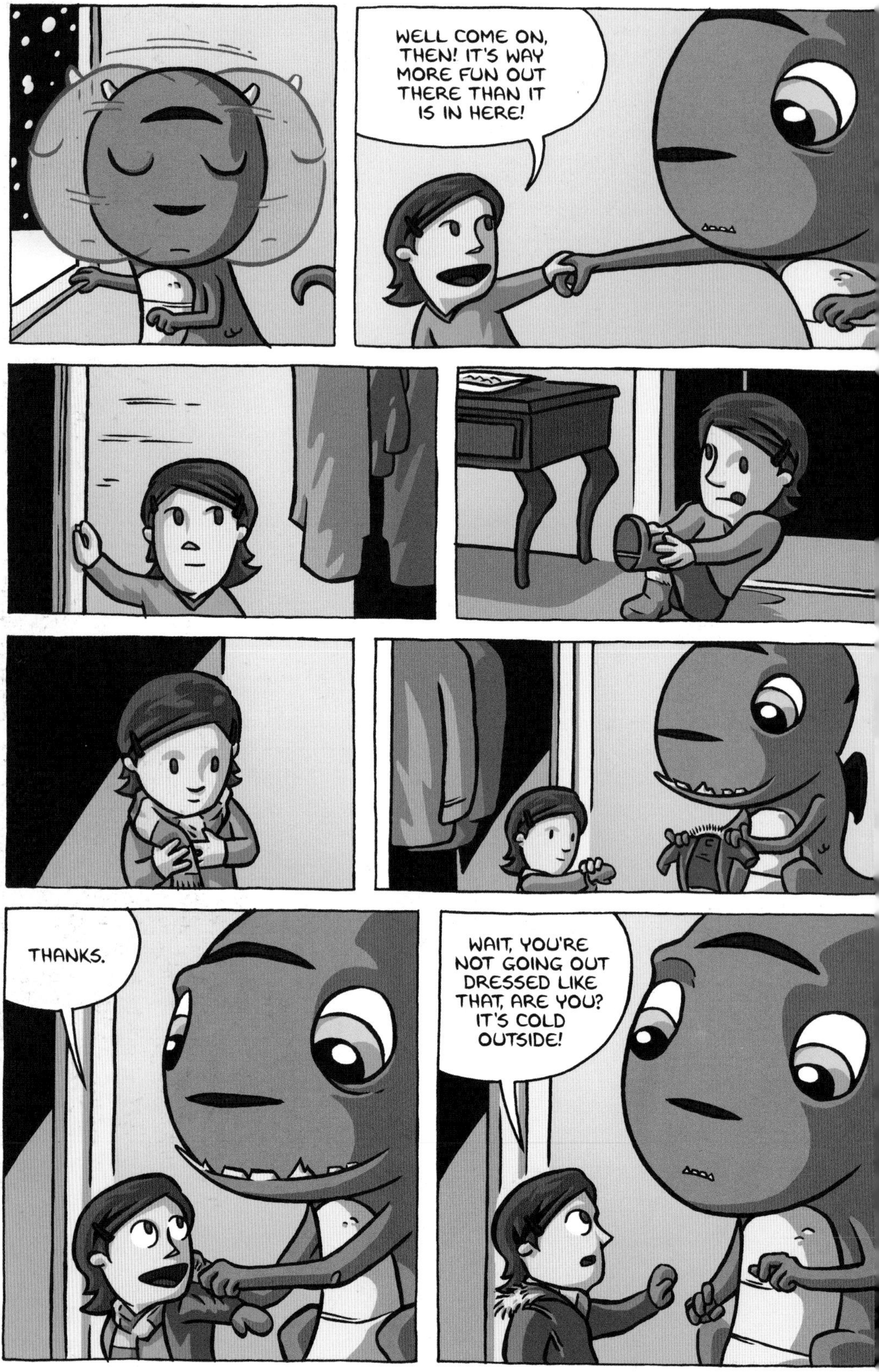
WELL COME ON, THEN! IT'S WAY MORE FUN OUT THERE THAN IT IS IN HERE!
THANKS.
WAIT, YOU'RE NOT GOING OUT DRESSED LIKE THAT, ARE YOU? IT'S COLD OUTSIDE!

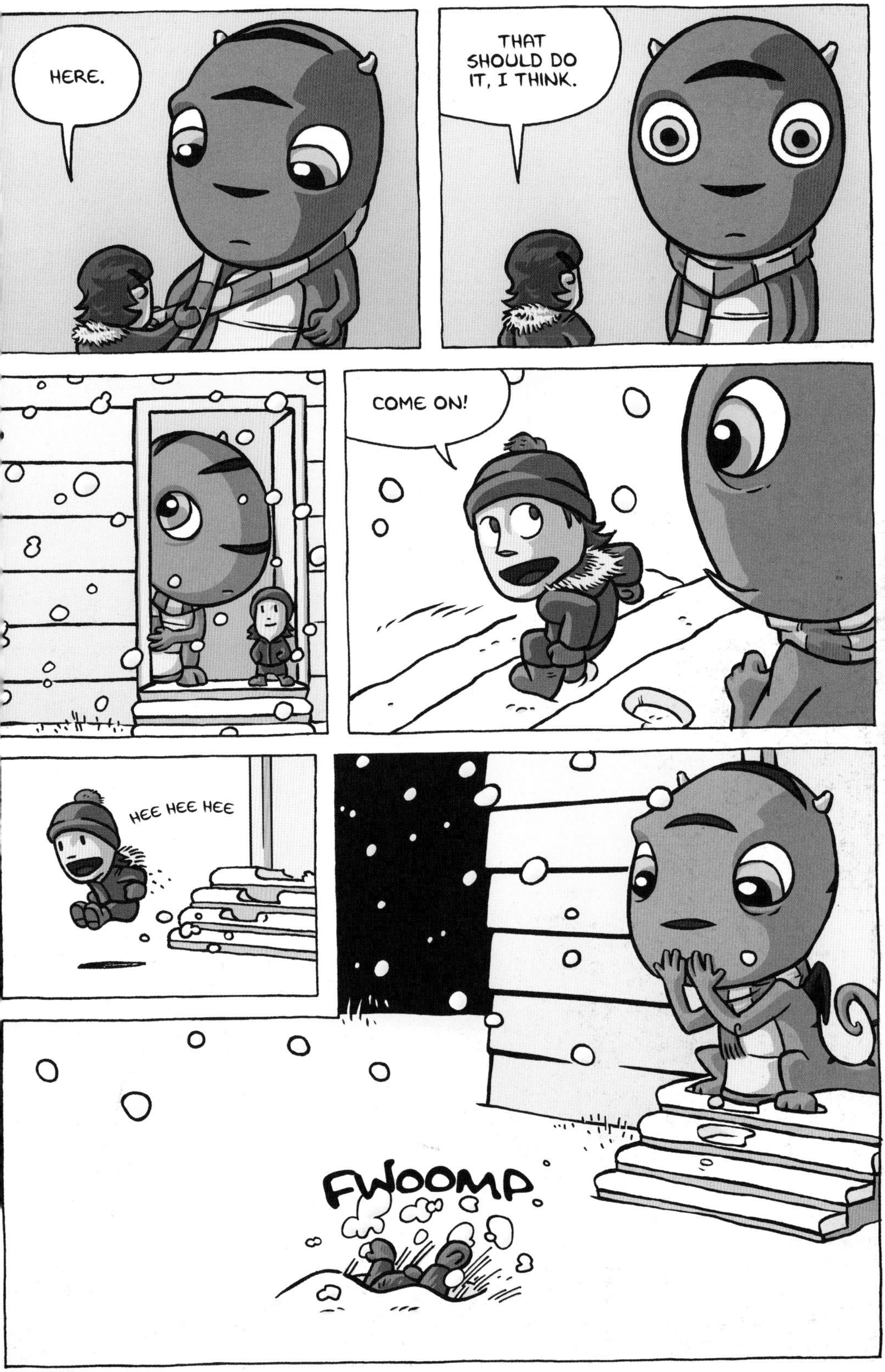
HERE.
THAT SHOULD DO IT, I THINK.
COME ON!
HEE HEE HEE
FWOOMP

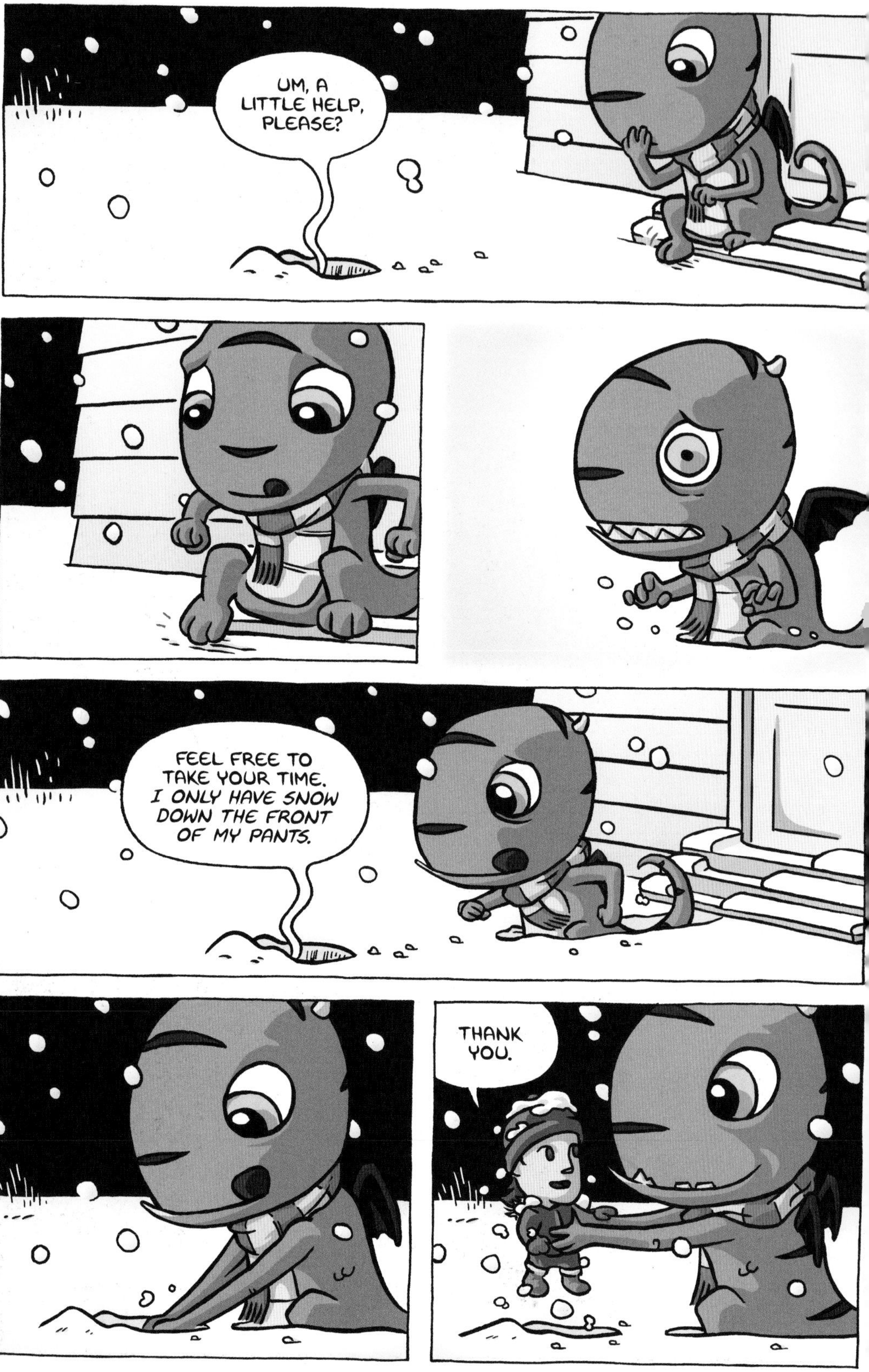
UM, A LITTLE HELP, PLEASE?
FEEL FREE TO TAKE YOUR TIME. I ONLY HAVE SNOW DOWN THE FRONT OF MY PANTS.
THANK YOU.

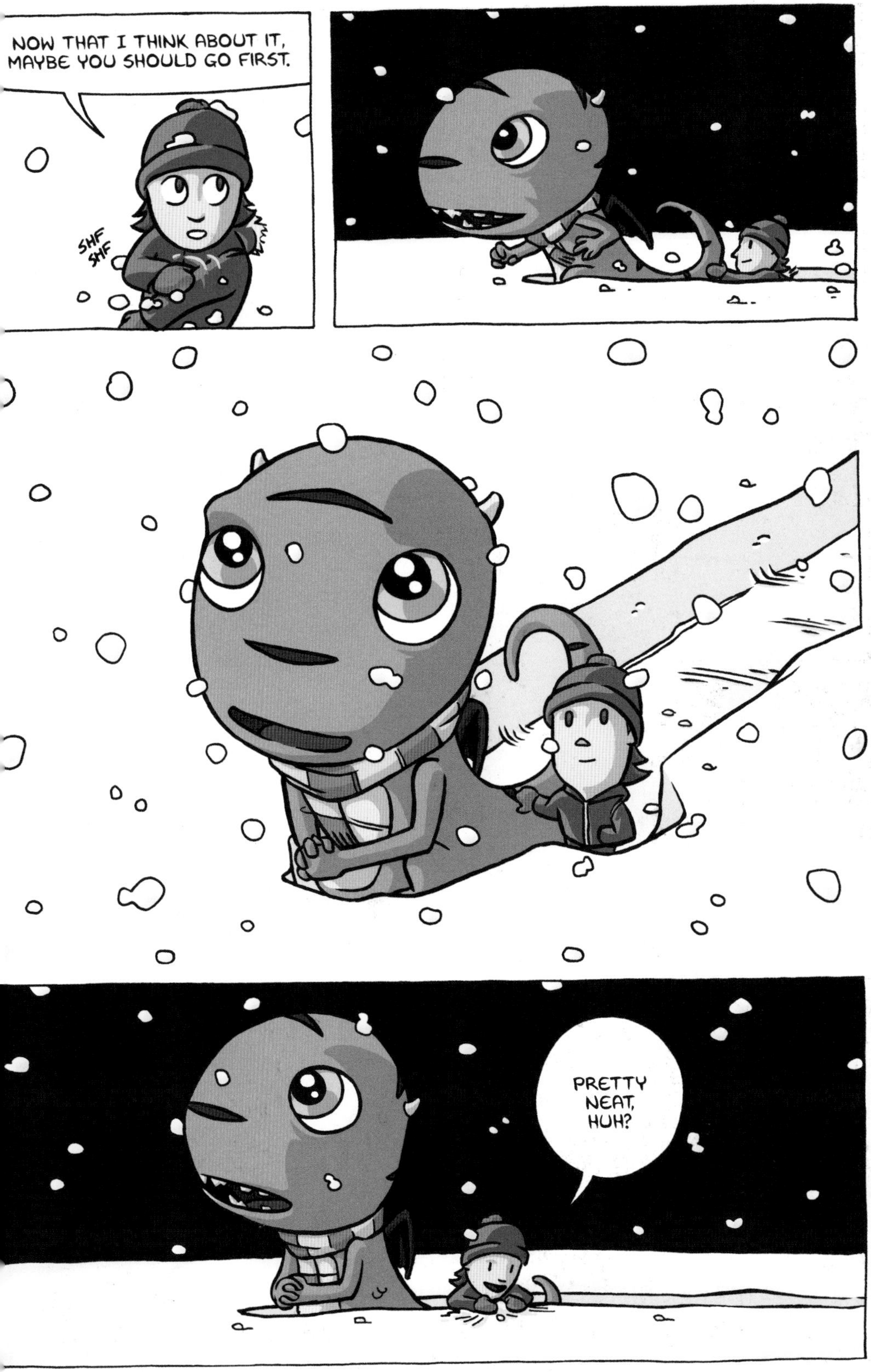
NOW THAT I THINK ABOUT IT, MAYBE YOU SHOULD GO FIRST.
SHF SHF
PRETTY NEAT, HUH?

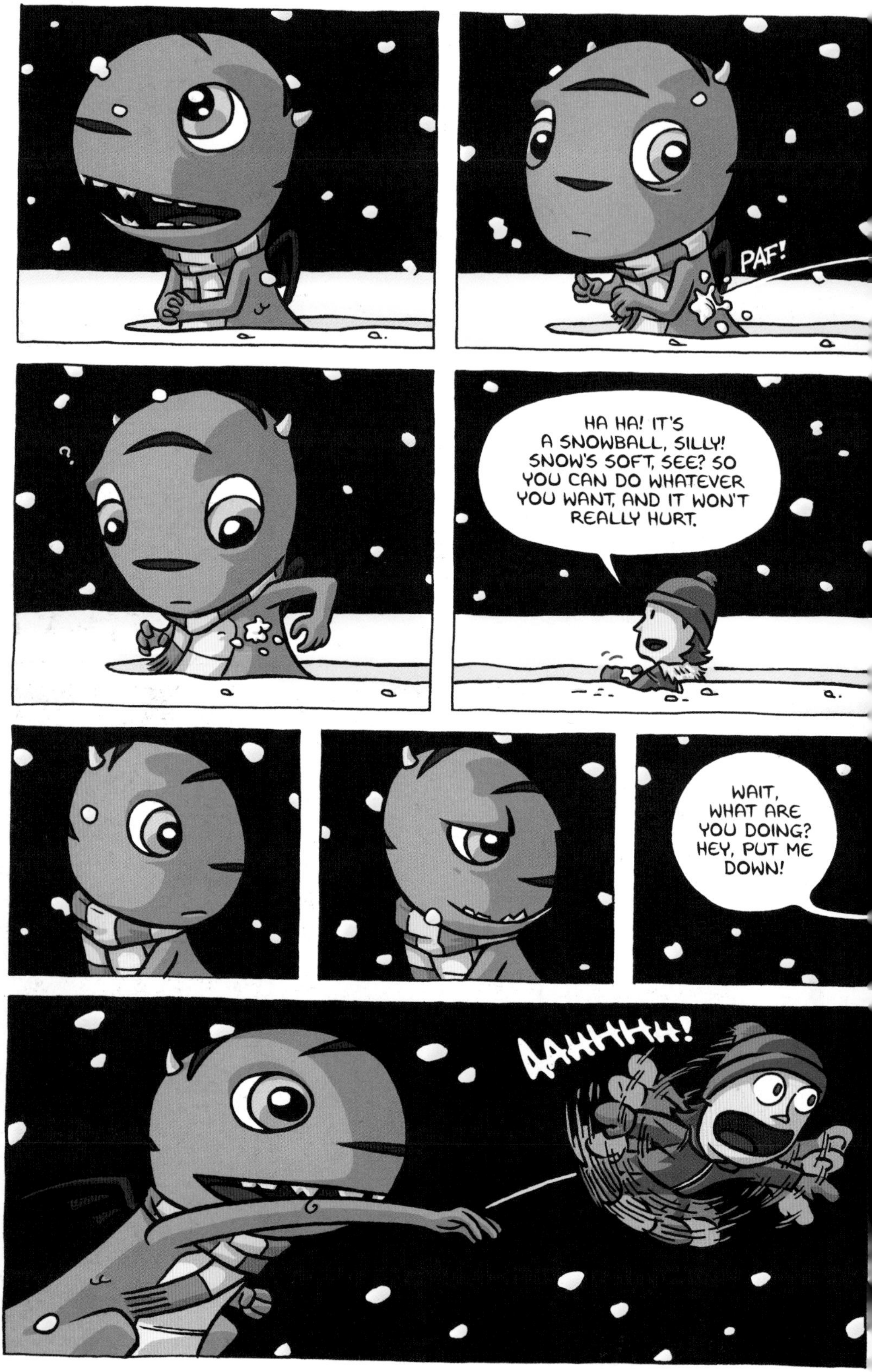
PAF!
?
HA HA! IT'S A SNOWBALL, SILLY! SNOW'S SOFT, SEE? SO YOU CAN DO WHATEVER YOU WANT, AND IT WON'T REALLY HURT.
WAIT, WHAT ARE YOU DOING? HEY, PUT ME DOWN!
AAHHHH!

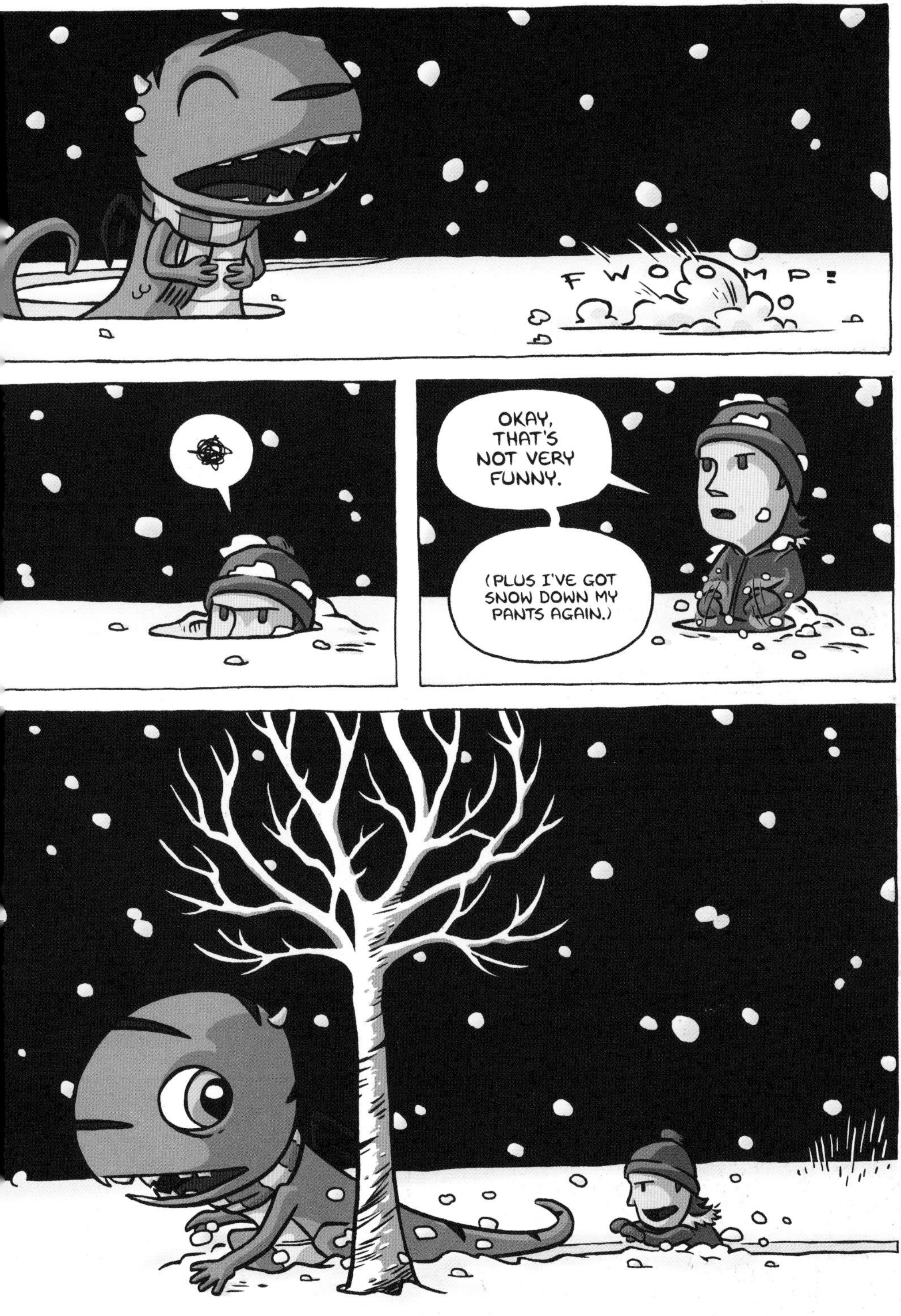
FWOOMP!
OKAY, THAT'S NOT VERY FUNNY.
(PLUS I'VE GOT SNOW DOWN MY PANTS AGAIN.)

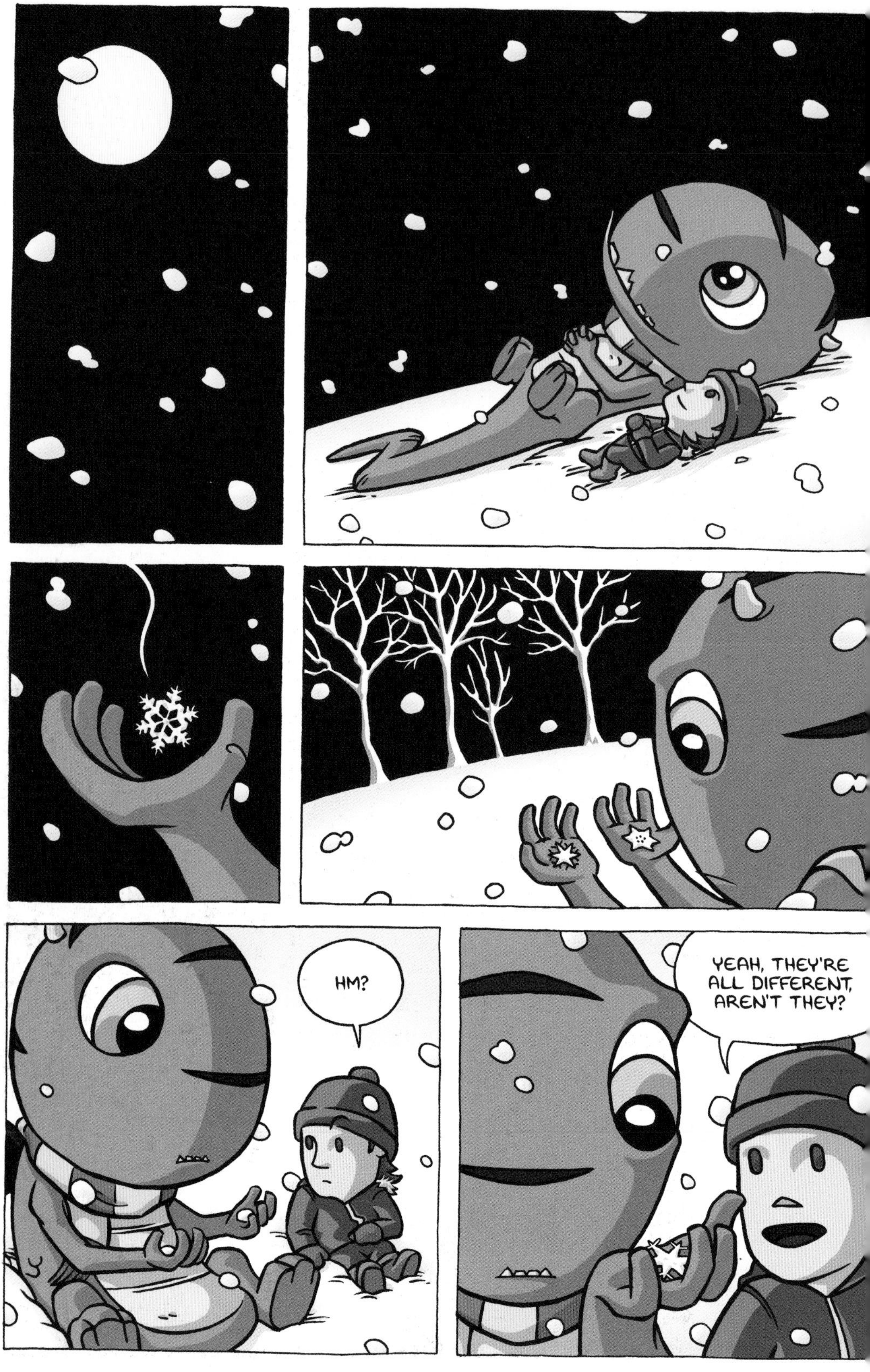
HM?
YEAH, THEY'RE ALL DIFFERENT, AREN'T THEY?

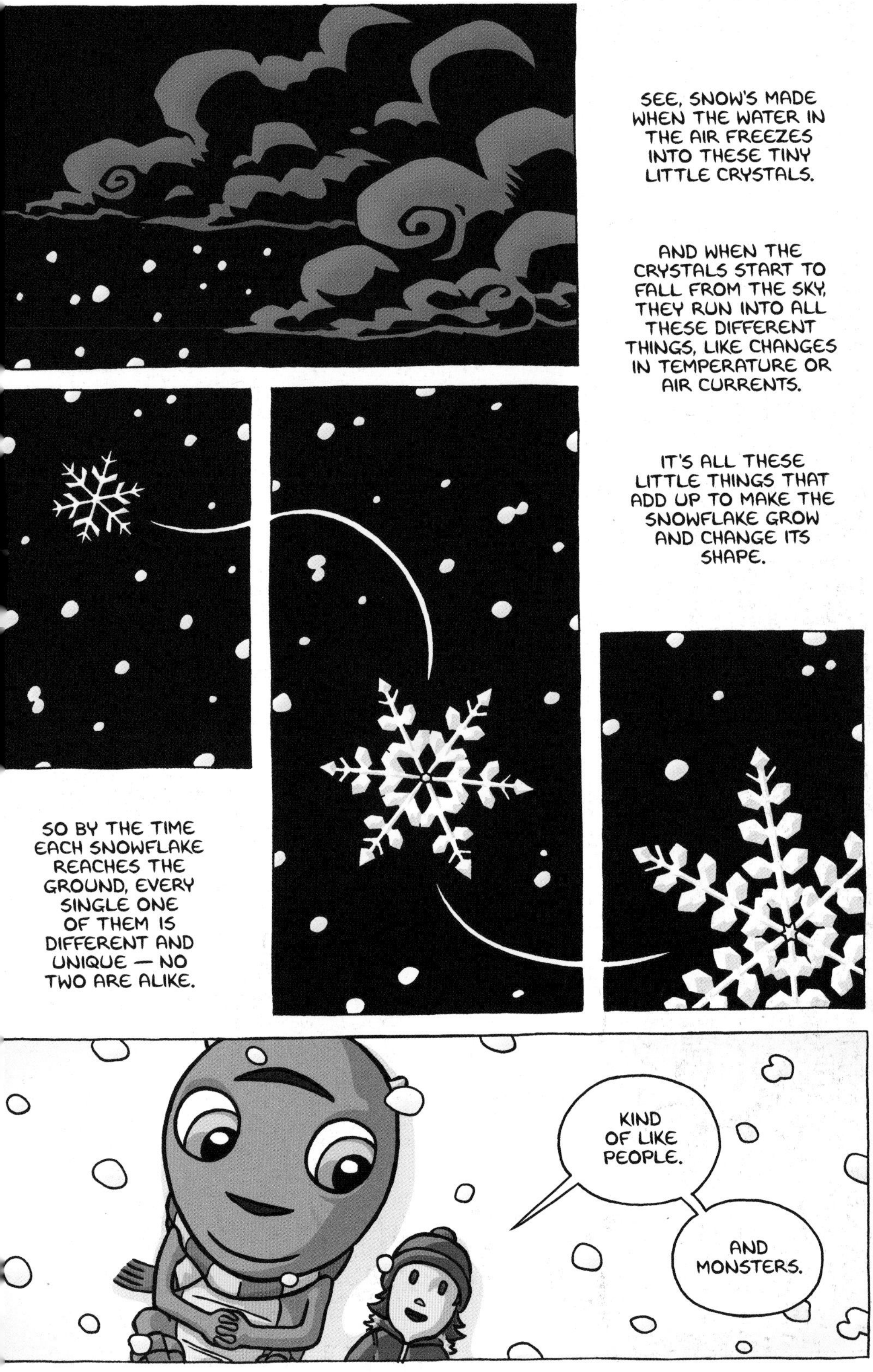
SEE, SNOW'S MADE WHEN THE WATER IN THE AIR FREEZES INTO THESE TINY LITTLE CRYSTALS.
AND WHEN THE CRYSTALS START TO FALL FROM THE SKY, THEY RUN INTO ALL THESE DIFFERENT THINGS, LIKE CHANGES IN TEMPERATURE OR AIR CURRENTS.
IT'S ALL THESE LITTLE THINGS THAT ADD UP TO MAKE THE SNOWFLAKE GROW AND CHANGE ITS SHAPE.
SO BY THE TIME EACH SNOWFLAKE REACHES THE GROUND, EVERY SINGLE ONE OF THEM IS DIFFERENT AND UNIQUE — NO TWO ARE ALIKE.
KIND OF LIKE PEOPLE.
AND MONSTERS.

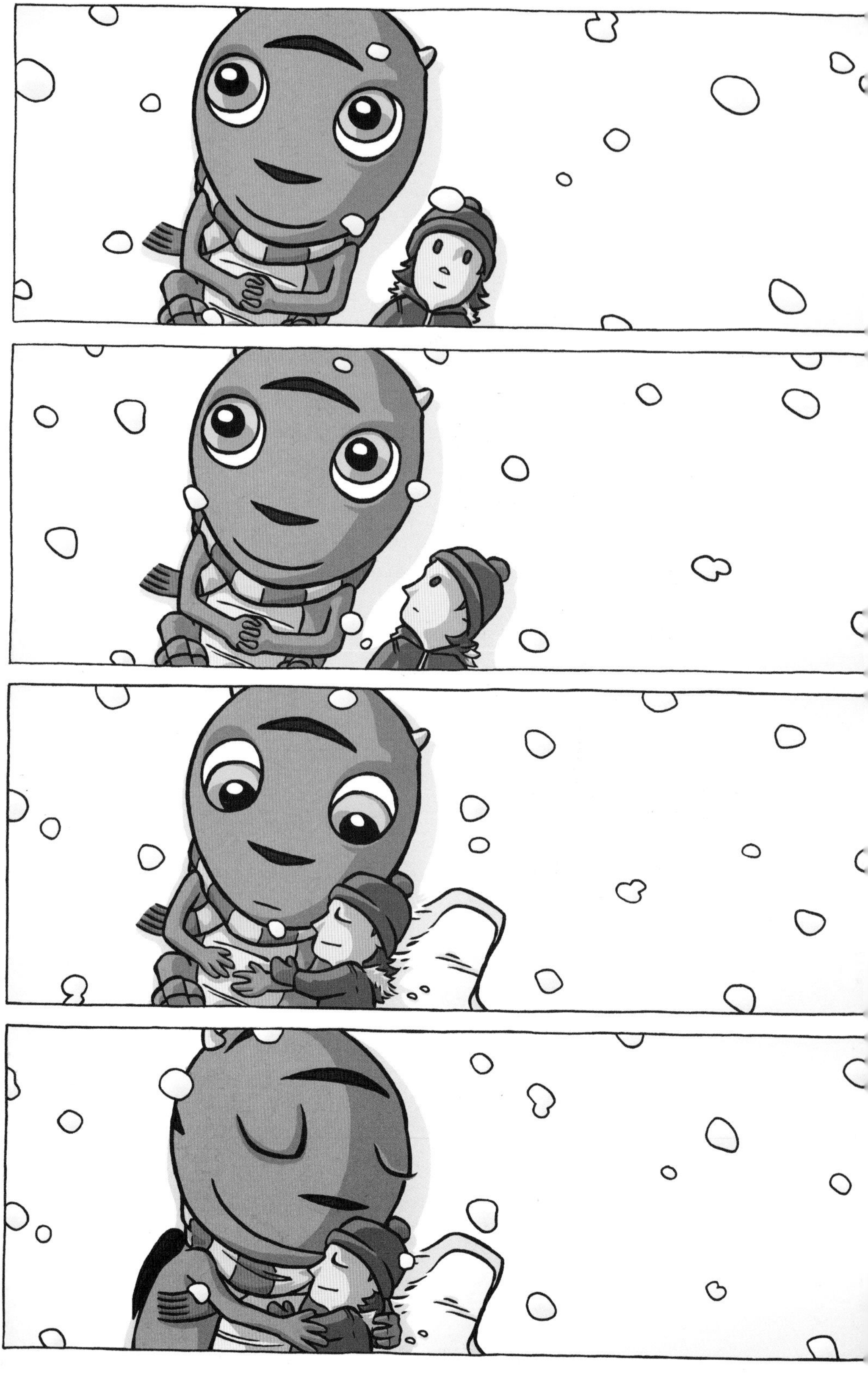

Big Mouth

by Philip Craven

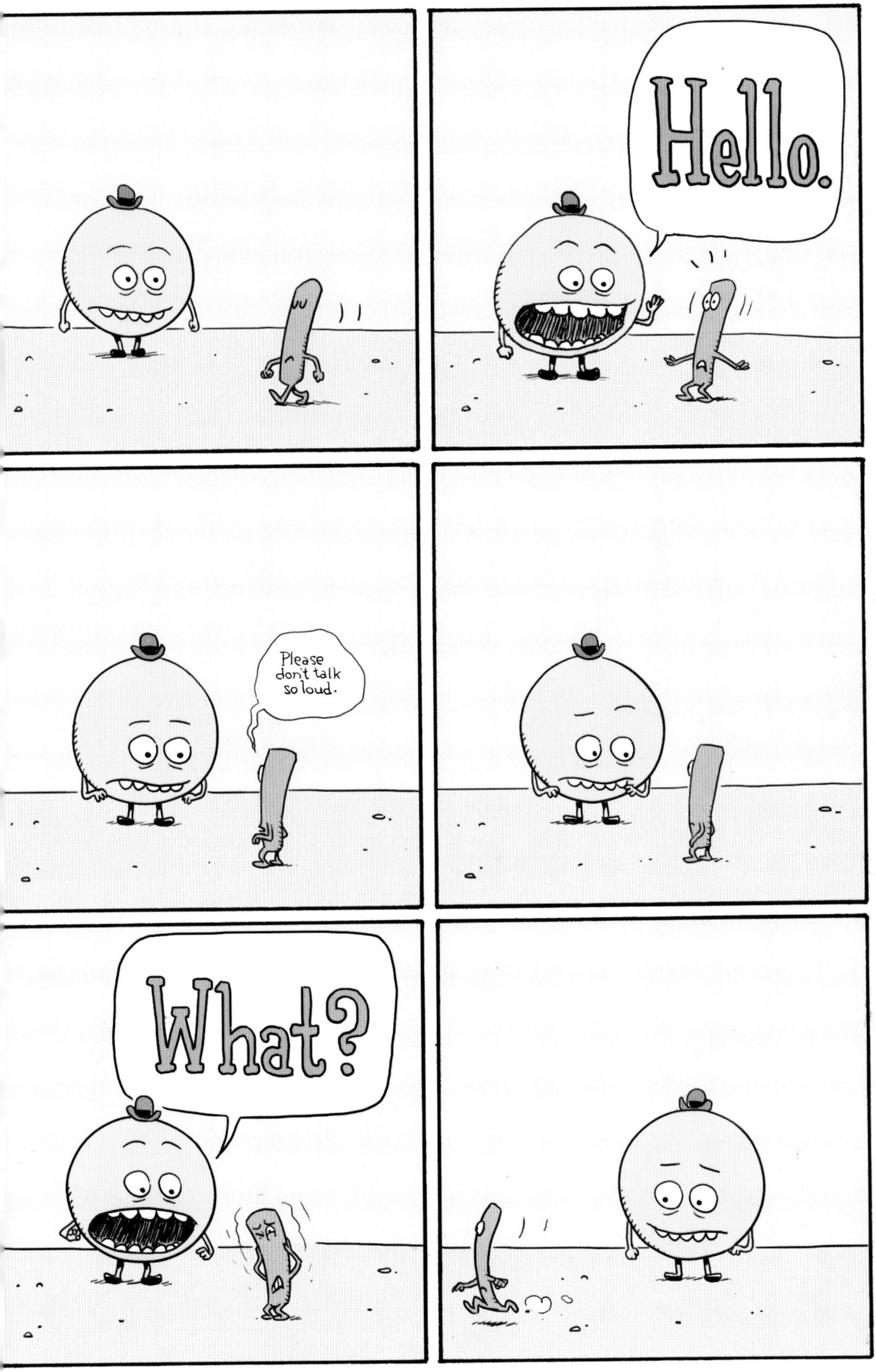
Hello.
Please don't talk so loud.
What?

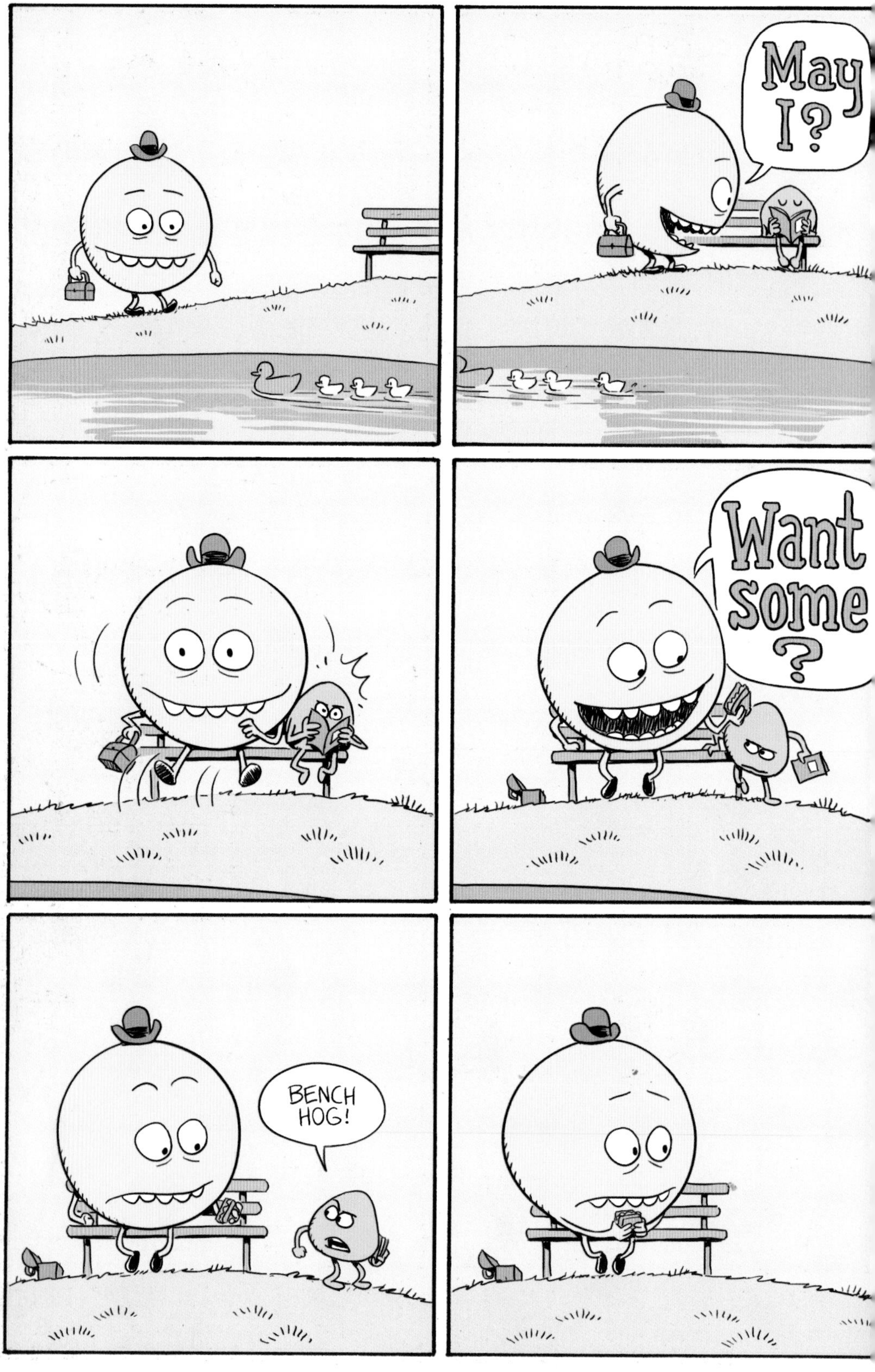
May I?
Want some?
BENCH HOG!

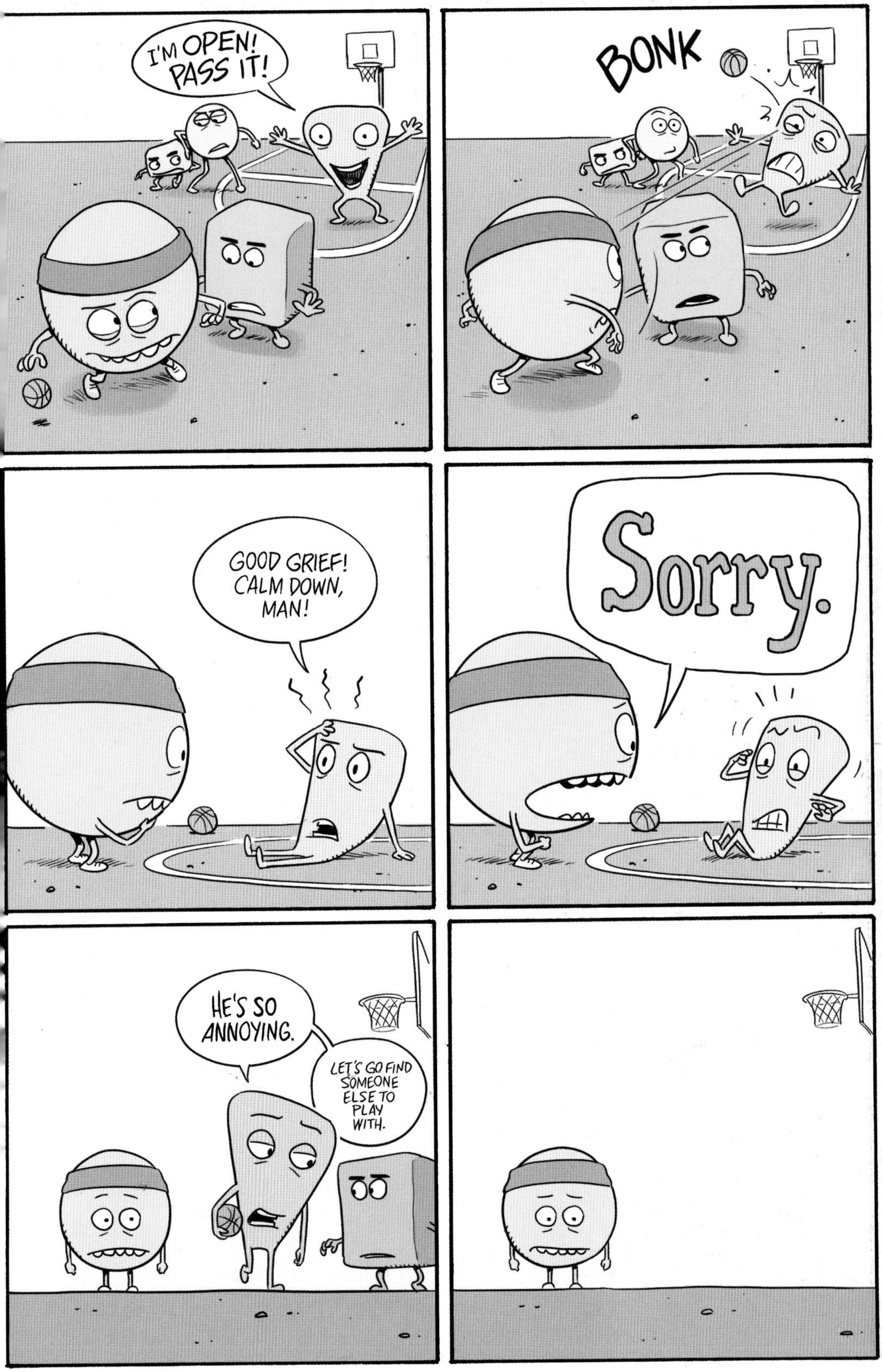
I'M OPEN! PASS IT!
BONK
GOOD GRIEF! CALM DOWN, MAN!
Sorry.
HE'S SO ANNOYING.
LET'S GO FIND SOMEONE ELSE TO PLAY WITH.

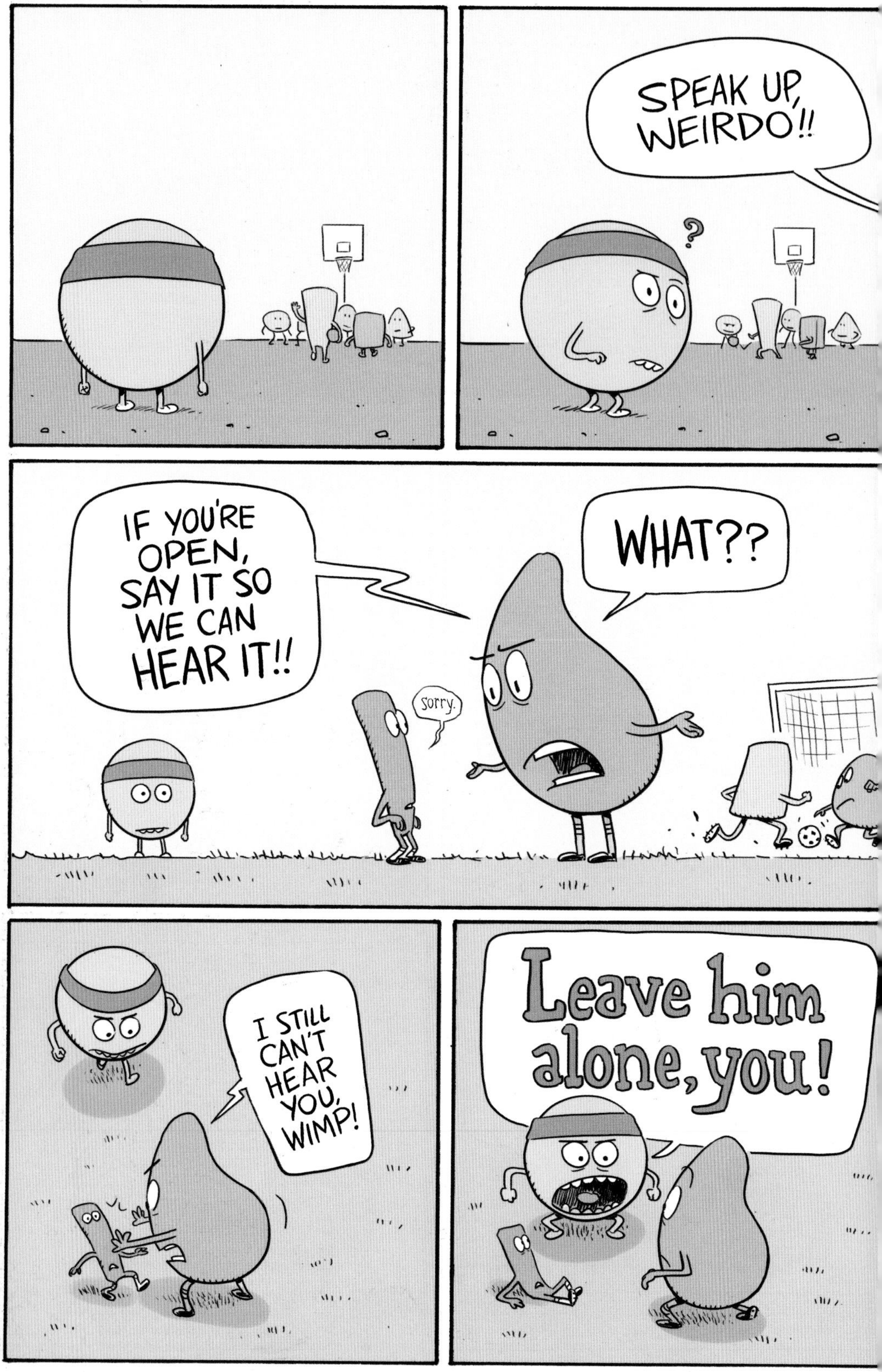
SPEAK UP, WEIRDO!!
IF YOU'RE OPEN, SAY IT SO WE CAN HEAR IT!!
WHAT??
Sorry.
I STILL CAN'T HEAR YOU, WIMP!
Leave him alone, you!

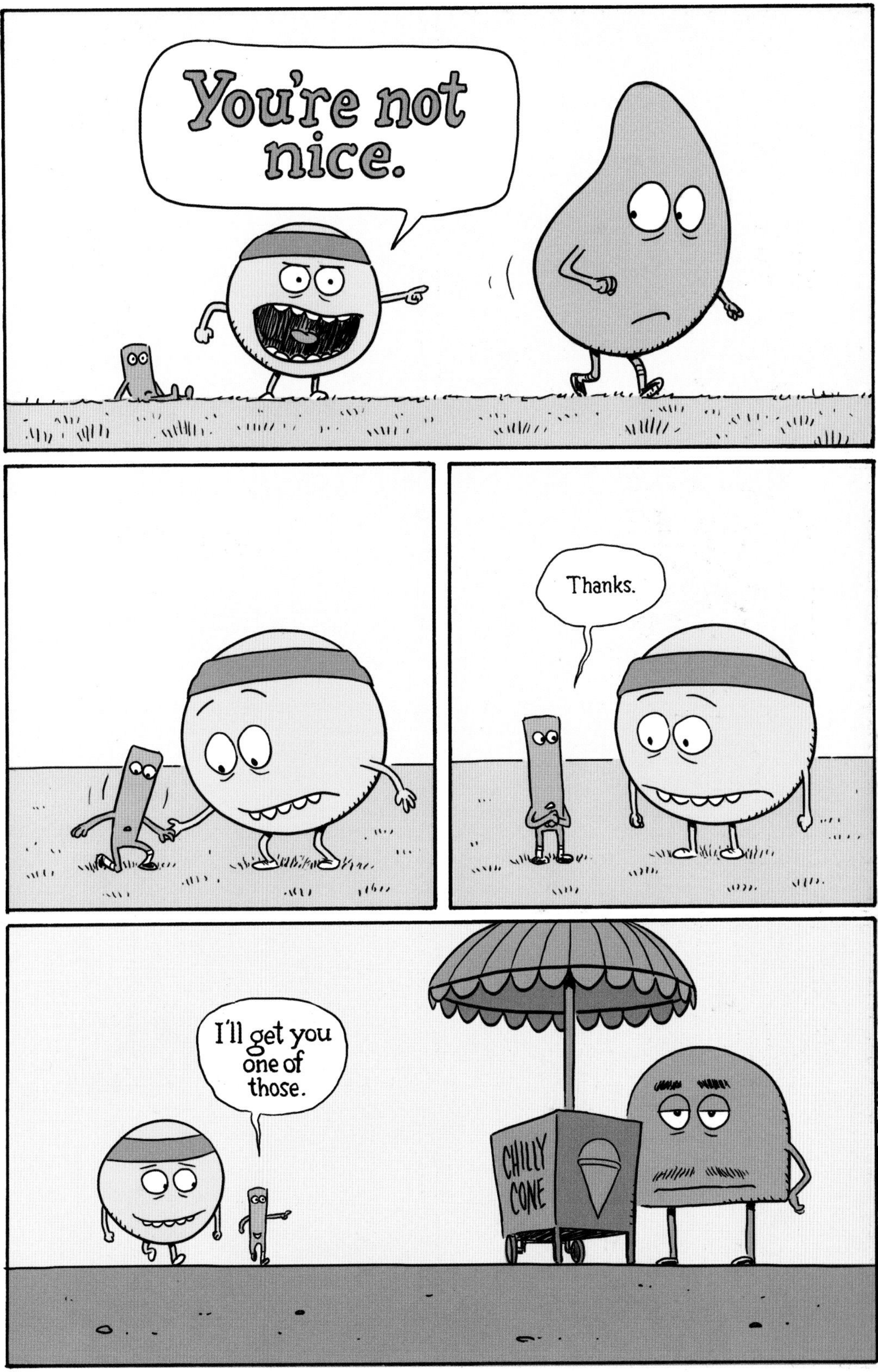
You're not nice.
Thanks.
I'll get you one of those.
CHILLY CONE

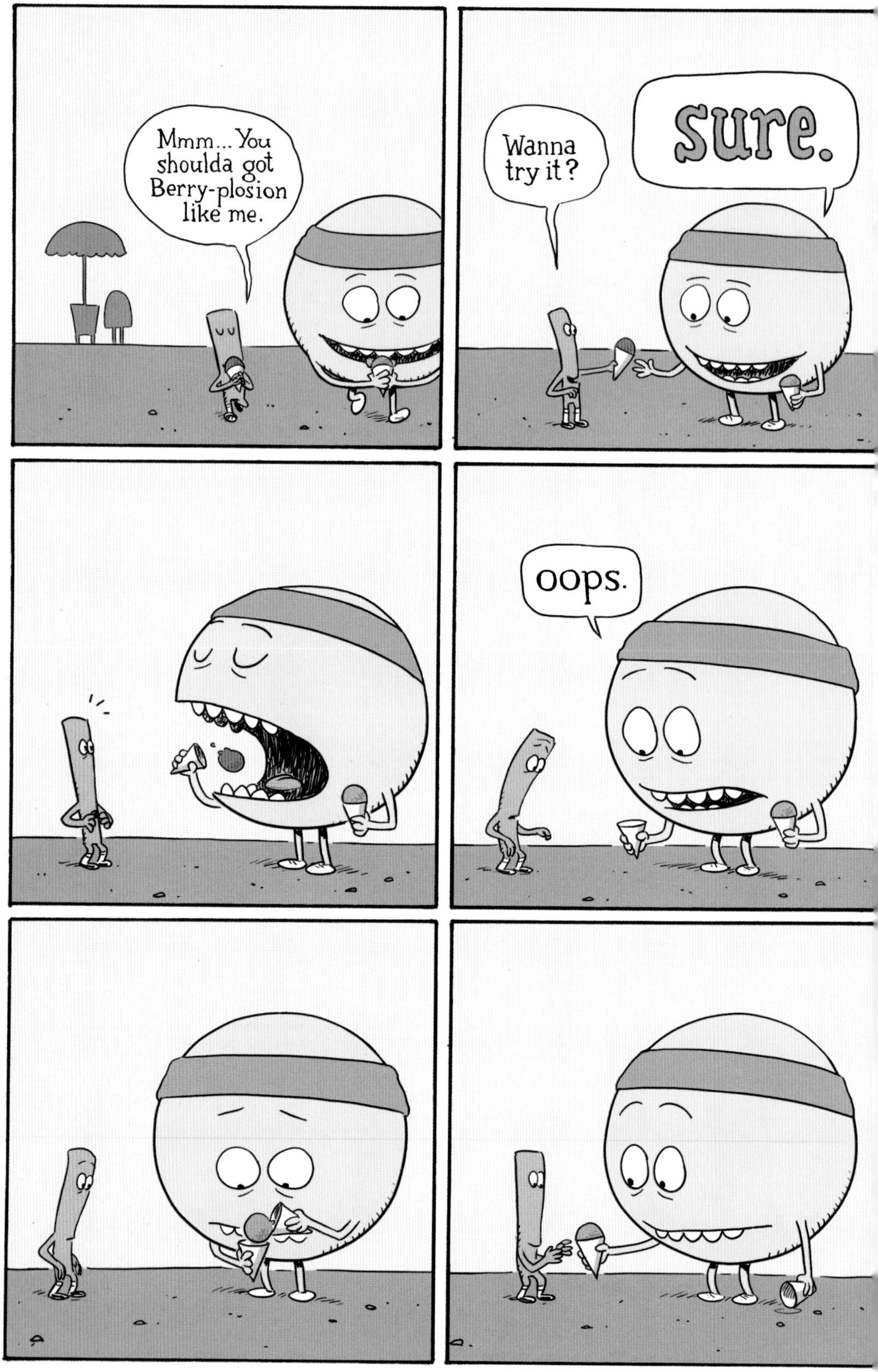
Mmm... You shoulda got Berry-plosion like me.
Wanna try it?
sure.
oops.

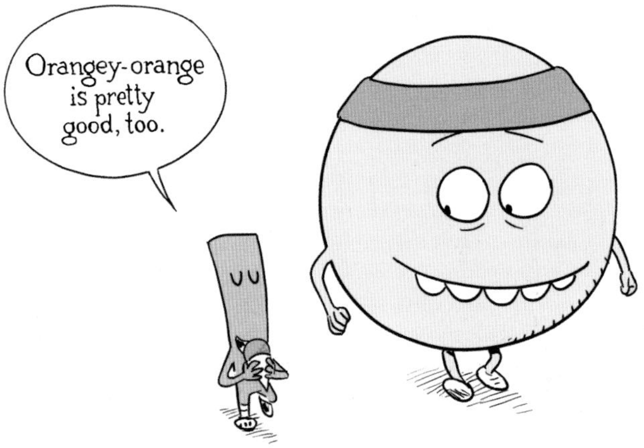
Orangey-orange is pretty good, too.

end

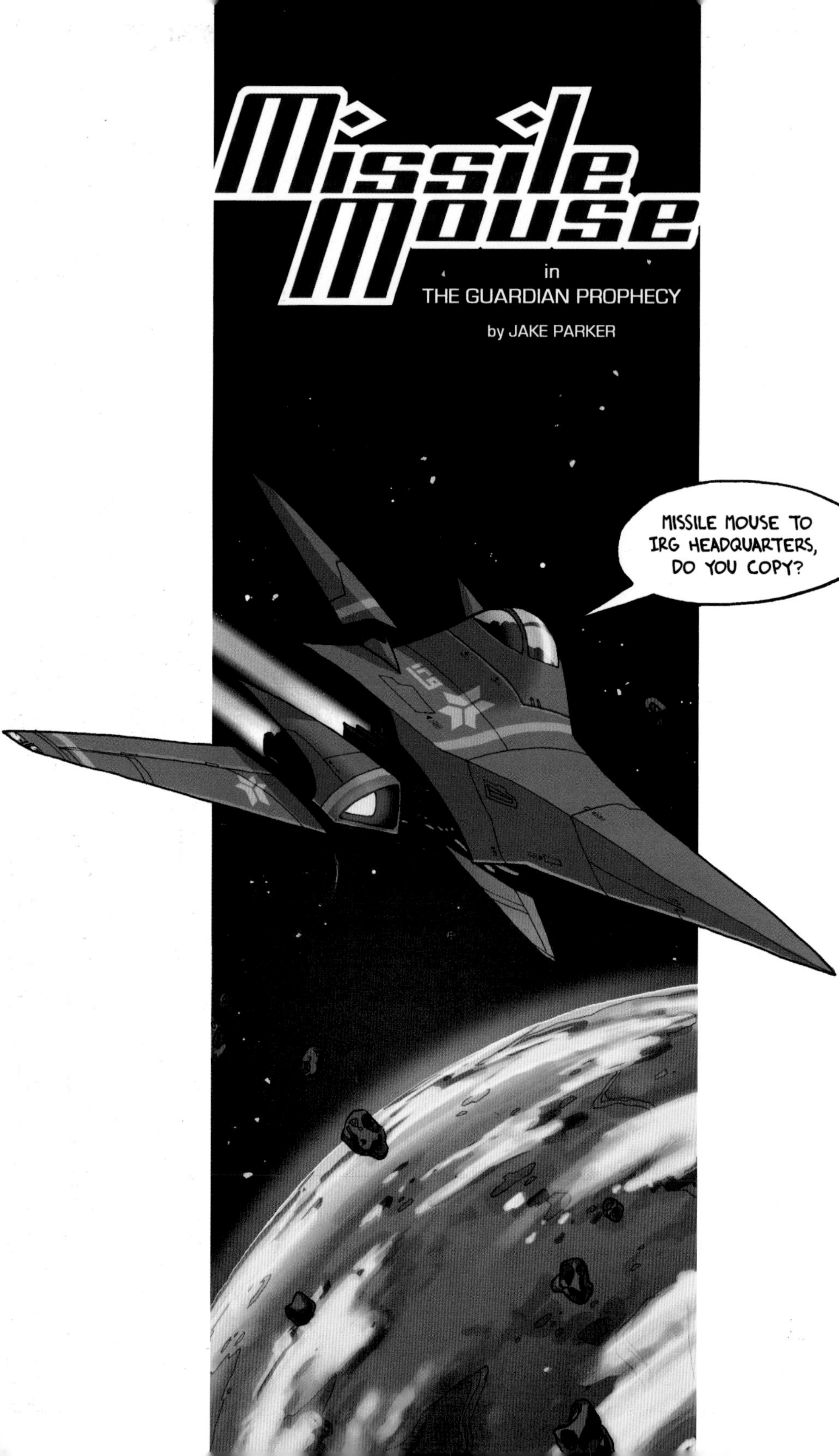
Missile Mouse
in
THE GUARDIAN PROPHECY
by JAKE PARKER
MISSILE MOUSE TO IRG HEADQUARTERS, DO YOU COPY?

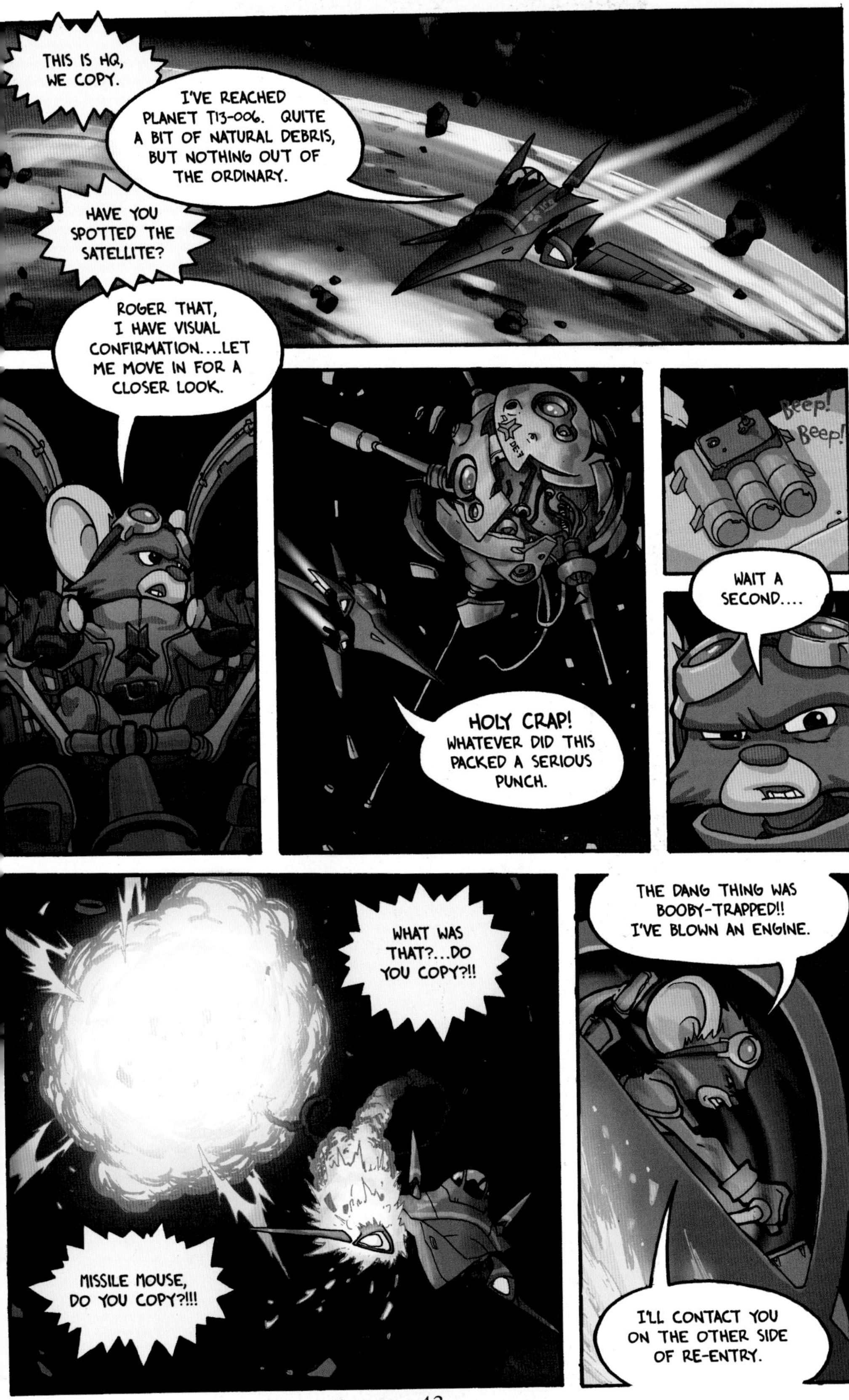
THIS IS HQ, WE COPY.
I'VE REACHED PLANET T13-006. QUITE A BIT OF NATURAL DEBRIS, BUT NOTHING OUT OF THE ORDINARY.
HAVE YOU SPOTTED THE SATELLITE?
ROGER THAT, I HAVE VISUAL CONFIRMATION....LET ME MOVE IN FOR A CLOSER LOOK.
HOLY CRAP! WHATEVER DID THIS PACKED A SERIOUS PUNCH.
Beep! Beep!
WAIT A SECOND....
WHAT WAS THAT?...DO YOU COPY?!!
MISSILE MOUSE, DO YOU COPY?!!!
THE DANG THING WAS BOOBY-TRAPPED!! I'VE BLOWN AN ENGINE.
I'LL CONTACT YOU ON THE OTHER SIDE OF RE-ENTRY.

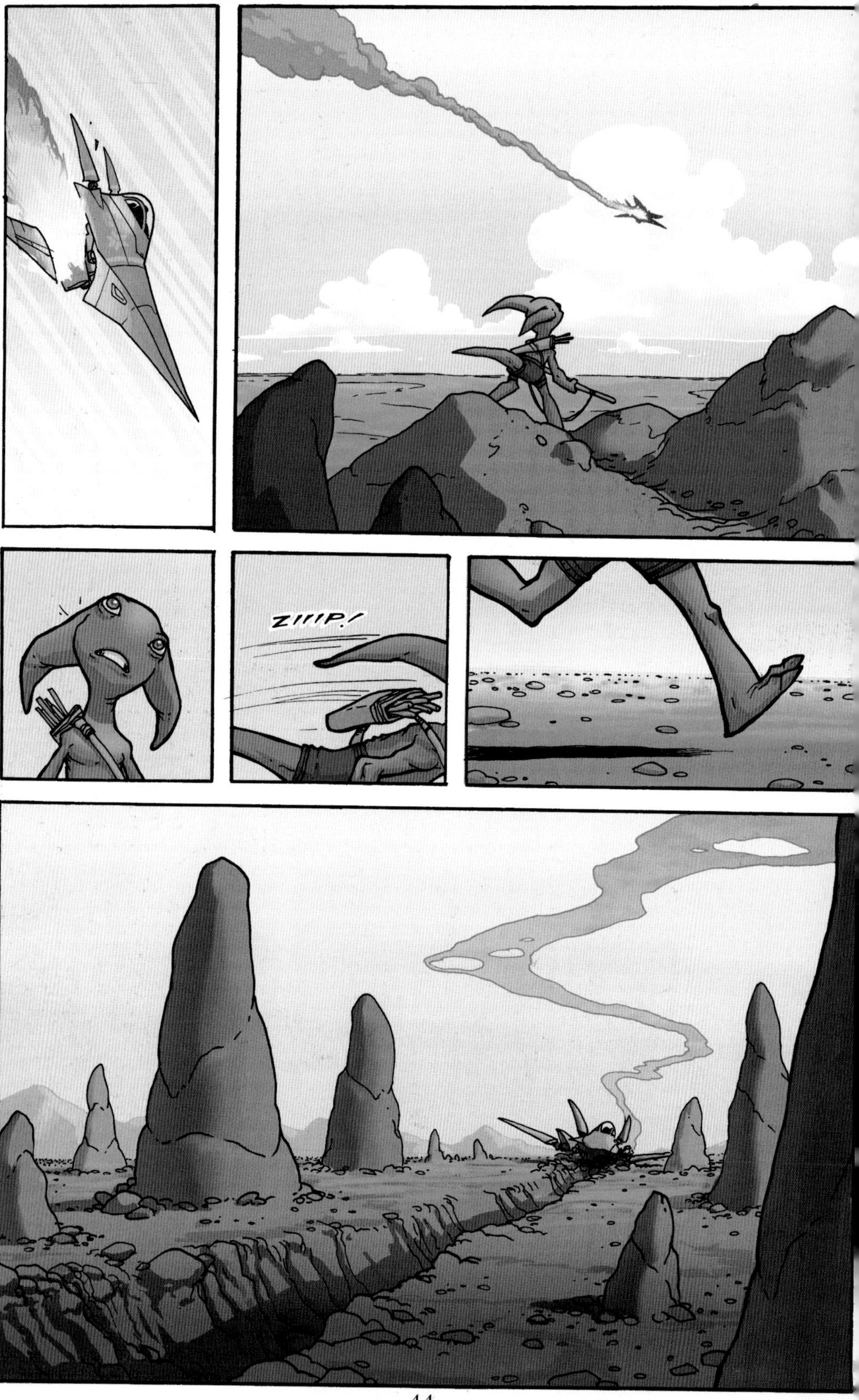
ZIIIP!

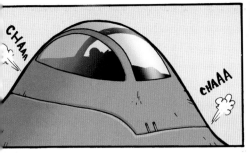

CHAAA

CHAAA

SSSSSS

SSSSSSSS

WELL NOW, THIS IS JUST GREAT. IT'LL TAKE ME DAYS TO REPAIR THIS.

ZIP

THAT WAS A WARNING SHOT.... MOVE AND I'LL PUT ONE THROUGH YOUR HEAD.

PANG!

ALL RIGHT, FREEZE!

CHACK

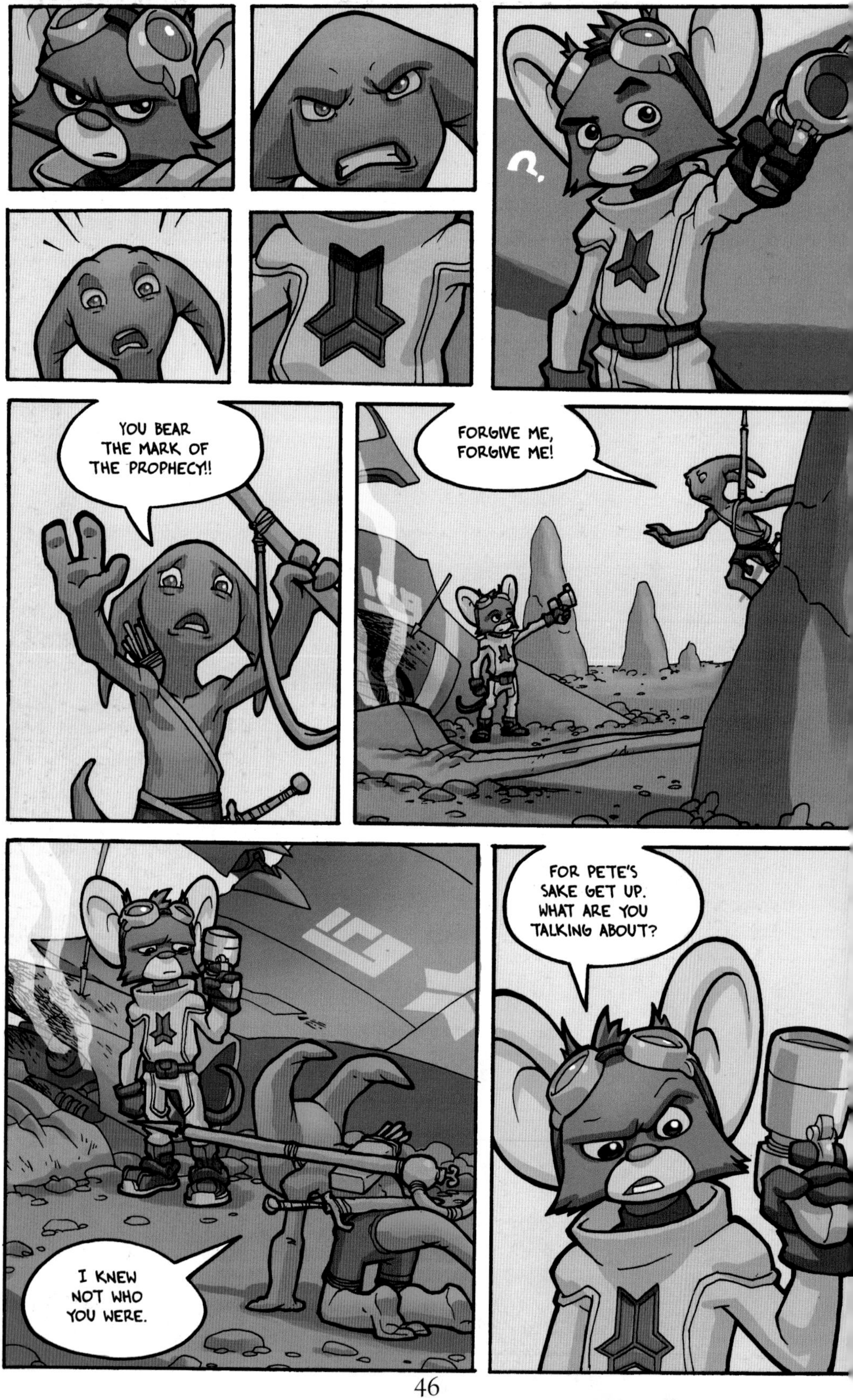
?
YOU BEAR THE MARK OF THE PROPHECY!!
FORGIVE ME, FORGIVE ME!
I KNEW NOT WHO YOU WERE.
FOR PETE'S SAKE GET UP. WHAT ARE YOU TALKING ABOUT?

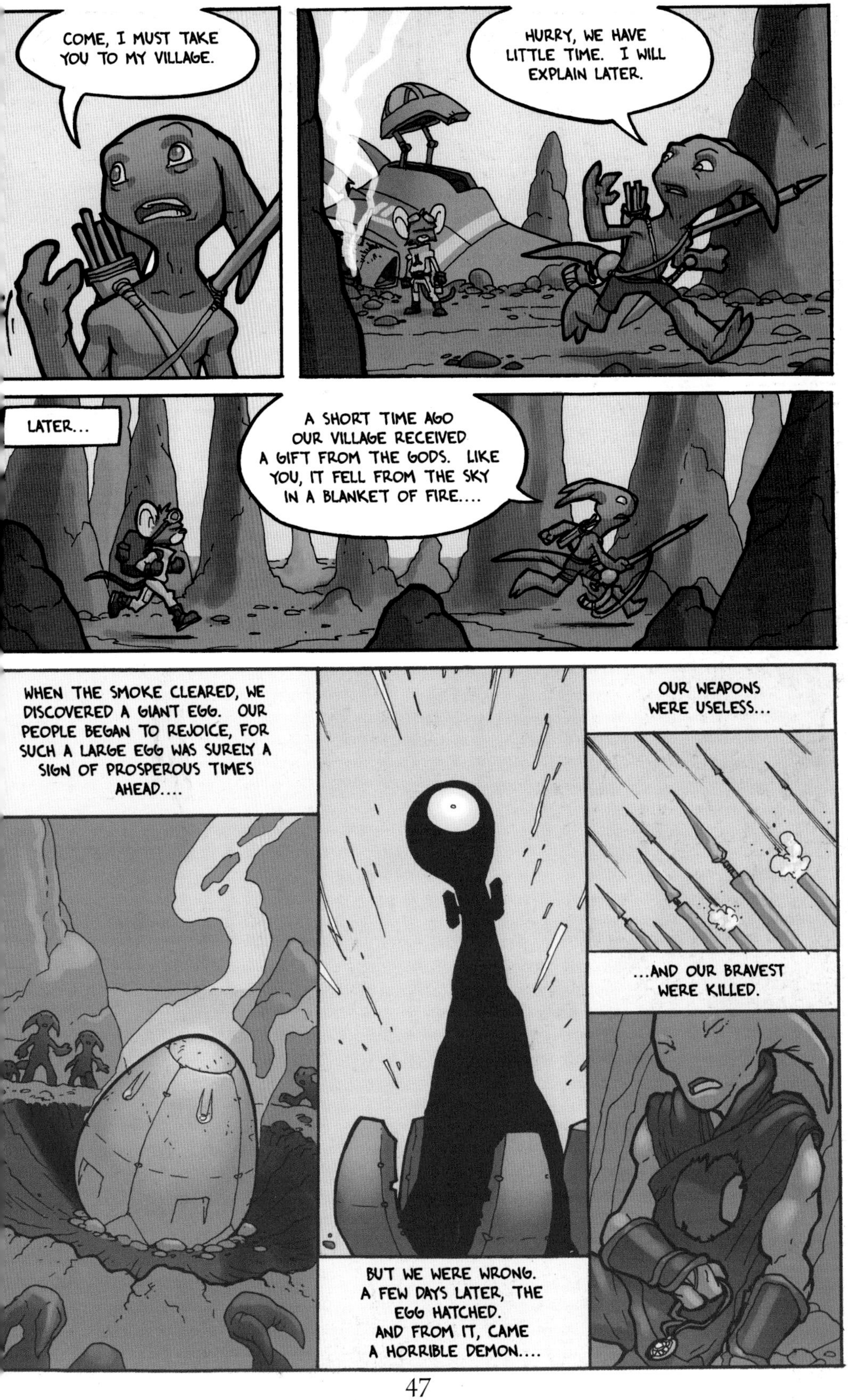
COME, I MUST TAKE YOU TO MY VILLAGE.
HURRY, WE HAVE LITTLE TIME. I WILL EXPLAIN LATER.
LATER...
A SHORT TIME AGO OUR VILLAGE RECEIVED A GIFT FROM THE GODS. LIKE YOU, IT FELL FROM THE SKY IN A BLANKET OF FIRE....
WHEN THE SMOKE CLEARED, WE DISCOVERED A GIANT EGG. OUR PEOPLE BEGAN TO REJOICE, FOR SUCH A LARGE EGG WAS SURELY A SIGN OF PROSPEROUS TIMES AHEAD....
BUT WE WERE WRONG. A FEW DAYS LATER, THE EGG HATCHED. AND FROM IT, CAME A HORRIBLE DEMON....
OUR WEAPONS WERE USELESS...
...AND OUR BRAVEST WERE KILLED.

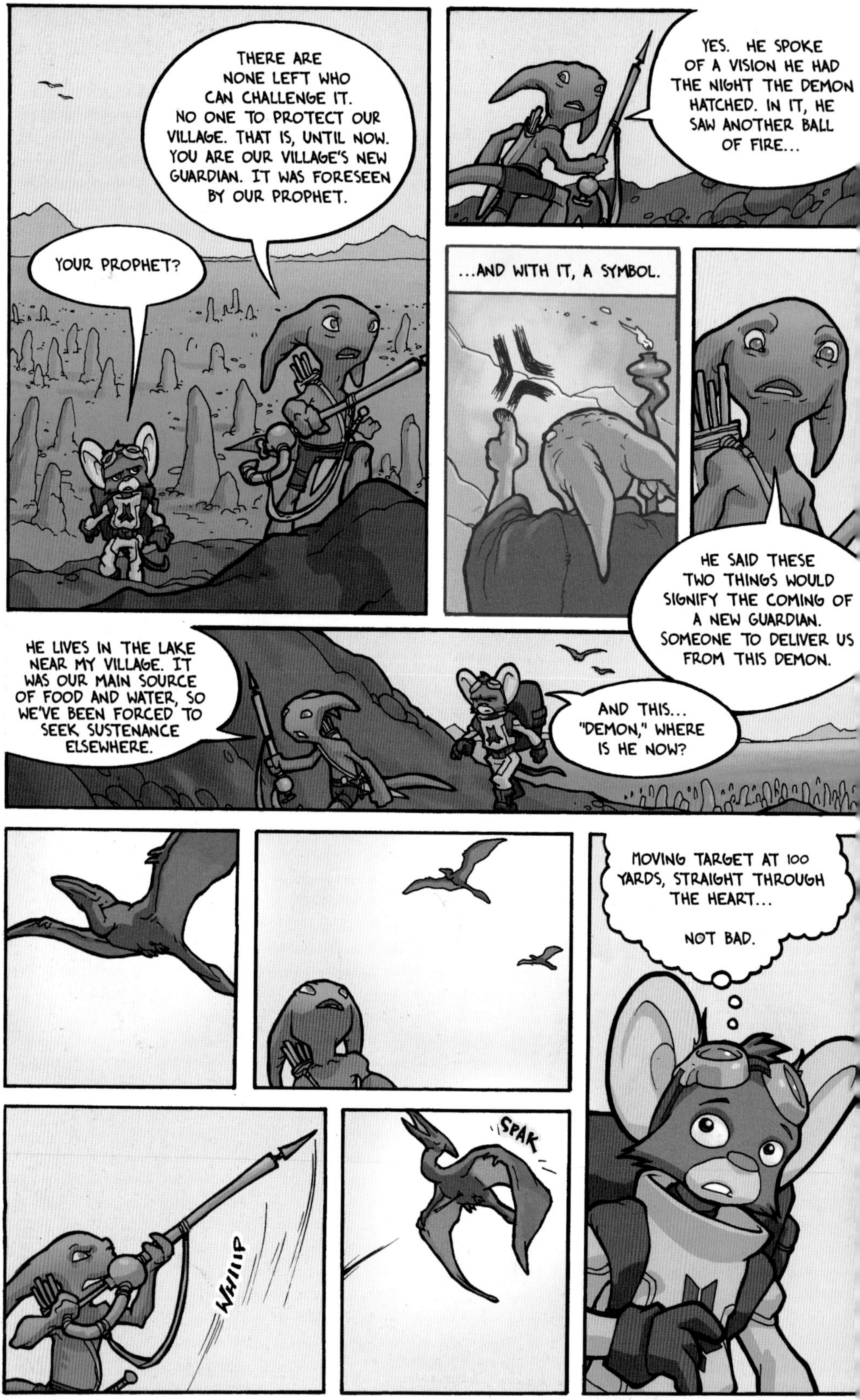
THERE ARE NONE LEFT WHO CAN CHALLENGE IT. NO ONE TO PROTECT OUR VILLAGE. THAT IS, UNTIL NOW. YOU ARE OUR VILLAGE'S NEW GUARDIAN. IT WAS FORESEEN BY OUR PROPHET.
YOUR PROPHET?
YES. HE SPOKE OF A VISION HE HAD THE NIGHT THE DEMON HATCHED. IN IT, HE SAW ANOTHER BALL OF FIRE...
...AND WITH IT, A SYMBOL.
HE SAID THESE TWO THINGS WOULD SIGNIFY THE COMING OF A NEW GUARDIAN. SOMEONE TO DELIVER US FROM THIS DEMON.
AND THIS... "DEMON," WHERE IS HE NOW?
HE LIVES IN THE LAKE NEAR MY VILLAGE. IT WAS OUR MAIN SOURCE OF FOOD AND WATER, SO WE'VE BEEN FORCED TO SEEK SUSTENANCE ELSEWHERE.
MOVING TARGET AT 100 YARDS, STRAIGHT THROUGH THE HEART...
NOT BAD.
WHIIIP
SPAK

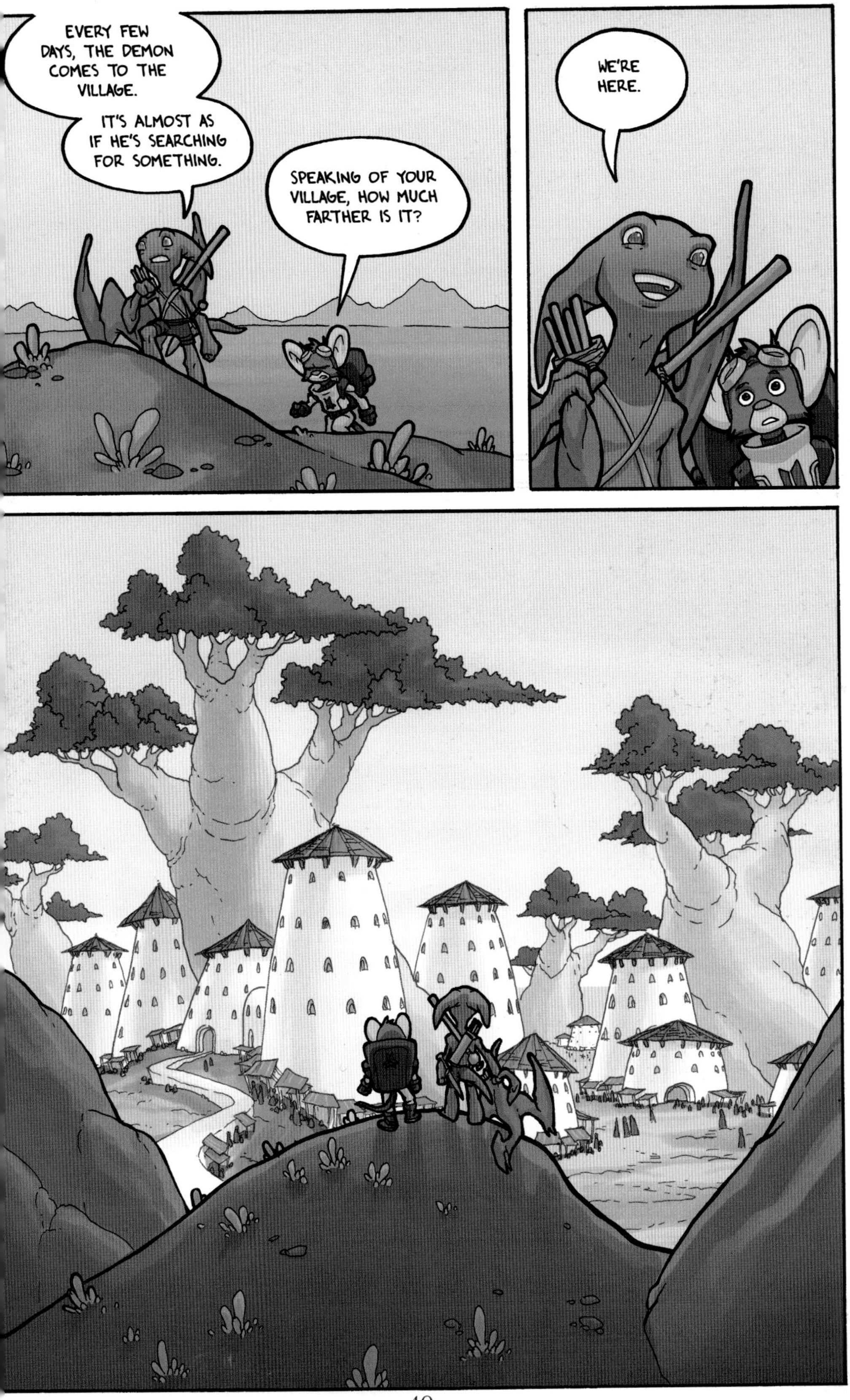

EVERY FEW DAYS, THE DEMON COMES TO THE VILLAGE.
IT'S ALMOST AS IF HE'S SEARCHING FOR SOMETHING.
SPEAKING OF YOUR VILLAGE, HOW MUCH FARTHER IS IT?
WE'RE HERE.

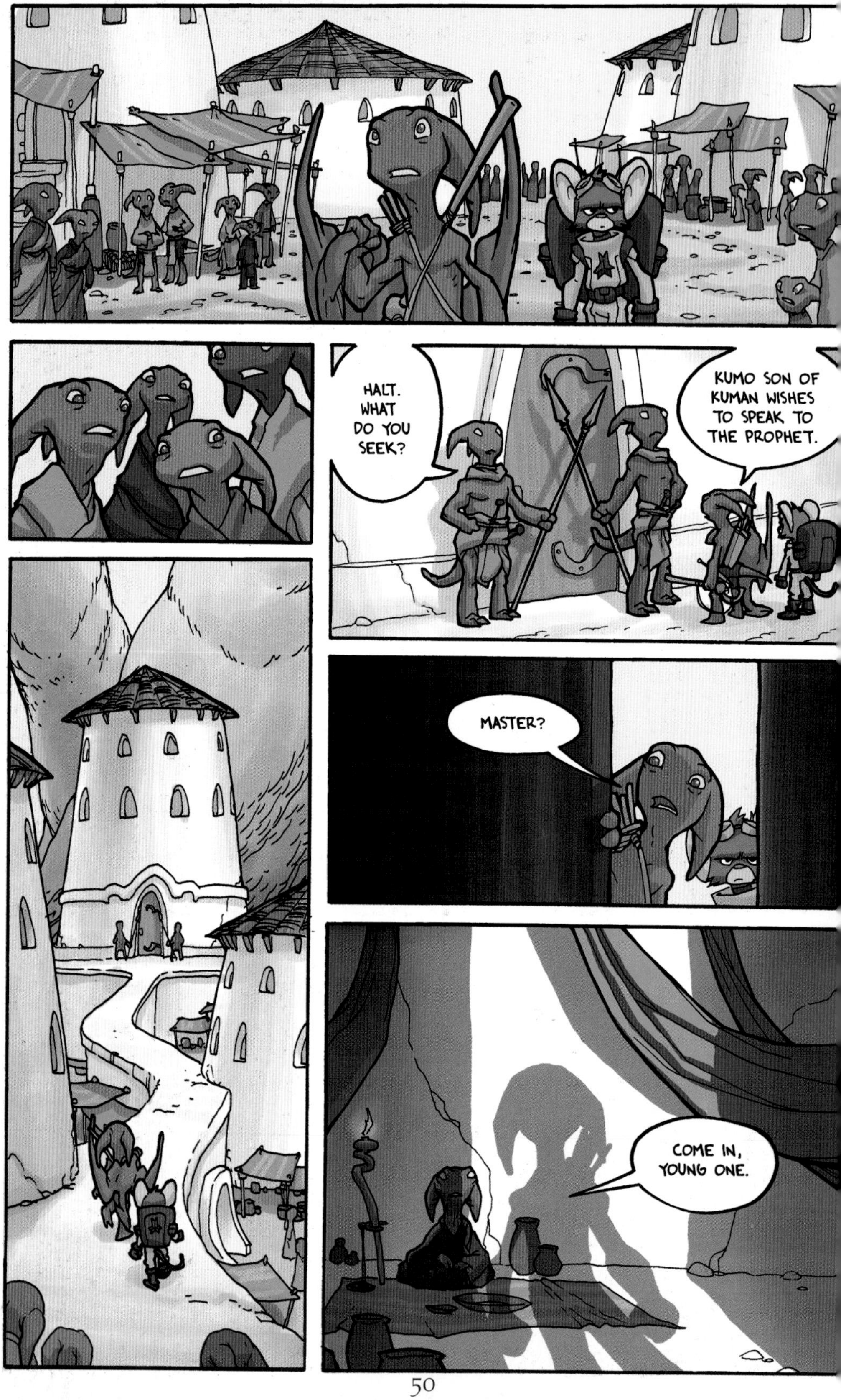
HALT. WHAT DO YOU SEEK?
KUMO SON OF KUMAN WISHES TO SPEAK TO THE PROPHET.
MASTER?
COME IN, YOUNG ONE.

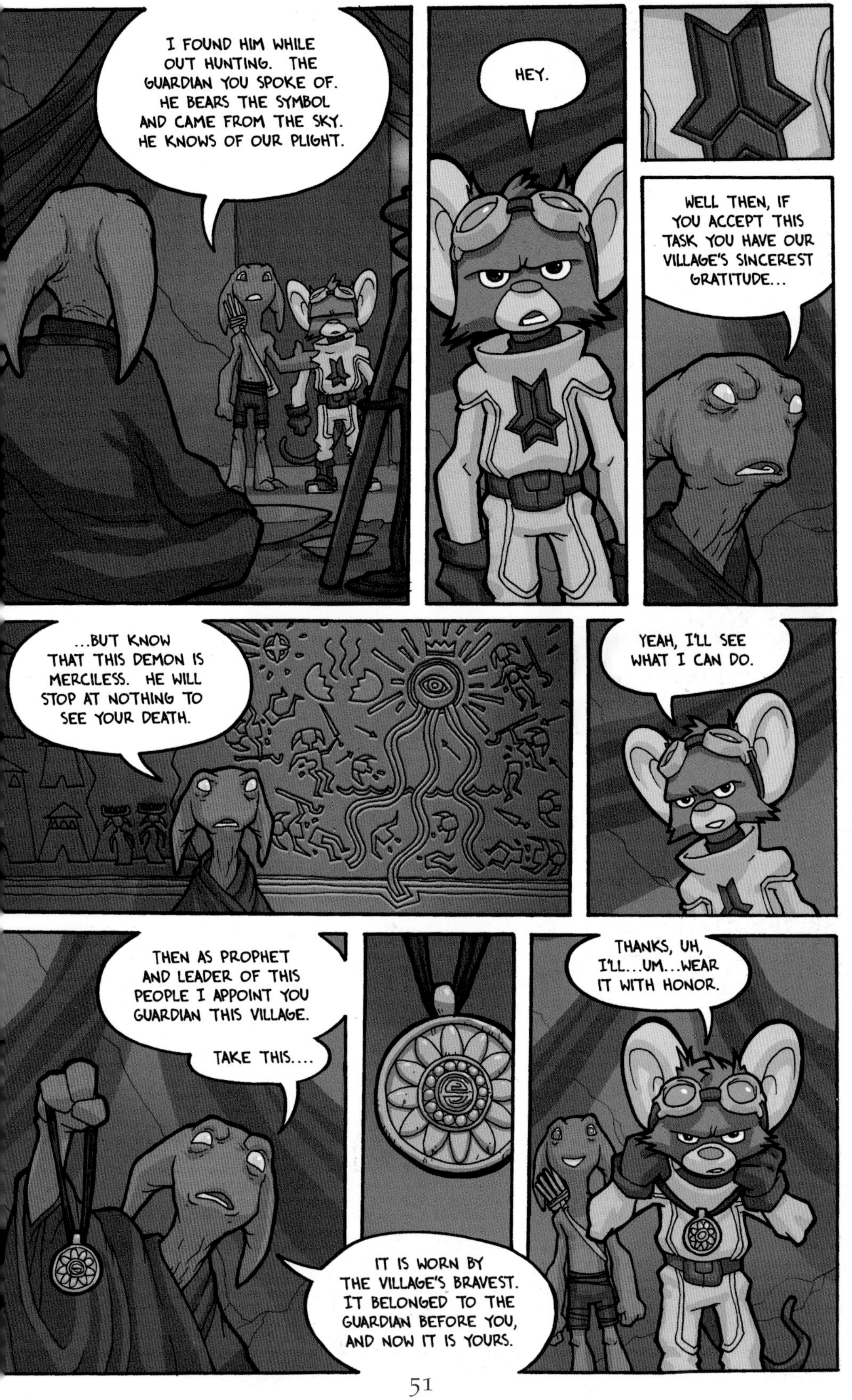
I FOUND HIM WHILE OUT HUNTING. THE GUARDIAN YOU SPOKE OF. HE BEARS THE SYMBOL AND CAME FROM THE SKY. HE KNOWS OF OUR PLIGHT.
HEY.
WELL THEN, IF YOU ACCEPT THIS TASK YOU HAVE OUR VILLAGE'S SINCEREST GRATITUDE...
...BUT KNOW THAT THIS DEMON IS MERCILESS. HE WILL STOP AT NOTHING TO SEE YOUR DEATH.
YEAH, I'LL SEE WHAT I CAN DO.
THEN AS PROPHET AND LEADER OF THIS PEOPLE I APPOINT YOU GUARDIAN THIS VILLAGE.
TAKE THIS....
IT IS WORN BY THE VILLAGE'S BRAVEST. IT BELONGED TO THE GUARDIAN BEFORE YOU, AND NOW IT IS YOURS.
THANKS, UH, I'LL...UM...WEAR IT WITH HONOR.

THAT NIGHT...

IRG HQ, DO YOU COPY?

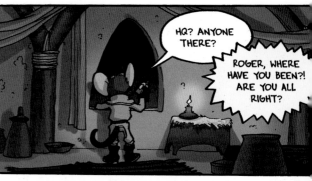

HQ? ANYONE THERE?

ROGER, WHERE HAVE YOU BEEN?! ARE YOU ALL RIGHT?

I'M FINE. LISTEN, I THINK I KNOW WHAT BOOBY-TRAPPED AND DESTROYED OUR RECON-SAT.

I'VE ESTABLISHED CONTACT WITH SOME LOCALS HERE, WHO ARE HAVING PROBLEMS WITH A "DEMON."

FROM THEIR CRUDE PAINTINGS IT LOOKS LIKE THEY HAVE A CCD* LURKING AROUND HERE.

A CCD? SURE ENOUGH, OUR CHARTS INDICATE A CEPHOLODIAN FRIGATE WAS SPOTTED IN THE T-13 QUADRANT TWO WEEKS AGO.... ALL RIGHT THEN, DO WHAT YOU MUST TO ELIMINATE THAT THING, AND THEN GET BACK HERE STAT. WE'VE GOT A KARCHARIAN SITUATION BREWING.

ROGER THAT, MM OUT.

ALL RIGHT BOYS, WE'VE GOT A JOB TO DO.

* CEPHOLODIAN COMMANDO DROID

52

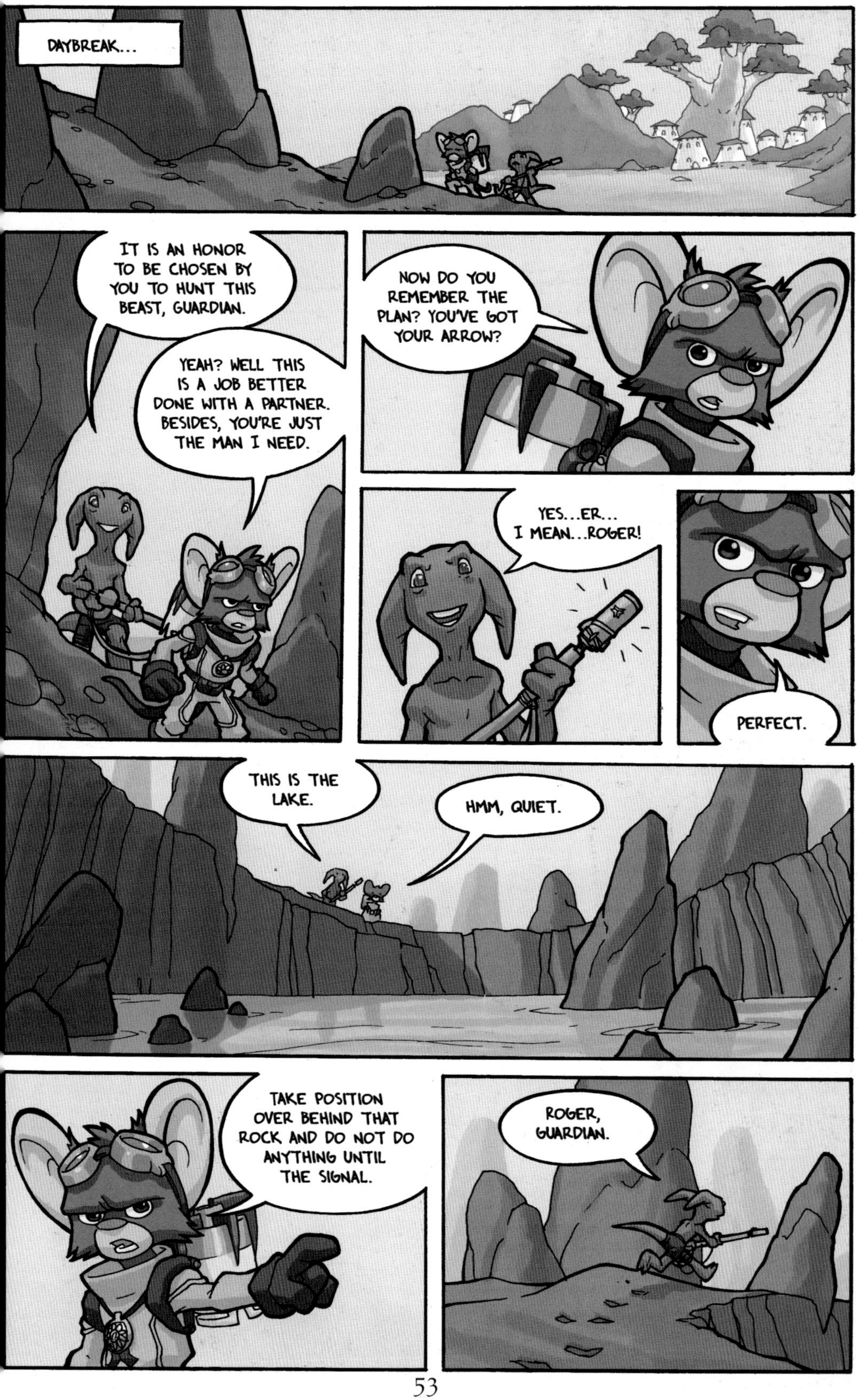
DAYBREAK...
IT IS AN HONOR TO BE CHOSEN BY YOU TO HUNT THIS BEAST, GUARDIAN.
YEAH? WELL THIS IS A JOB BETTER DONE WITH A PARTNER. BESIDES, YOU'RE JUST THE MAN I NEED.
NOW DO YOU REMEMBER THE PLAN? YOU'VE GOT YOUR ARROW?
YES...ER... I MEAN...ROGER!
PERFECT.
THIS IS THE LAKE.
HMM, QUIET.
TAKE POSITION OVER BEHIND THAT ROCK AND DO NOT DO ANYTHING UNTIL THE SIGNAL.
ROGER, GUARDIAN.

KNOCK KNOCK, ANYBODY HOME?

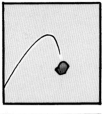

PLOOP

YOU SURE THIS IS THE RIGHT LAKE?

WELL, LET'S KNOCK A LITTLE LOUDER THEN....

CHACK!

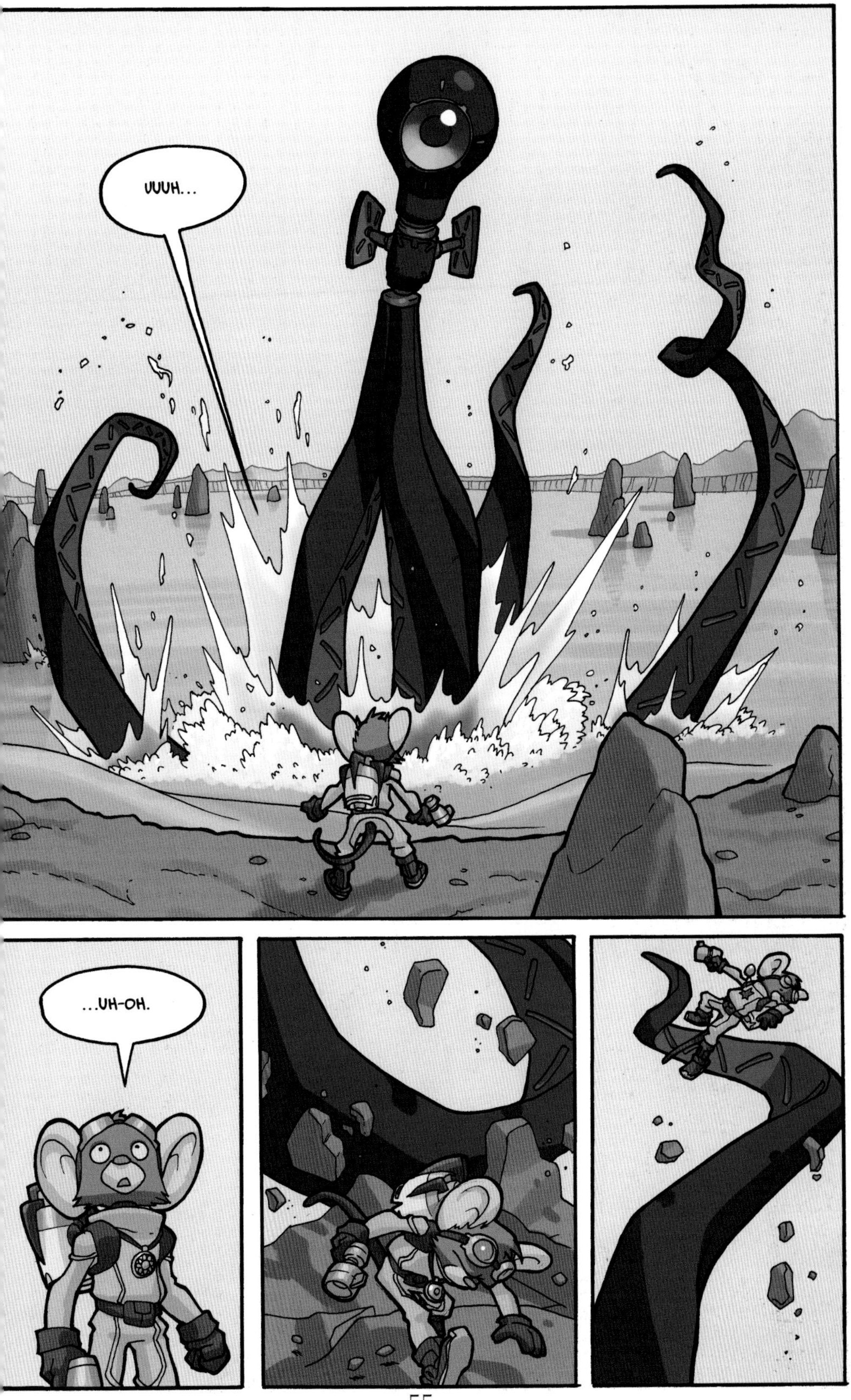
UUUH...
...UH-OH.

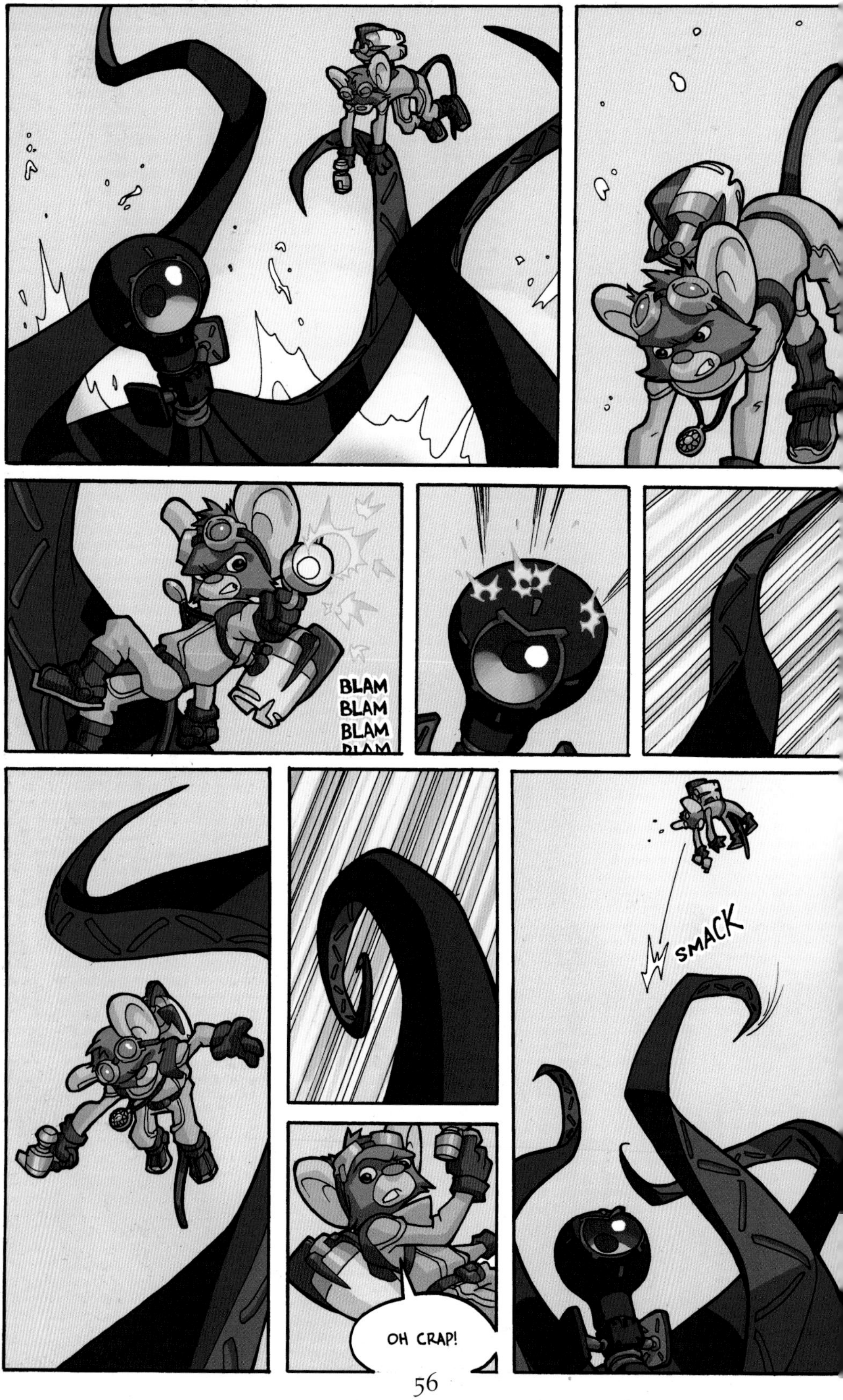
BLAM
BLAM
BLAM
BLAM
SMACK
OH CRAP!

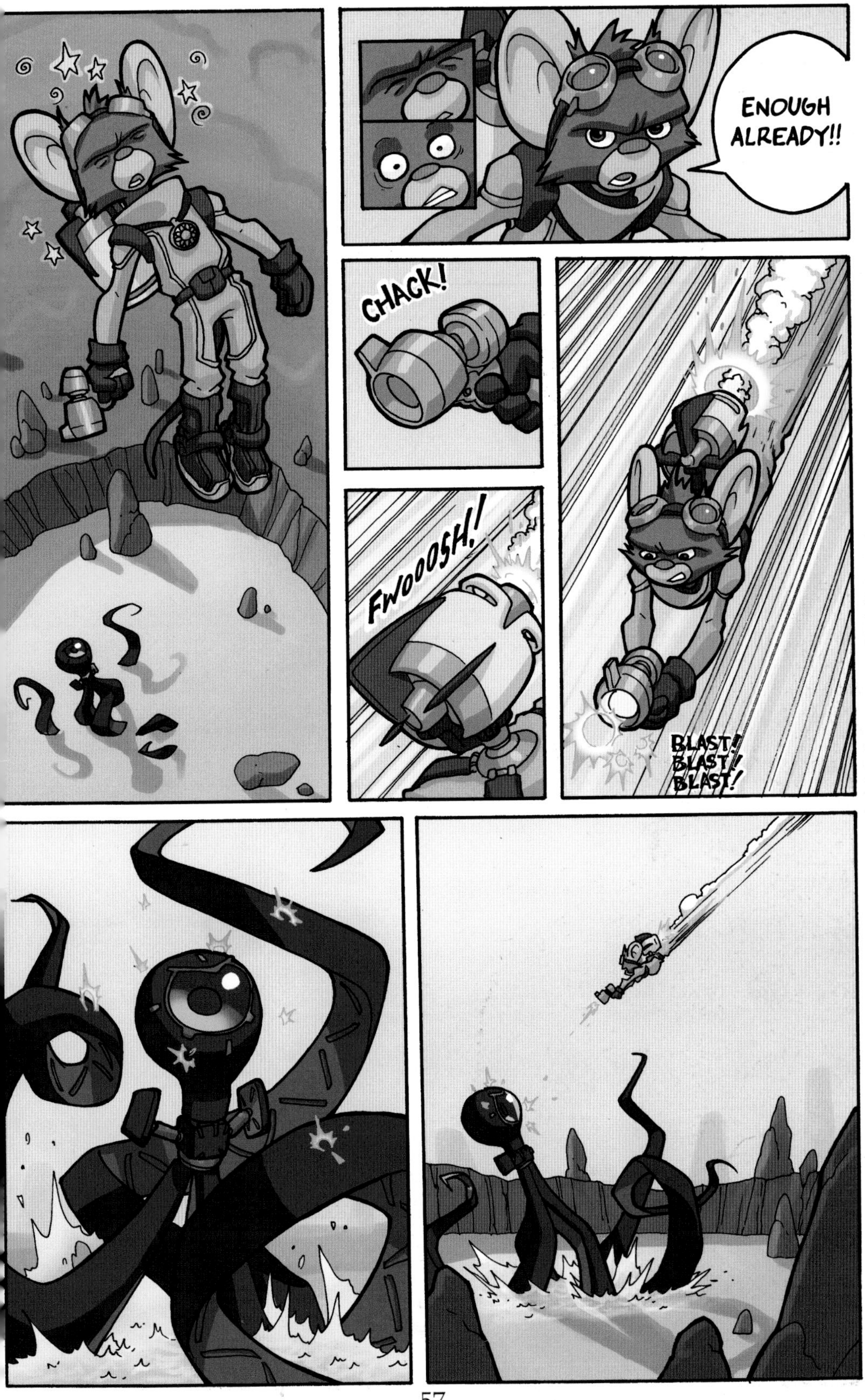
ENOUGH ALREADY!!
CHACK!
FWOOOSH!
BLAST!
BLAST!
BLAST!

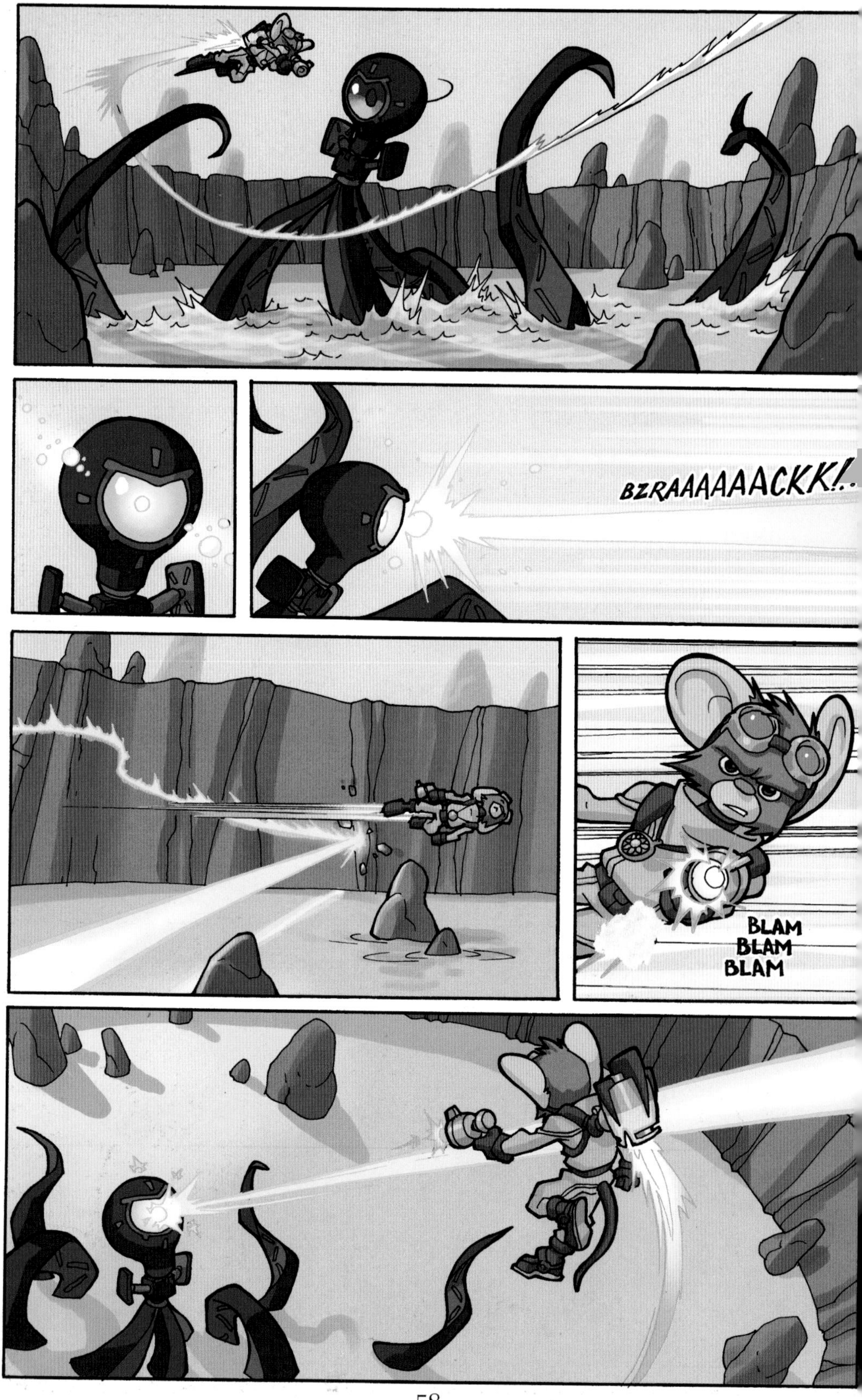
BZRAAAAAACKK!..
BLAM
BLAM
BLAM

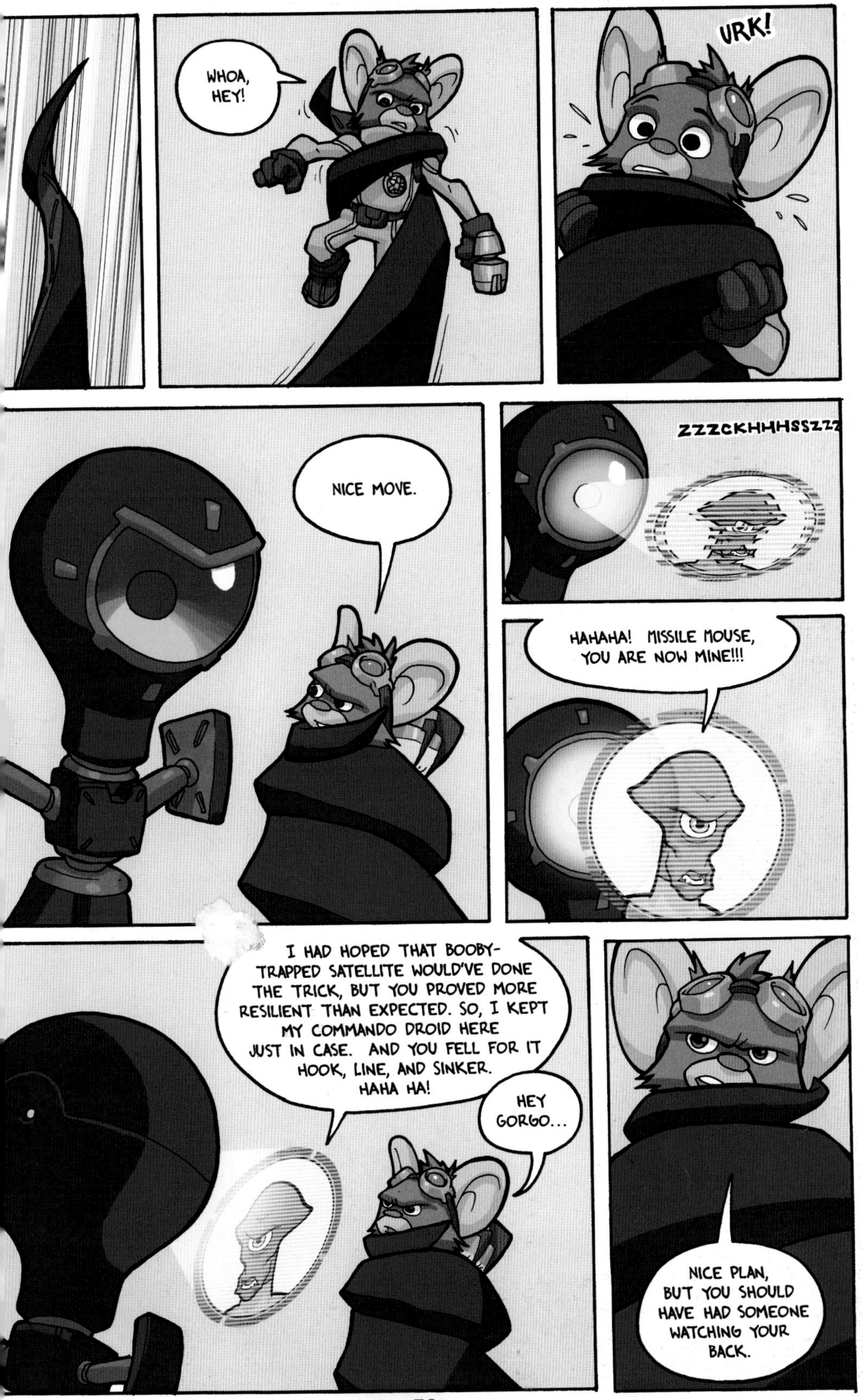
WHOA, HEY!
URK!
NICE MOVE.
ZZZCKHHHSSZZZ
HAHAHA! MISSILE MOUSE, YOU ARE NOW MINE!!!
I HAD HOPED THAT BOOBY-TRAPPED SATELLITE WOULD'VE DONE THE TRICK, BUT YOU PROVED MORE RESILIENT THAN EXPECTED. SO, I KEPT MY COMMANDO DROID HERE JUST IN CASE. AND YOU FELL FOR IT HOOK, LINE, AND SINKER. HAHA HA!
HEY GORGO...
NICE PLAN, BUT YOU SHOULD HAVE HAD SOMEONE WATCHING YOUR BACK.

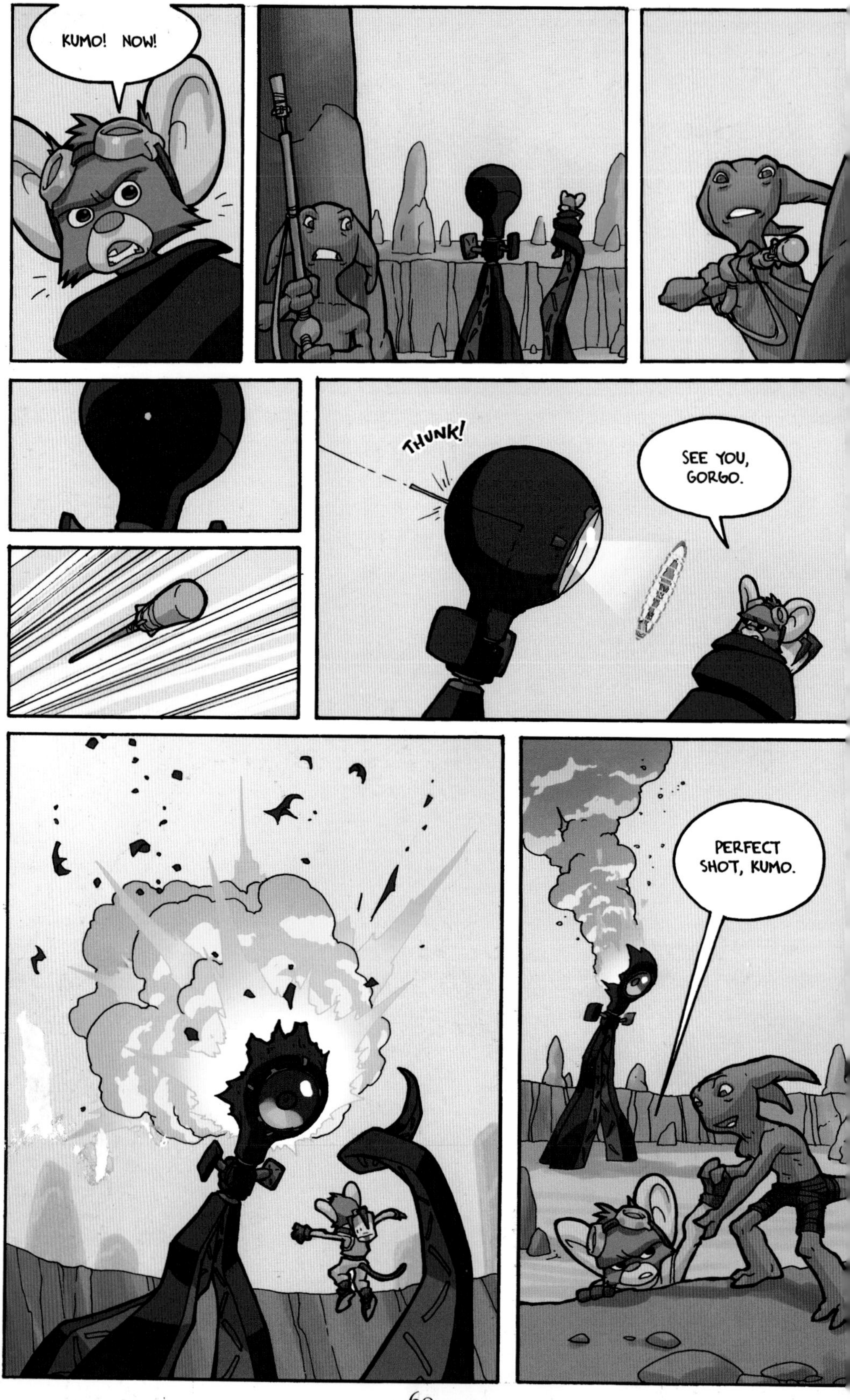
KUMO! NOW!
THUNK!
SEE YOU, GORGO.
PERFECT SHOT, KUMO.

LATER THAT DAY...

FAREWELL. WE ARE FOREVER IN YOUR DEBT.

GLAD I COULD HELP. AND THANKS AGAIN FOR THE PROVISIONS.

PROPHET, WHO WILL PROTECT OUR VILLAGE NOW? WE ARE LEFT VULNERABLE AGAIN.

BEFORE HE LEFT HE TOLD ME HOW THE DEMON WAS DESTROYED. IT WAS NOT ALL HIS DOING.

HE ALSO GAVE ME THIS, TO PASS ON TO YOU

YOU HAVE PROVEN YOURSELF WORTHY TO PROTECT THIS VILLAGE.

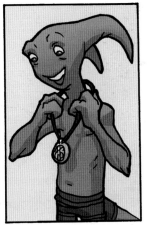

SPECIAL THANKS TO TOM SAVILLE

THE END

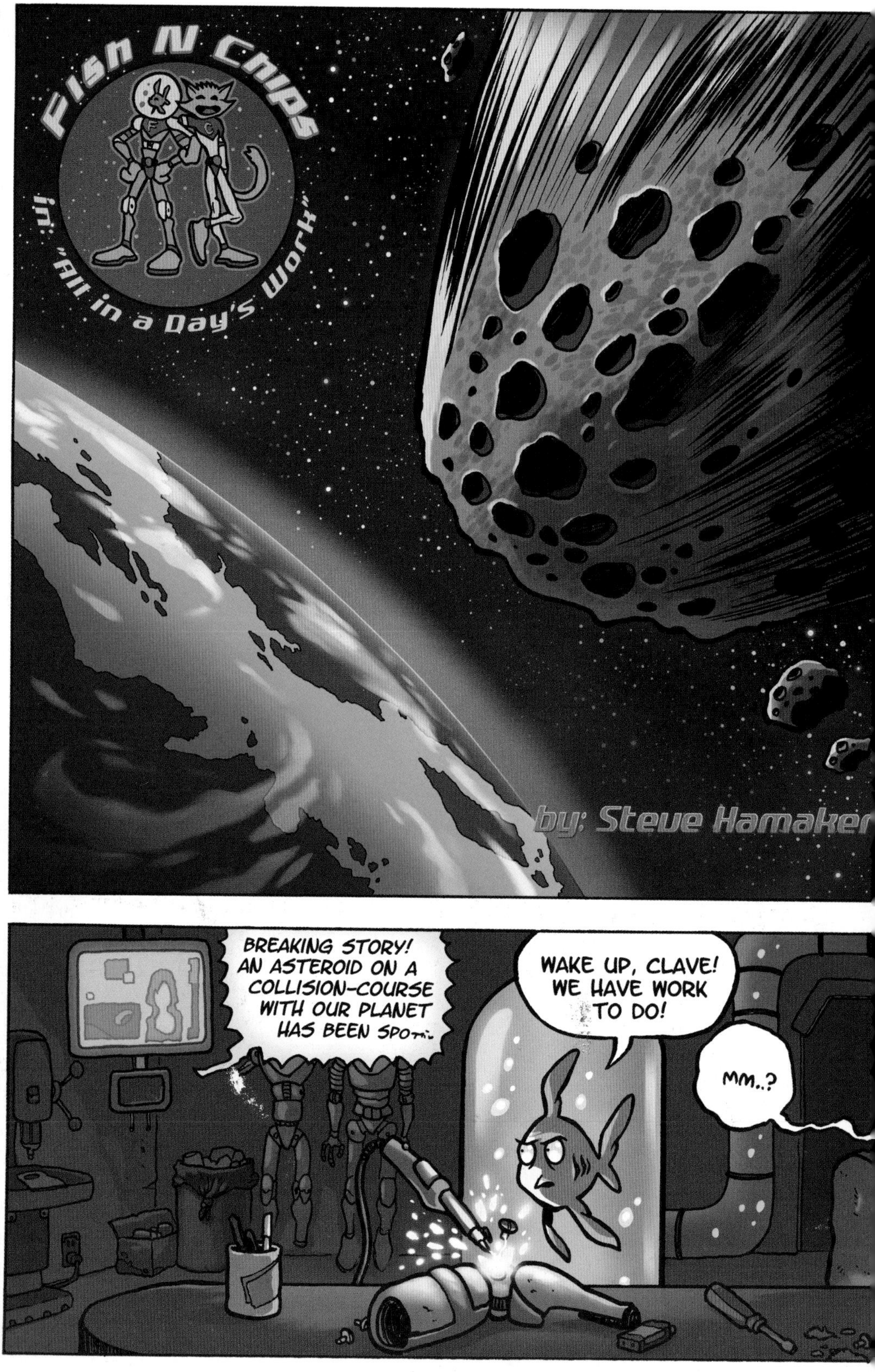
Fish N Chips
in: "All in a Day's Work"
by: Steve Hamaker
BREAKING STORY! AN ASTEROID ON A COLLISION-COURSE WITH OUR PLANET HAS BEEN SPO
WAKE UP, CLAVE! WE HAVE WORK TO DO!
MM..?

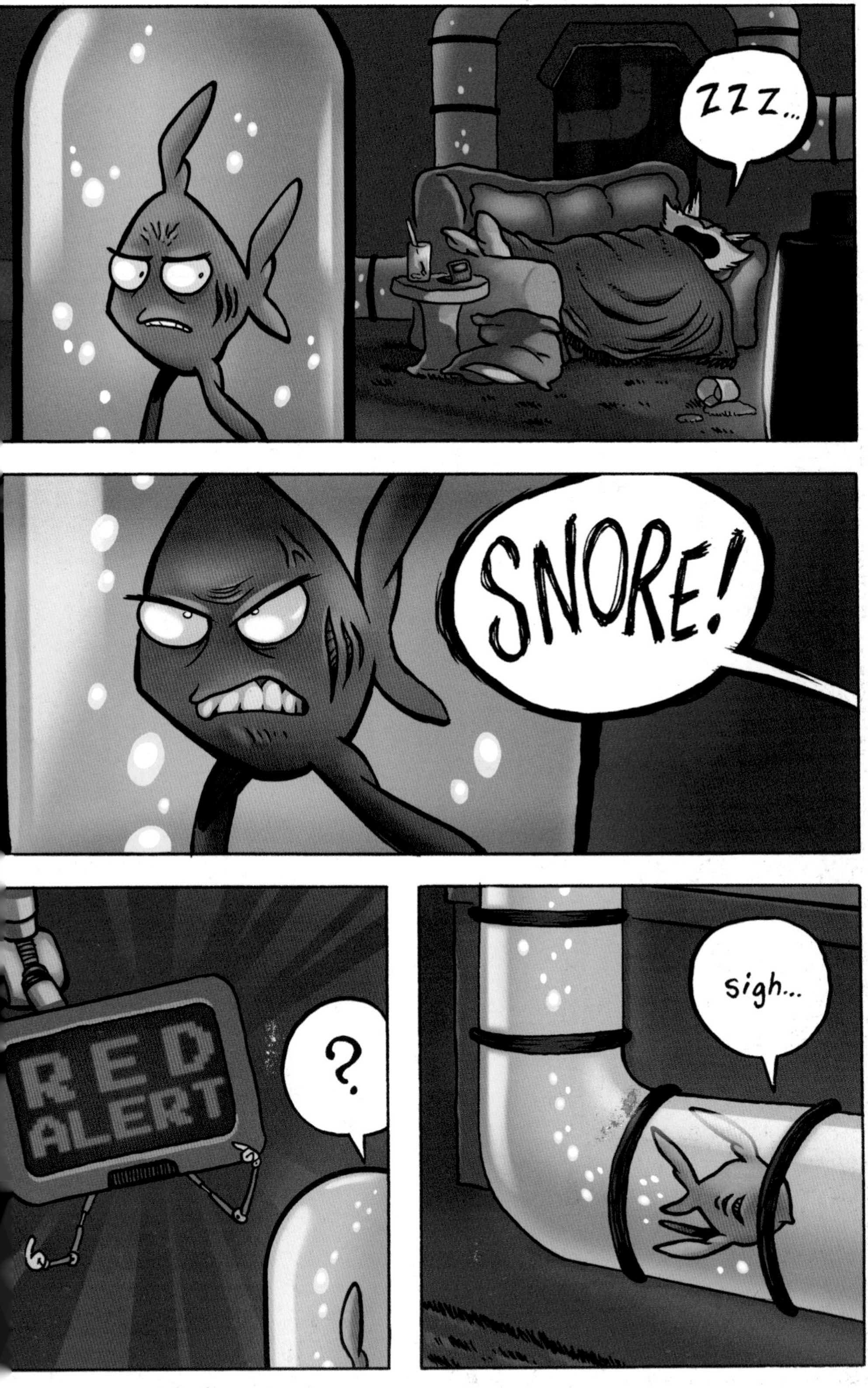
ZZZ...
SNORE!
RED ALERT
?
sigh...

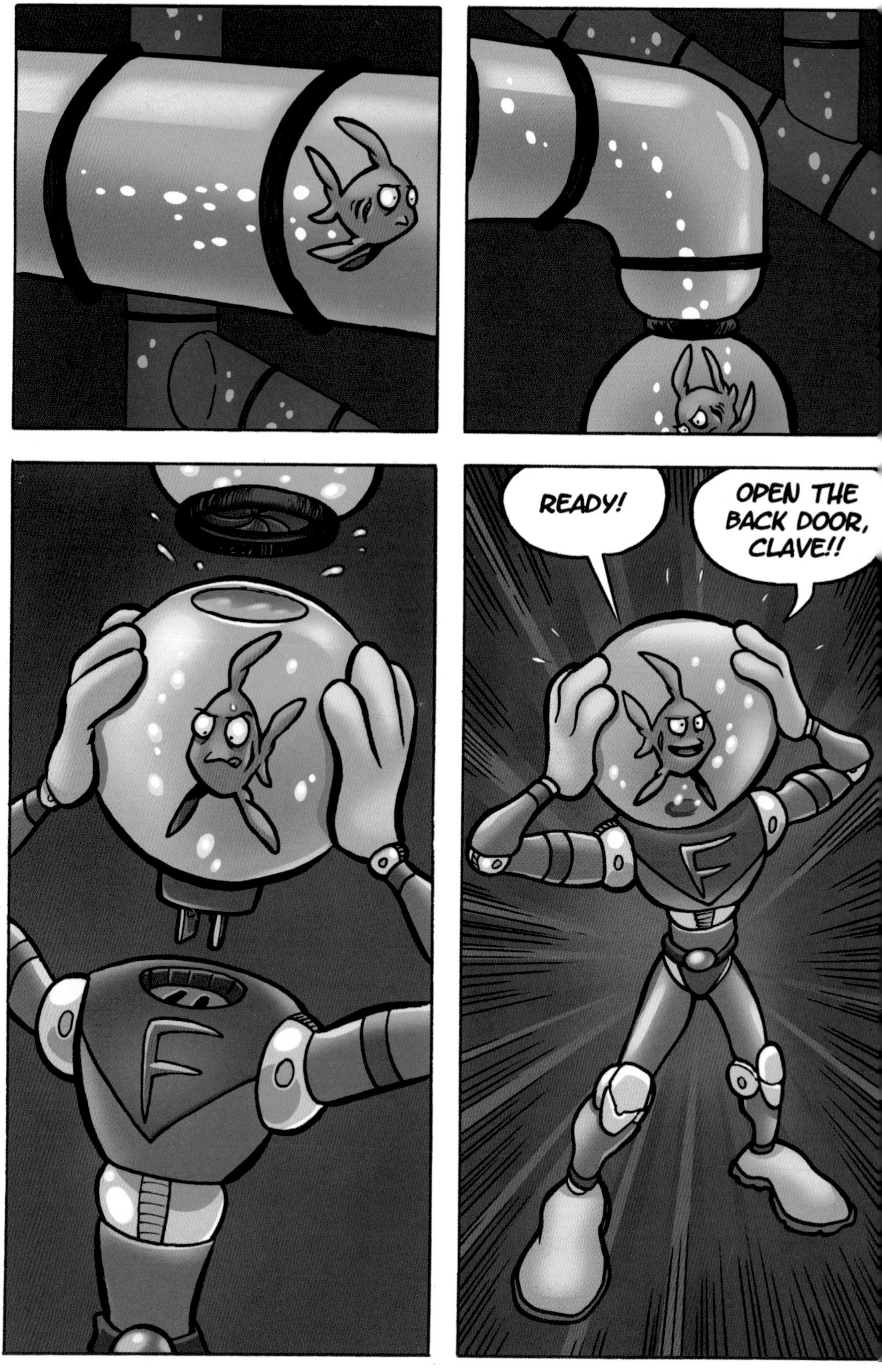
READY!
OPEN THE BACK DOOR, CLAVE!!

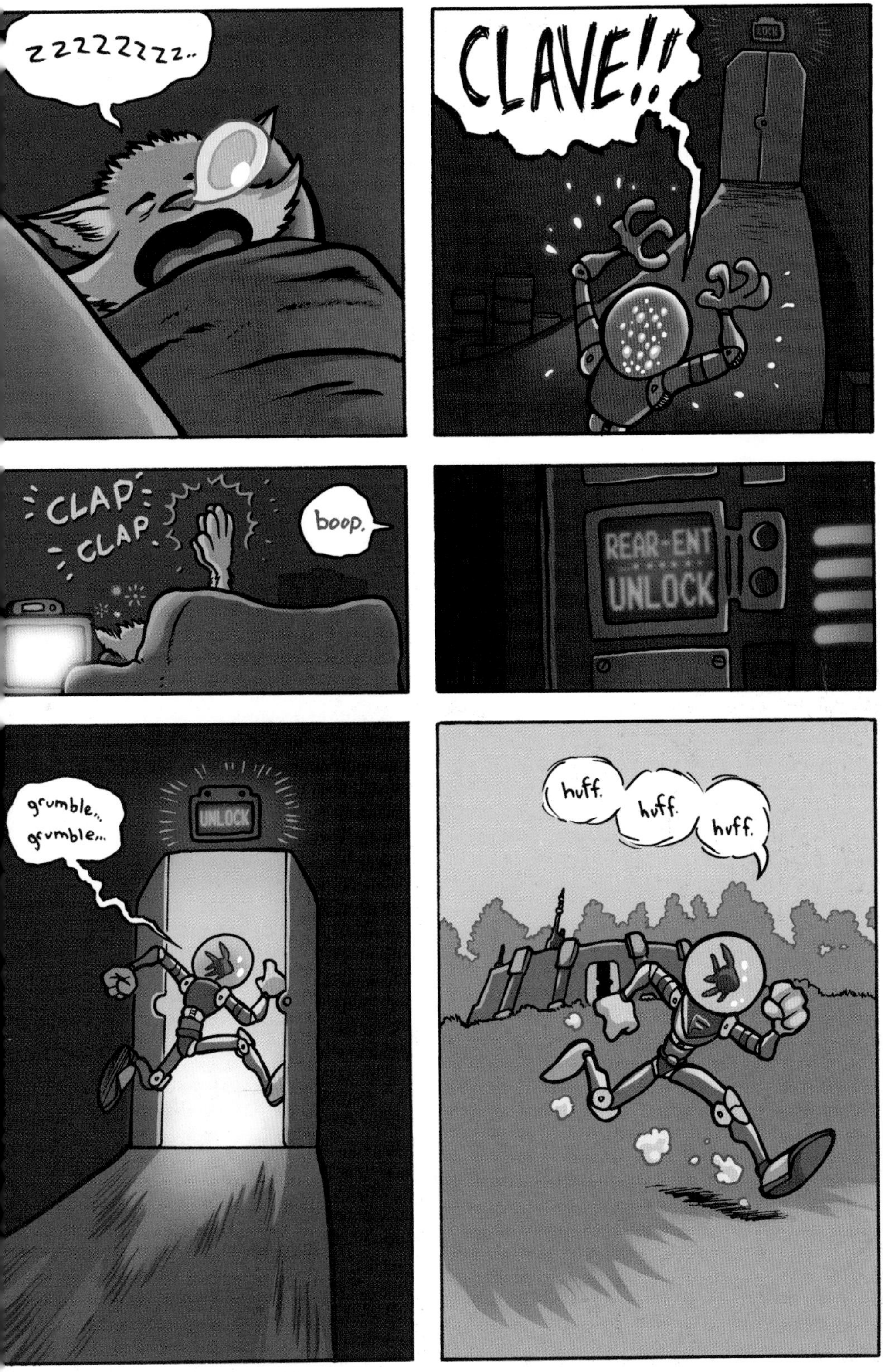

zzzzzzzz..
CLAVE!!
CLAP
CLAP
boop.
REAR-ENT
UNLOCK
grumble...
grumble...
UNLOCK
huff.
huff.
huff.

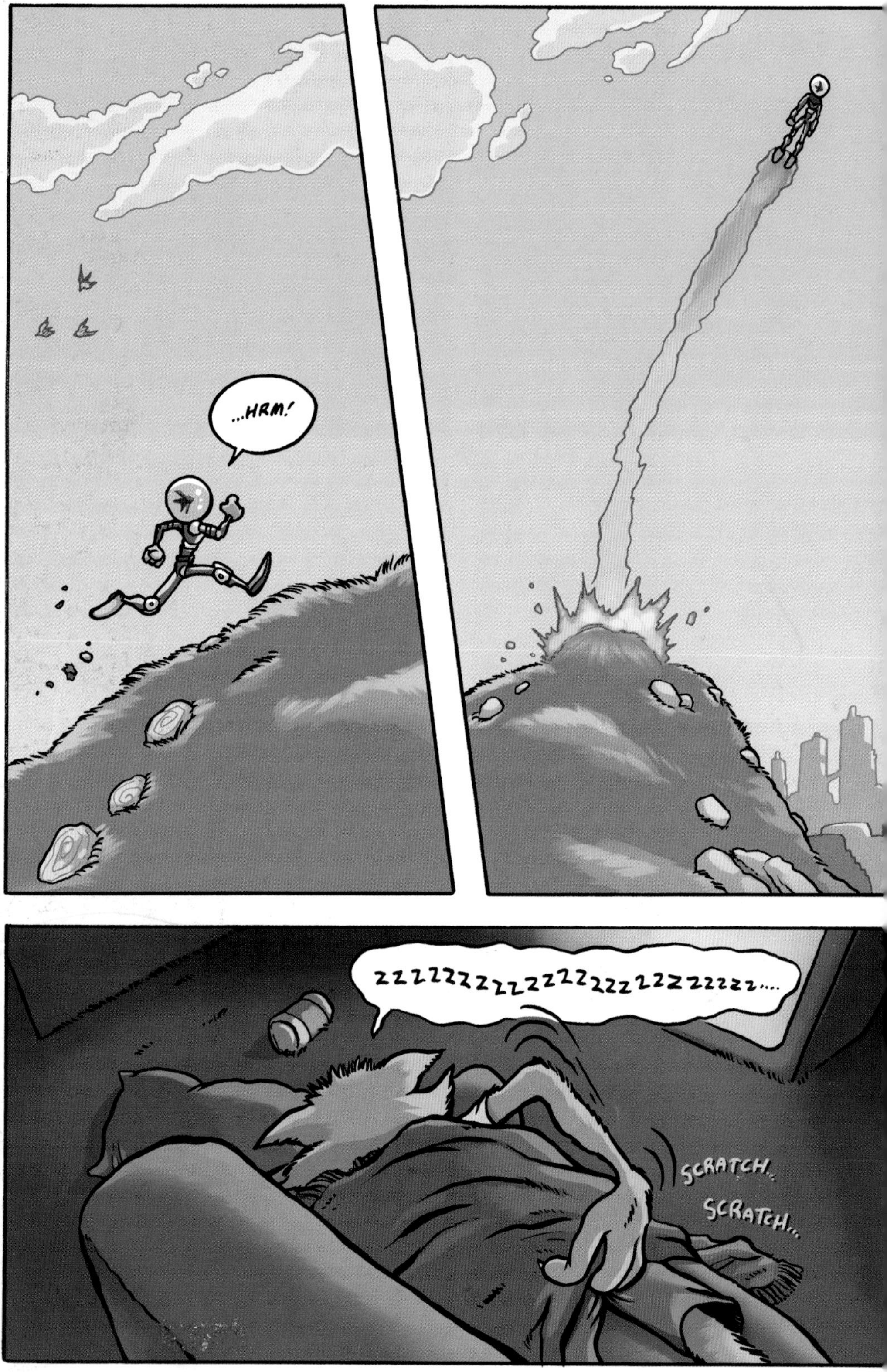
...HRM!
ZZZZZZZZZZZZZZZZZZZZZZZZ....
SCRATCH...
SCRATCH...

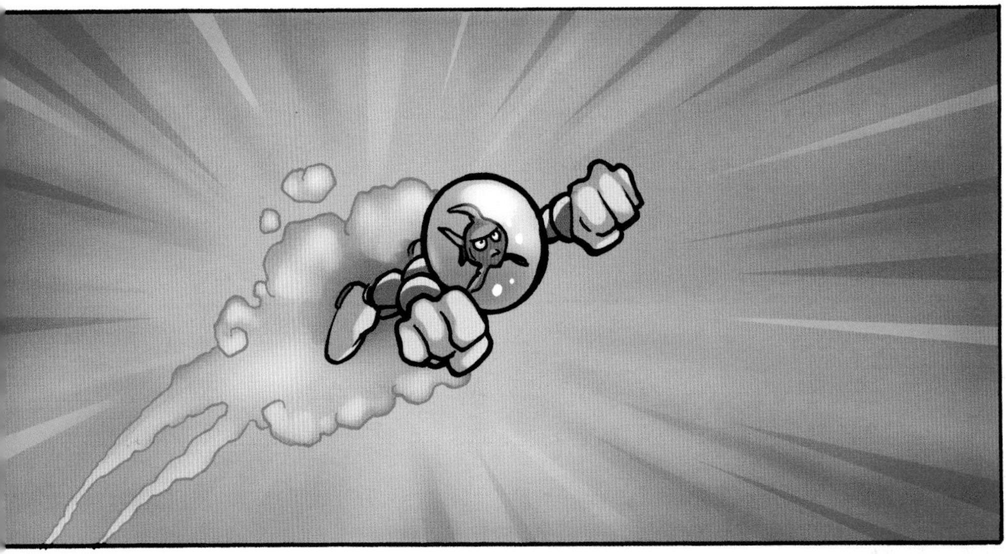

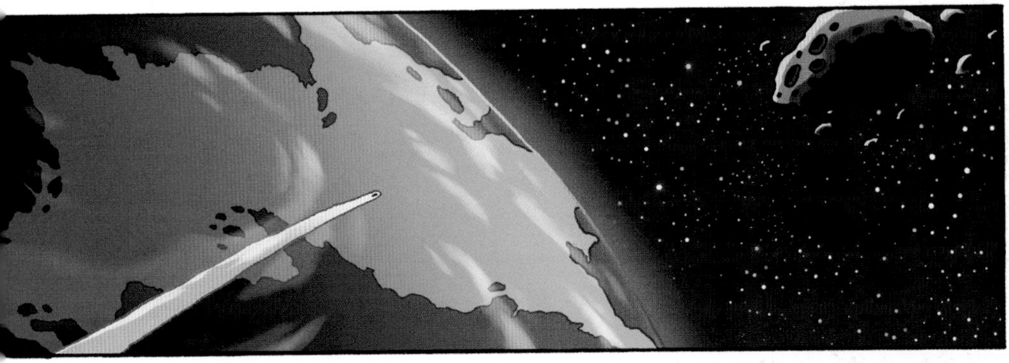

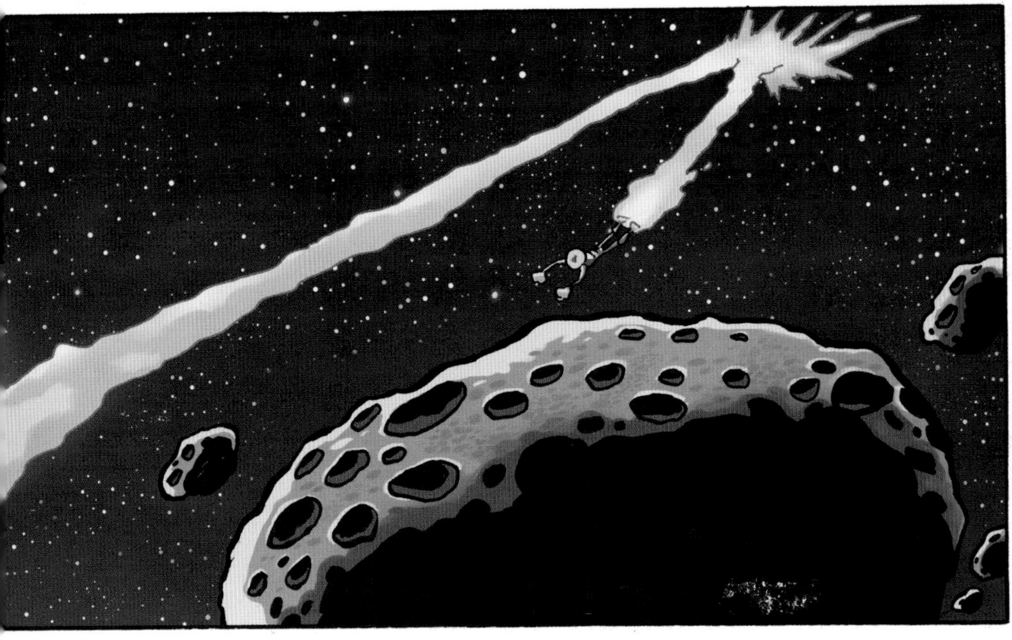

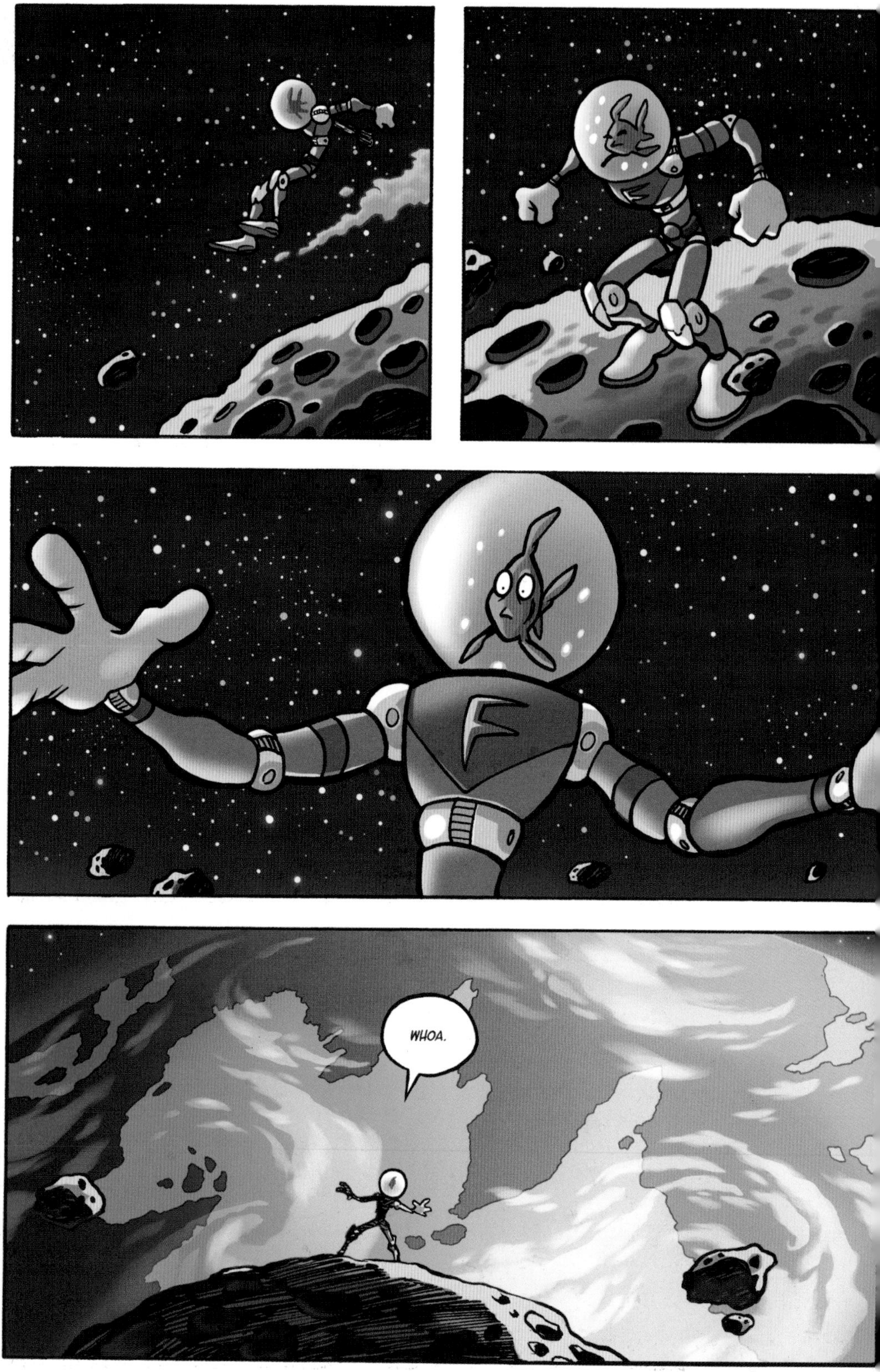
WHOA.

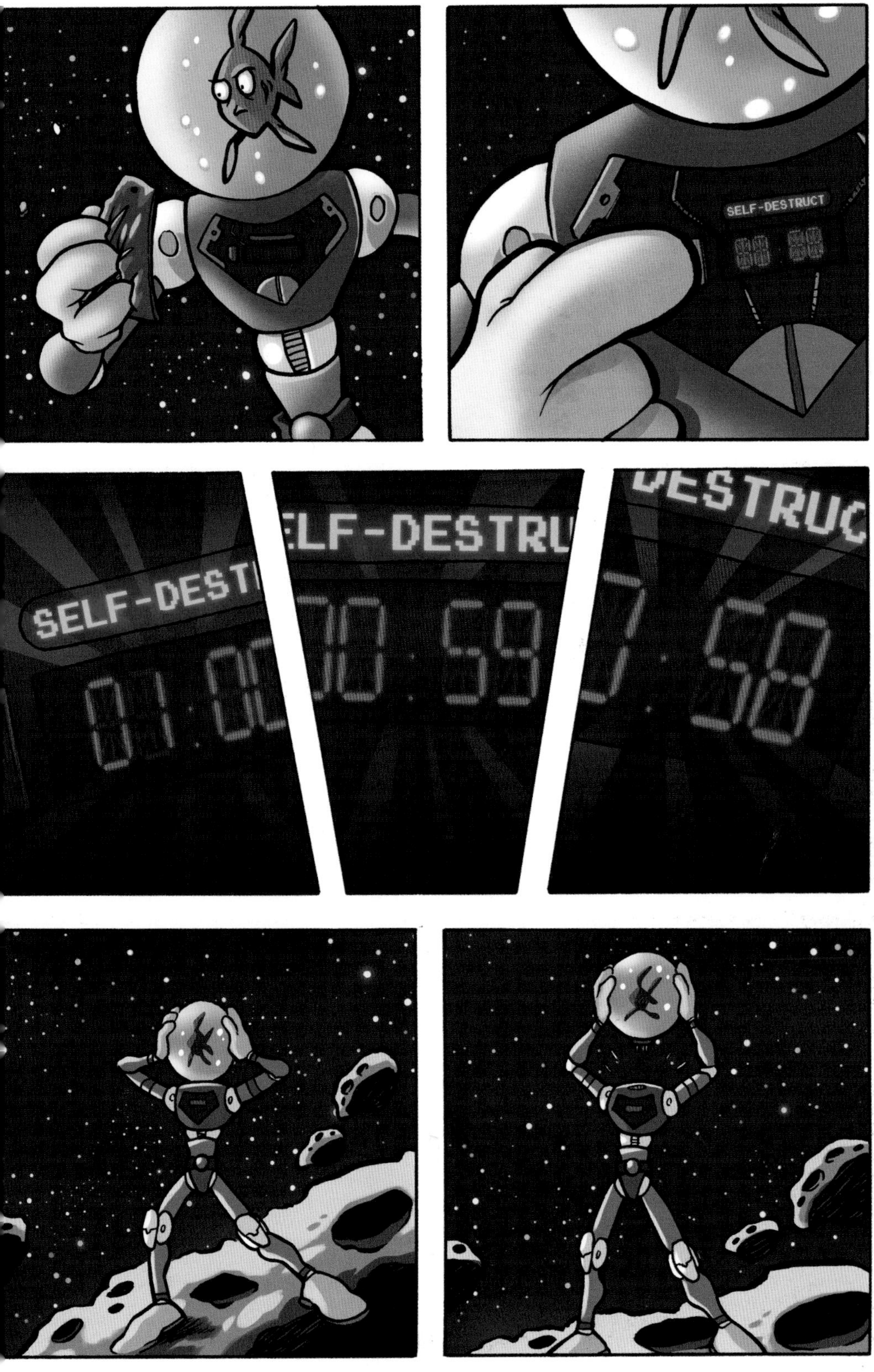
SELF-DESTRUCT
SELF-DEST
01 00
ELF-DESTRU
00 59
DESTRUC
58

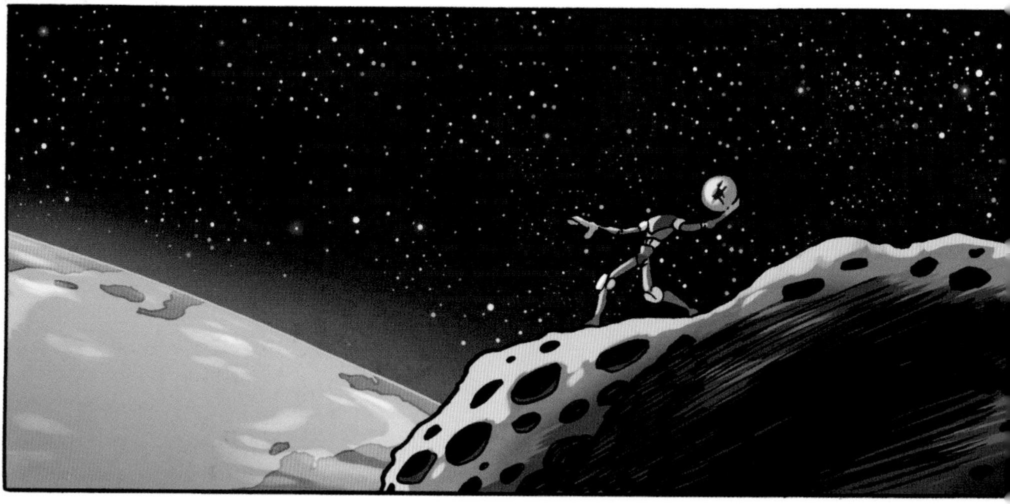

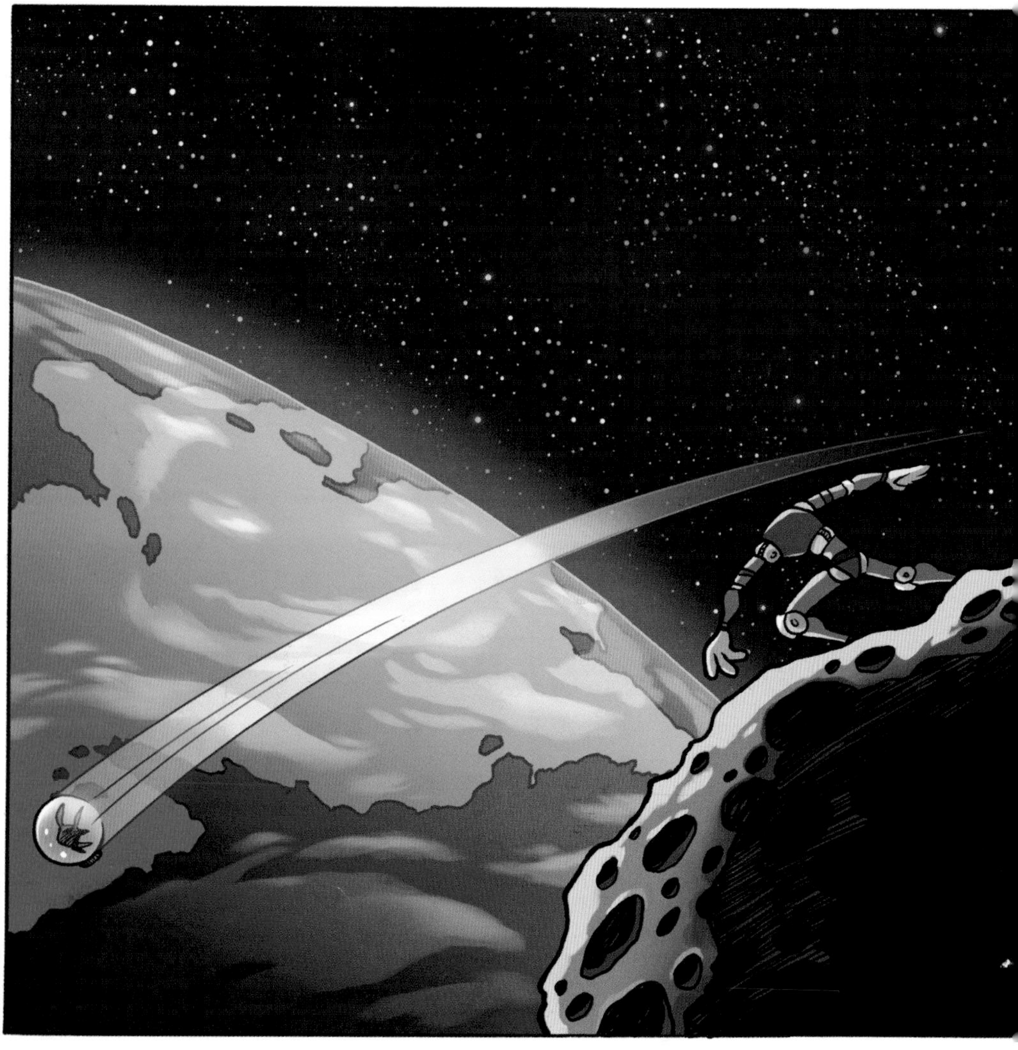

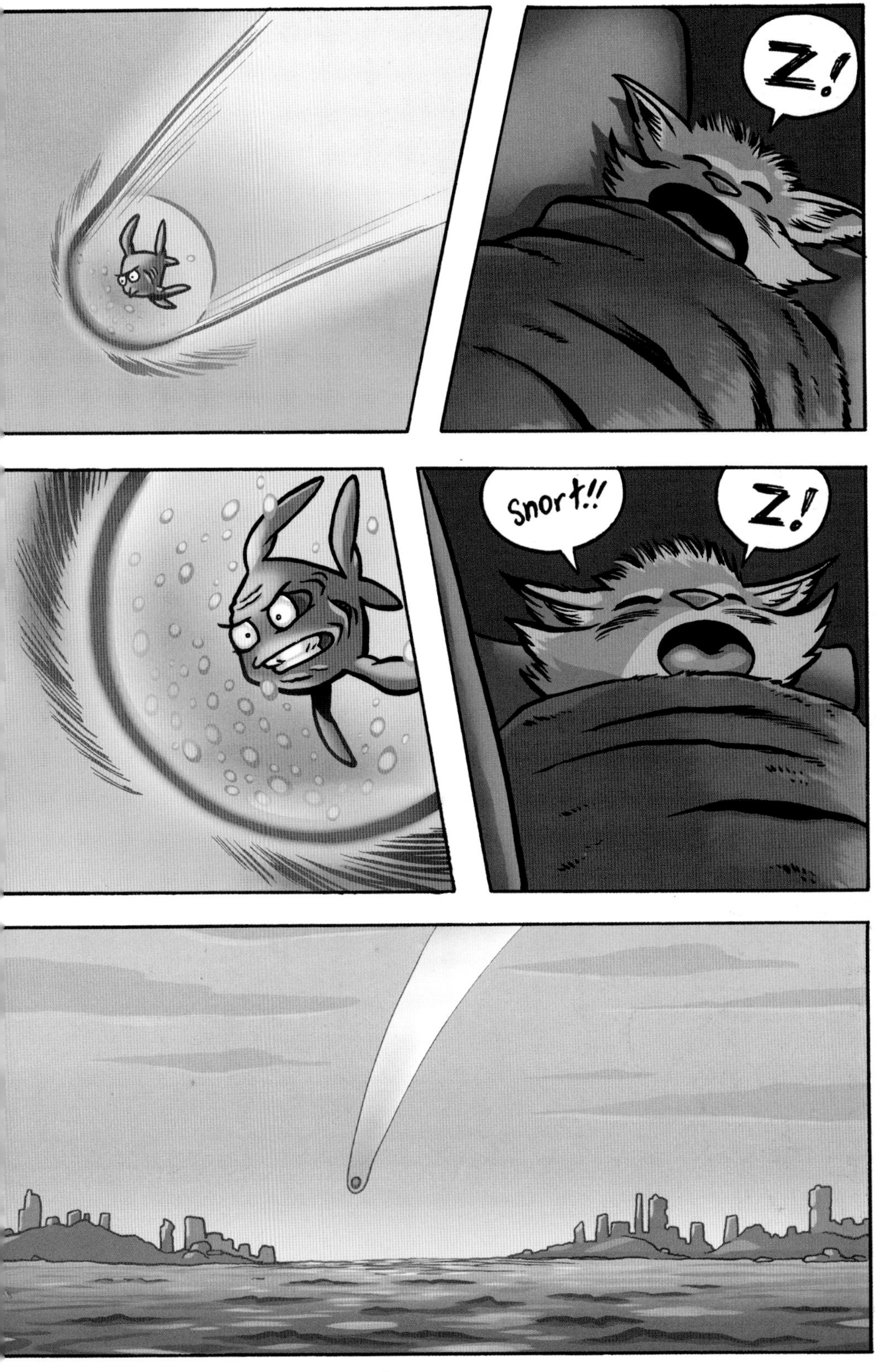
Z!
Snort!!
Z!

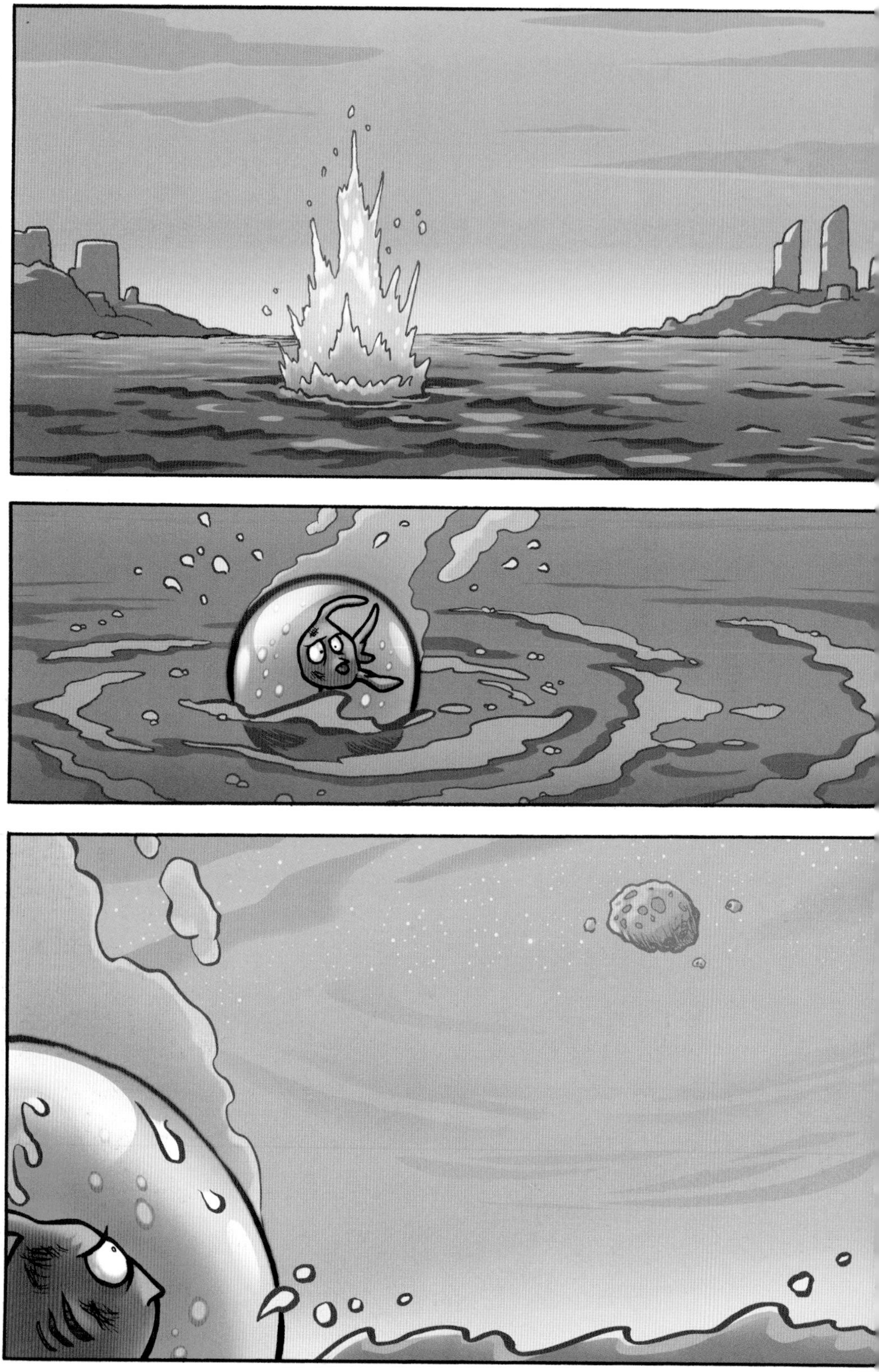

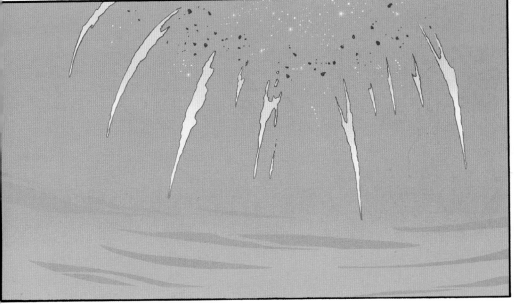

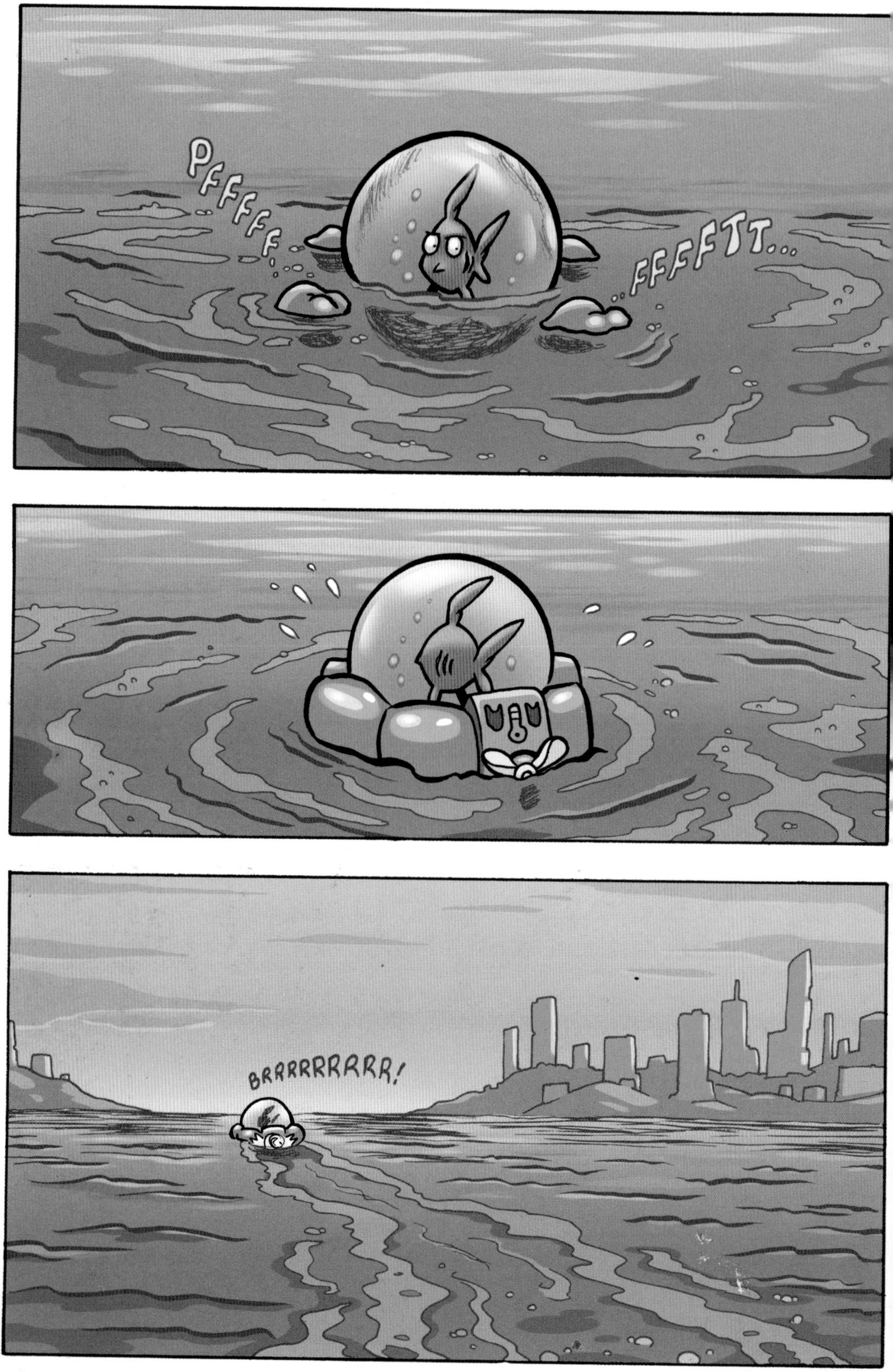
PFFFFF
FFFFTT...
BRRRRRRRRR!

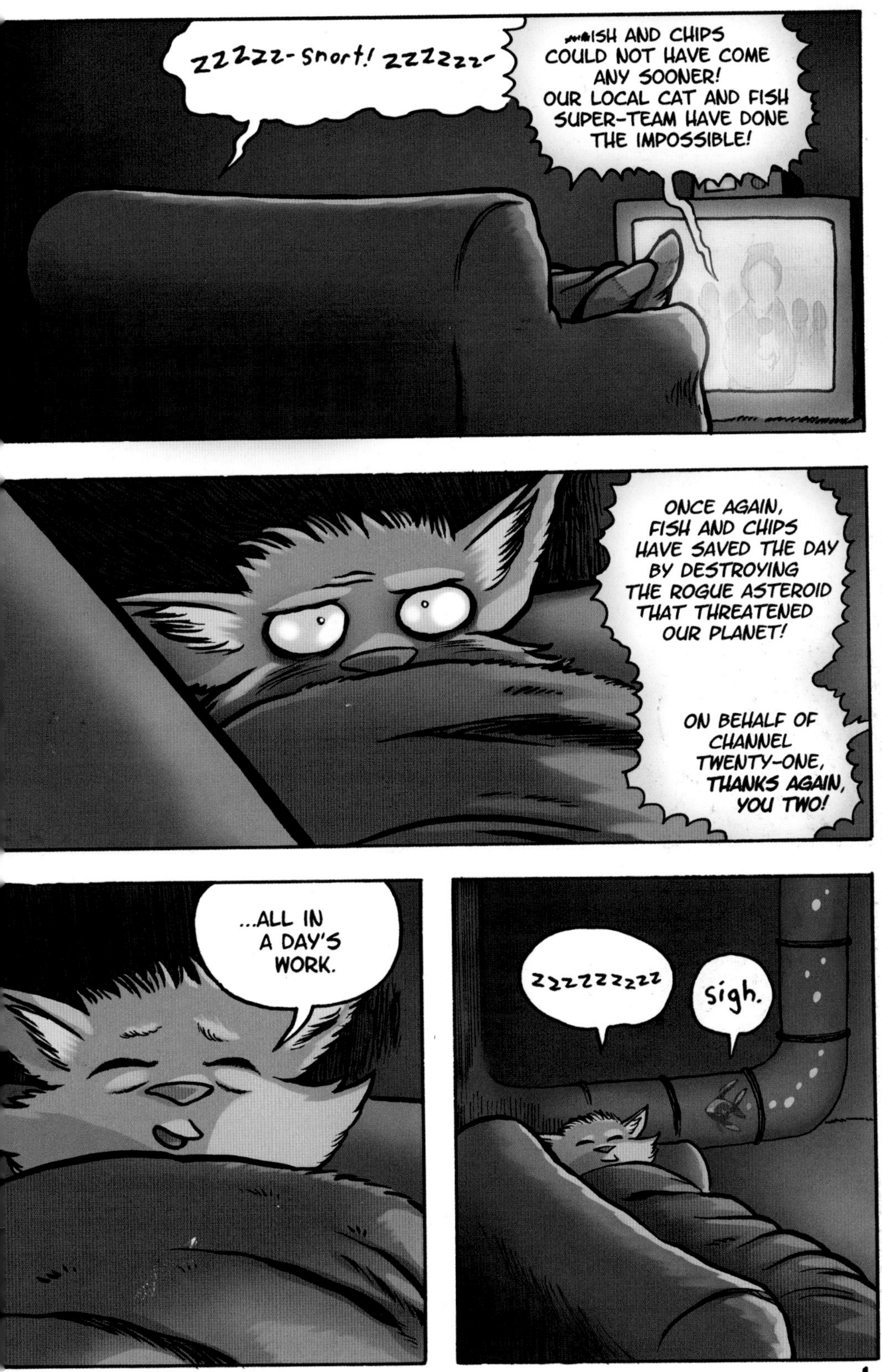
ZZZZZ-Snort! ZZZZZZ-
...ISH AND CHIPS COULD NOT HAVE COME ANY SOONER! OUR LOCAL CAT AND FISH SUPER-TEAM HAVE DONE THE IMPOSSIBLE!
ONCE AGAIN, FISH AND CHIPS HAVE SAVED THE DAY BY DESTROYING THE ROGUE ASTEROID THAT THREATENED OUR PLANET!
ON BEHALF OF CHANNEL TWENTY-ONE, THANKS AGAIN, YOU TWO!
...ALL IN A DAY'S WORK.
ZZZZZZZZZ
sigh.

end.

ZITA THE SPACEGIRL

in

"If Wishes Were Socks"

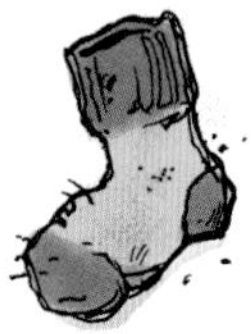

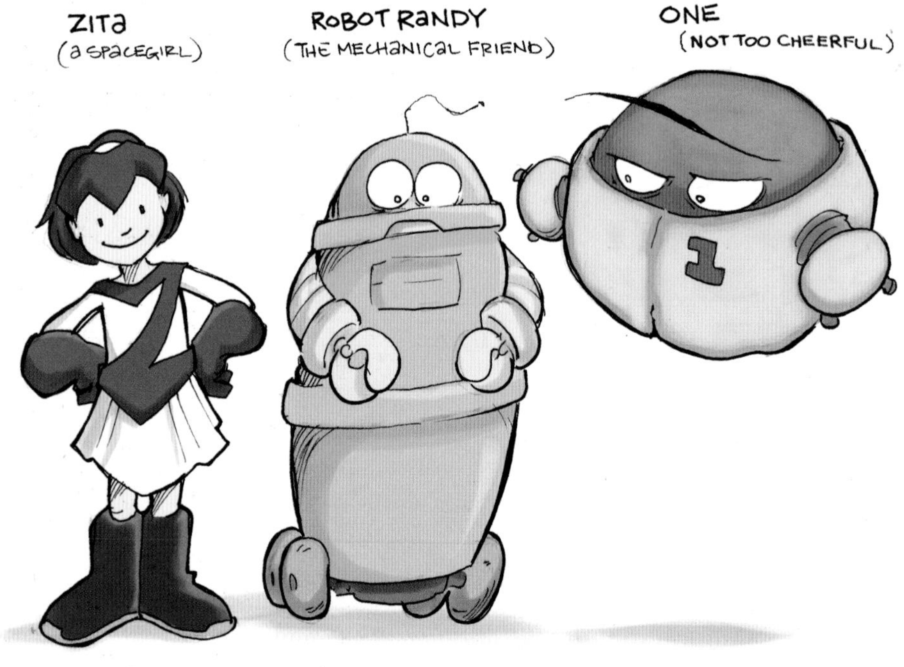

ZITA
(A SPACEGIRL)
ROBOT RANDY
(THE MECHANICAL FRIEND)
ONE
(NOT TOO CHEERFUL)

By Ben Hatke

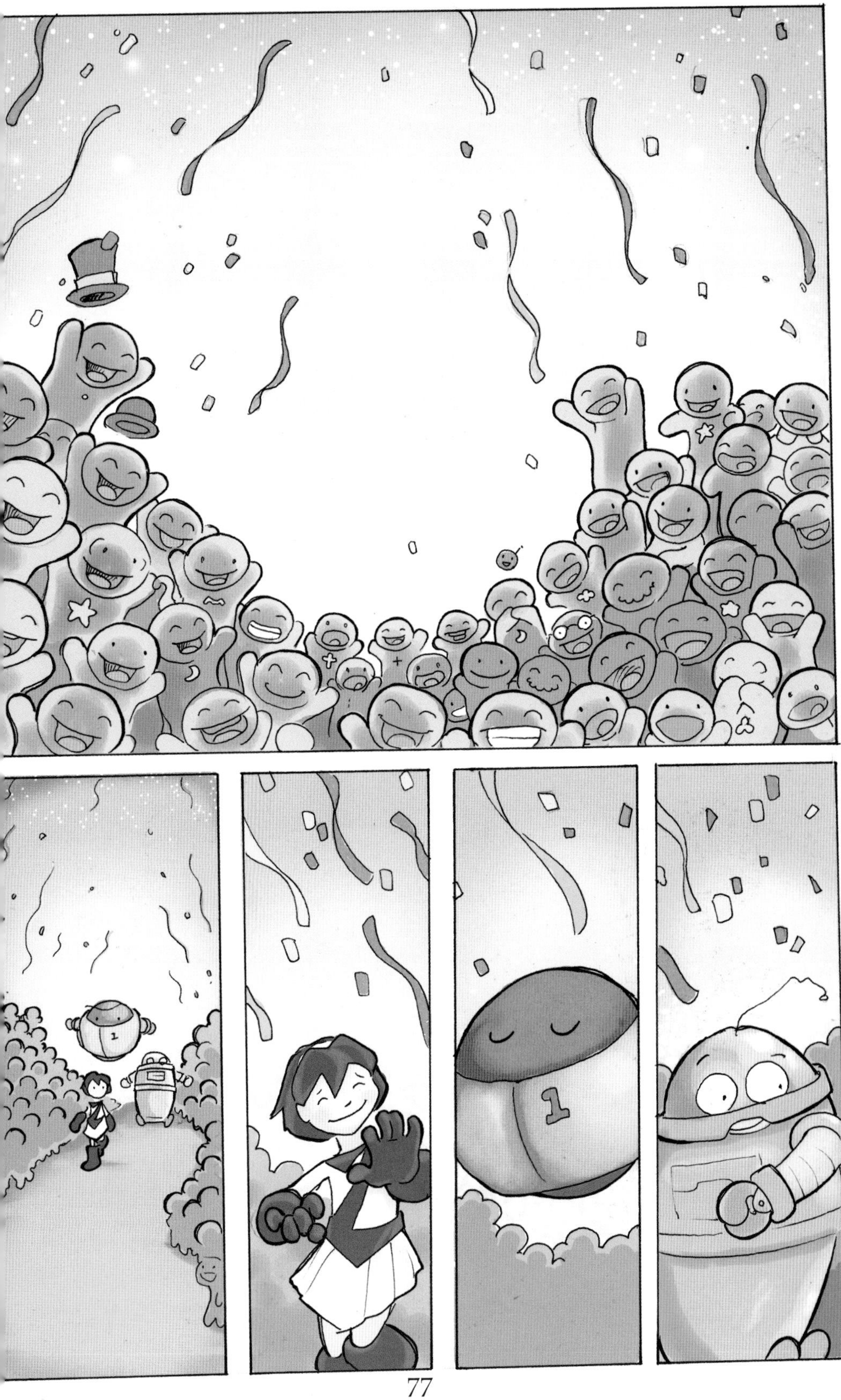

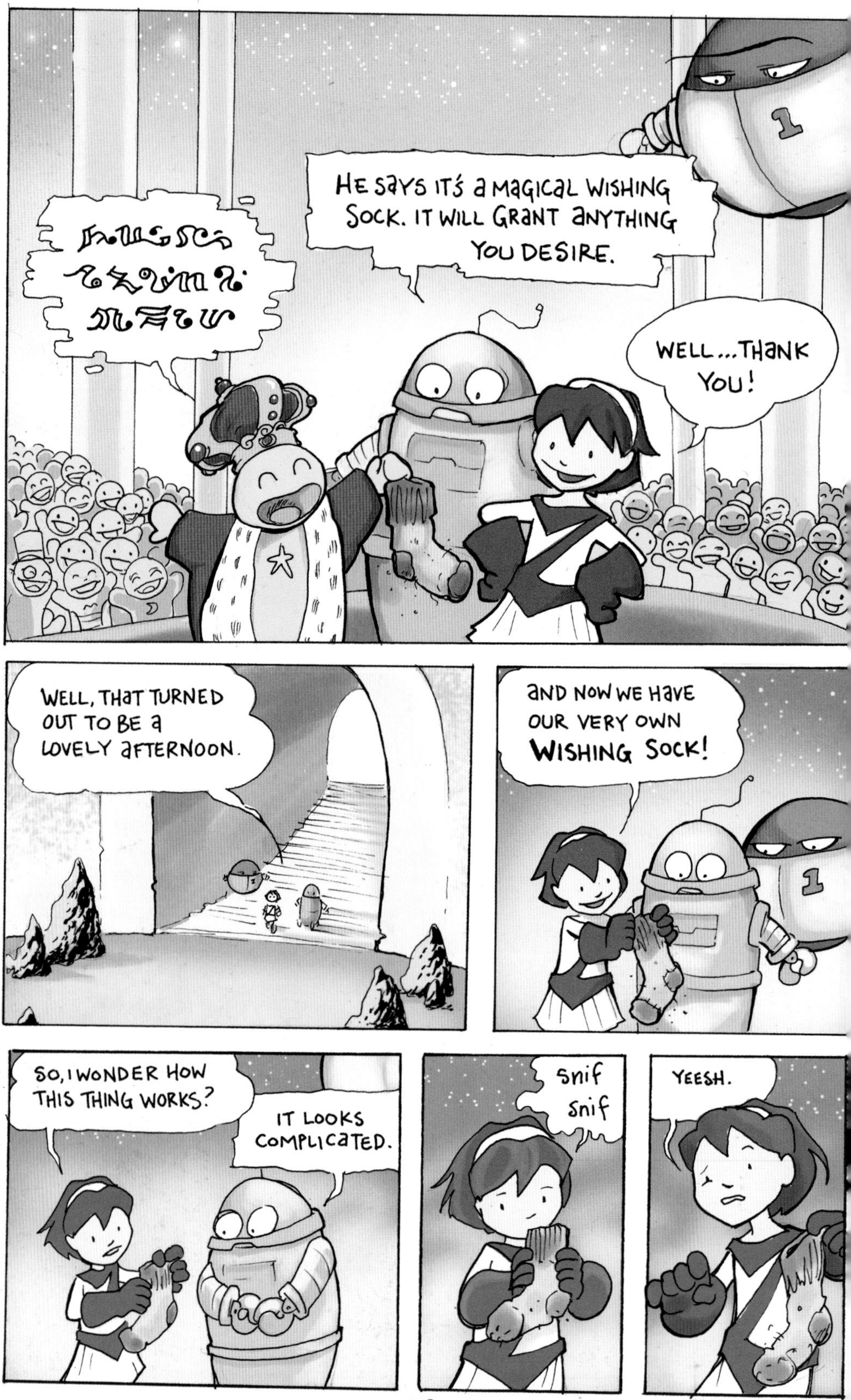
HE SAYS IT'S A MAGICAL WISHING SOCK. IT WILL GRANT ANYTHING YOU DESIRE.
WELL...THANK YOU!
WELL, THAT TURNED OUT TO BE A LOVELY AFTERNOON.
AND NOW WE HAVE OUR VERY OWN WISHING SOCK!
SO, I WONDER HOW THIS THING WORKS?
IT LOOKS COMPLICATED.
snif
snif
YEESH.

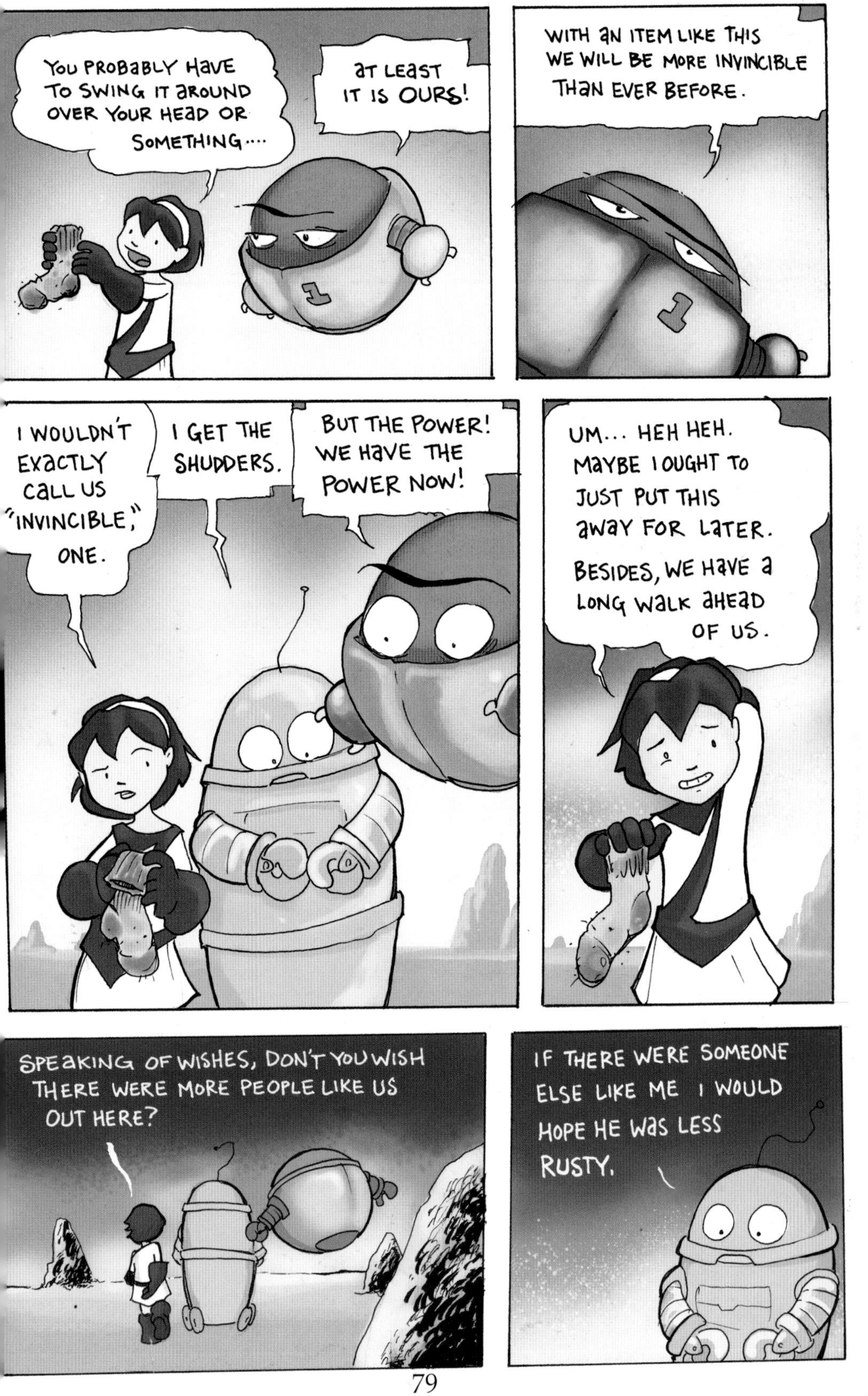
YOU PROBABLY HAVE TO SWING IT AROUND OVER YOUR HEAD OR SOMETHING....
AT LEAST IT IS OURS!
WITH AN ITEM LIKE THIS WE WILL BE MORE INVINCIBLE THAN EVER BEFORE.
I WOULDN'T EXACTLY CALL US "INVINCIBLE," ONE.
I GET THE SHUDDERS.
BUT THE POWER! WE HAVE THE POWER NOW!
UM... HEH HEH. MAYBE I OUGHT TO JUST PUT THIS AWAY FOR LATER.
BESIDES, WE HAVE A LONG WALK AHEAD OF US.
SPEAKING OF WISHES, DON'T YOU WISH THERE WERE MORE PEOPLE LIKE US OUT HERE?
IF THERE WERE SOMEONE ELSE LIKE ME I WOULD HOPE HE WAS LESS RUSTY.

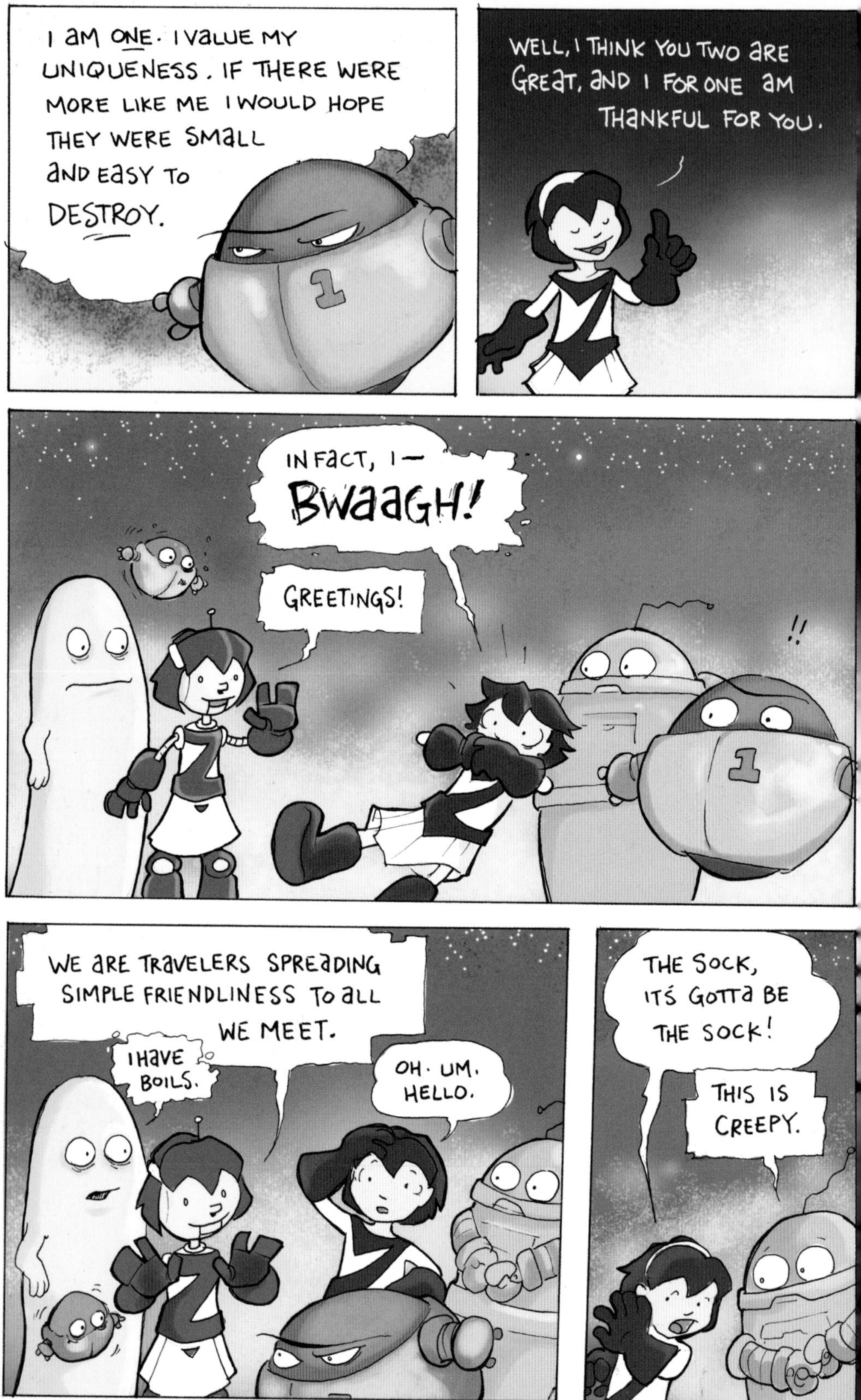
I AM ONE. I VALUE MY UNIQUENESS. IF THERE WERE MORE LIKE ME I WOULD HOPE THEY WERE SMALL AND EASY TO DESTROY.
WELL, I THINK YOU TWO ARE GREAT, AND I FOR ONE AM THANKFUL FOR YOU.
IN FACT, I—
BWAAGH!
GREETINGS!
!!
WE ARE TRAVELERS SPREADING SIMPLE FRIENDLINESS TO ALL WE MEET.
I HAVE BOILS.
OH. UM. HELLO.
THE SOCK, IT'S GOTTA BE THE SOCK!
THIS IS CREEPY.

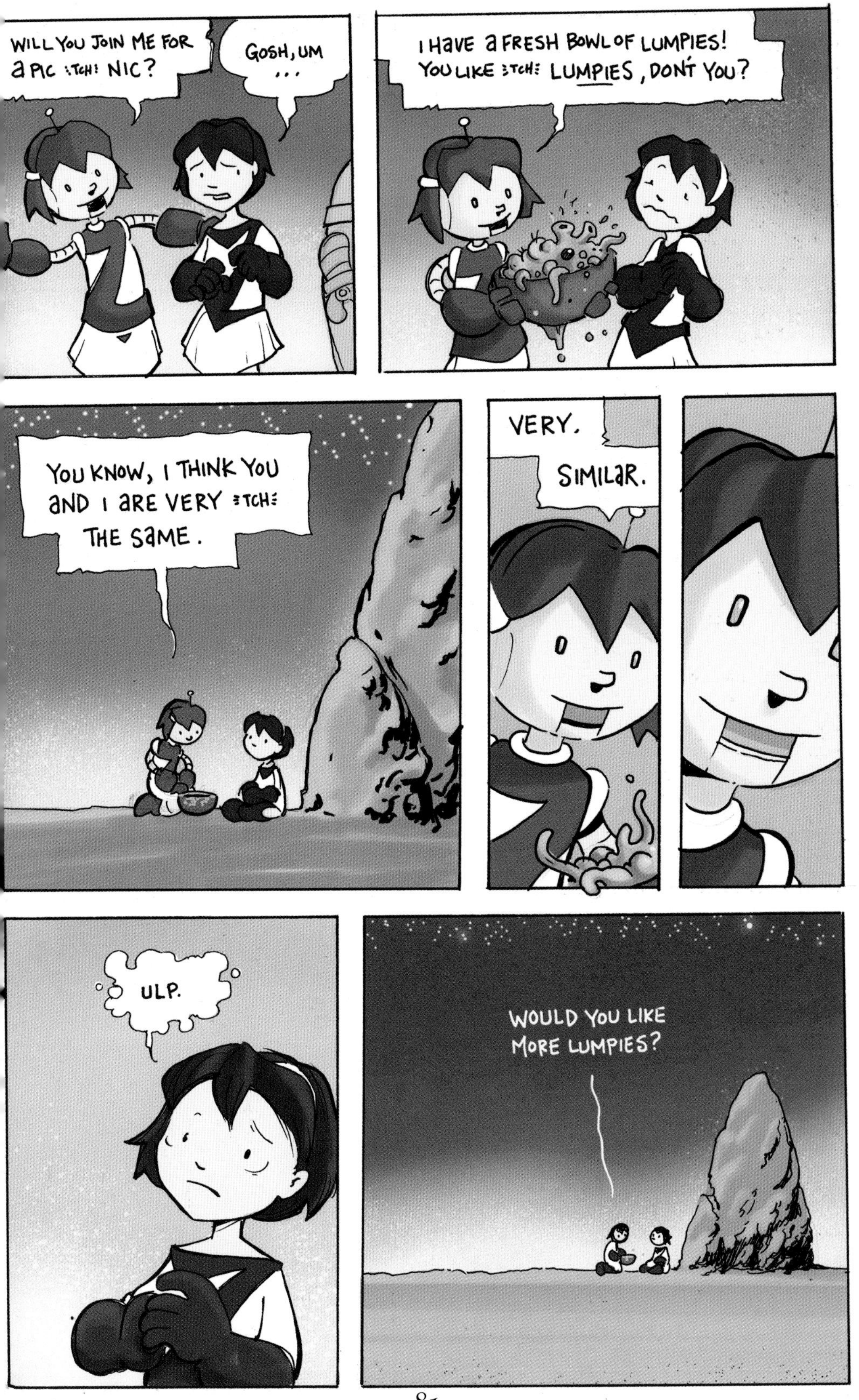
WILL YOU JOIN ME FOR a PIC :TCH: NIC?
GOSH, UM ...
I HaVE a FRESH BOWL OF LUMPIES! YOU LIKE :TCH: LUMPIES, DON'T YOU?
YOU KNOW, I THINK YOU aND I aRE VERY :TCH: THE SaME.
VERY.
SIMILaR.
ULP.
WOULD YOU LIKE MORE LUMPIES?

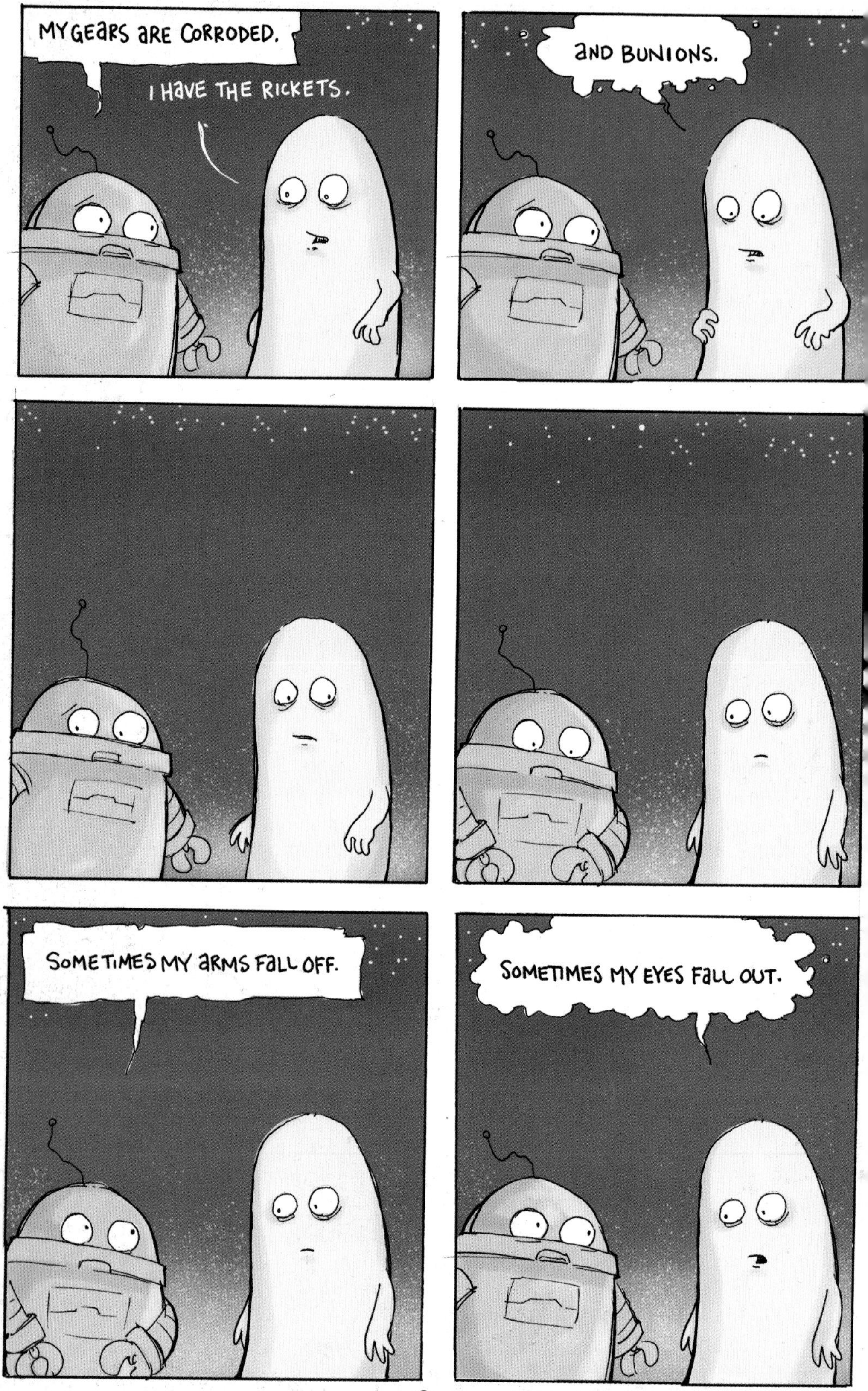
MY GEARS ARE CORRODED.
I HAVE THE RICKETS.
AND BUNIONS.
SOMETIMES MY ARMS FALL OFF.
SOMETIMES MY EYES FALL OUT.

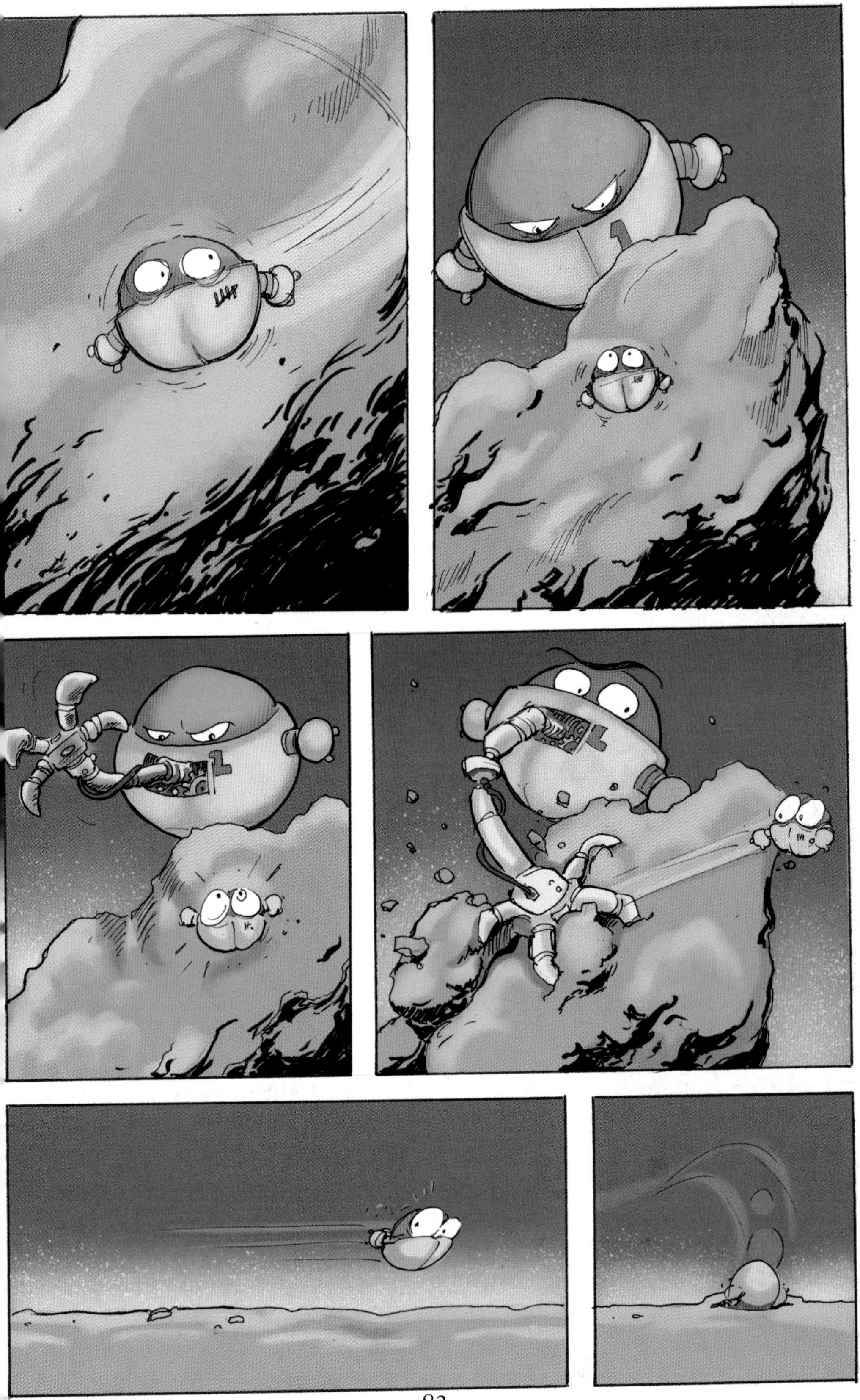

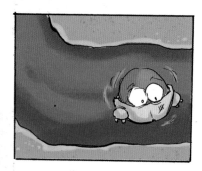
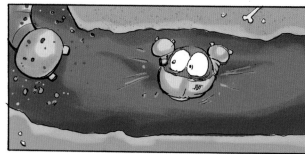
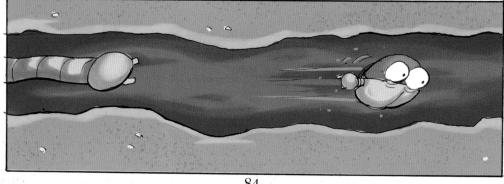

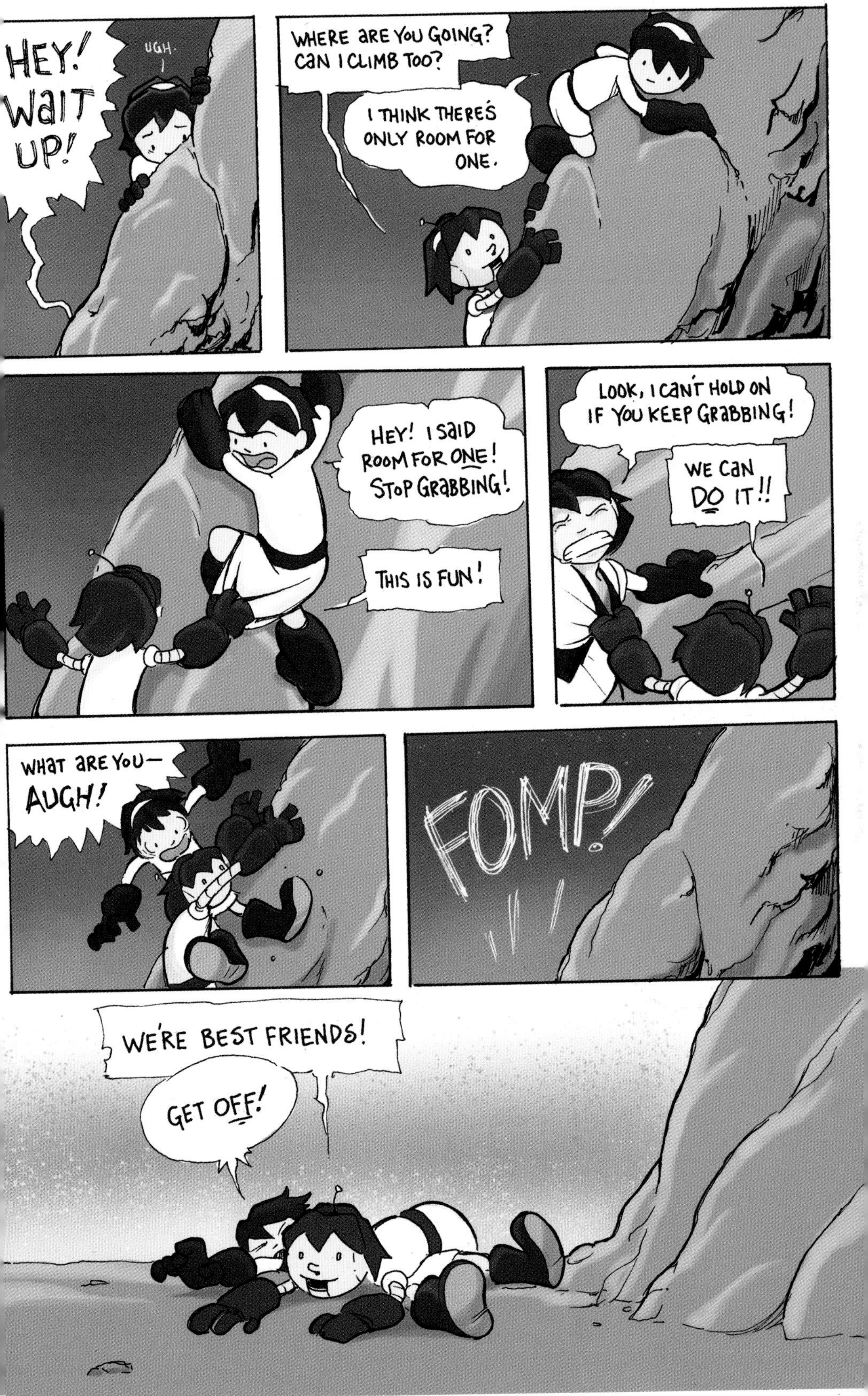
HEY! WAIT UP!
UGH.
WHERE ARE YOU GOING? CAN I CLIMB TOO?
I THINK THERE'S ONLY ROOM FOR ONE.
HEY! I SAID ROOM FOR ONE! STOP GRABBING!
THIS IS FUN!
LOOK, I CAN'T HOLD ON IF YOU KEEP GRABBING!
WE CAN DO IT!!
WHAT ARE YOU— AUGH!
FOMP!
WE'RE BEST FRIENDS!
GET OFF!

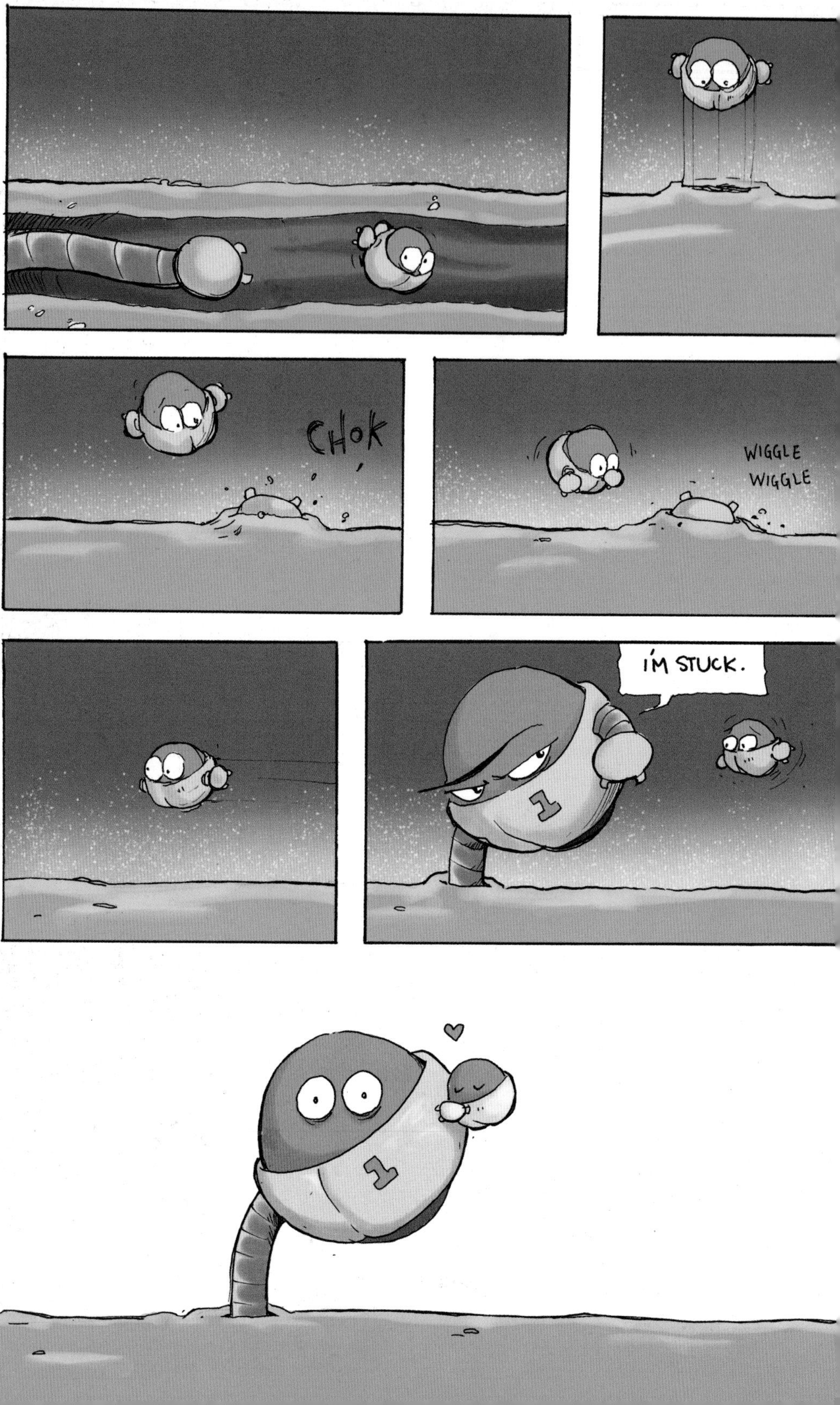
CHOK
WIGGLE WIGGLE
I'M STUCK.

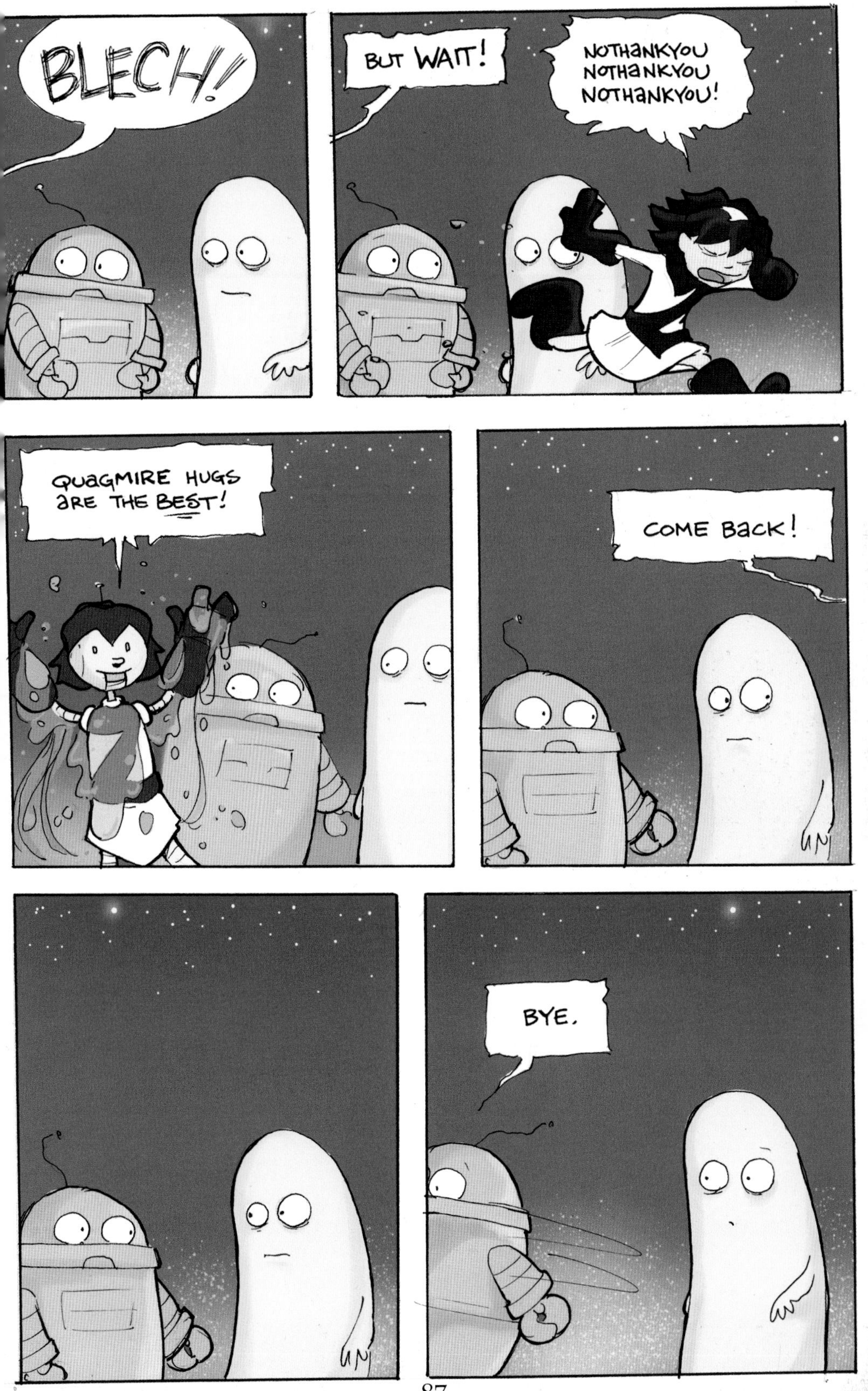
BLECH!
BUT WAIT!
NOTHANKYOU NOTHANKYOU NOTHANKYOU!
QUAGMIRE HUGS ARE THE BEST!
COME BACK!
BYE.

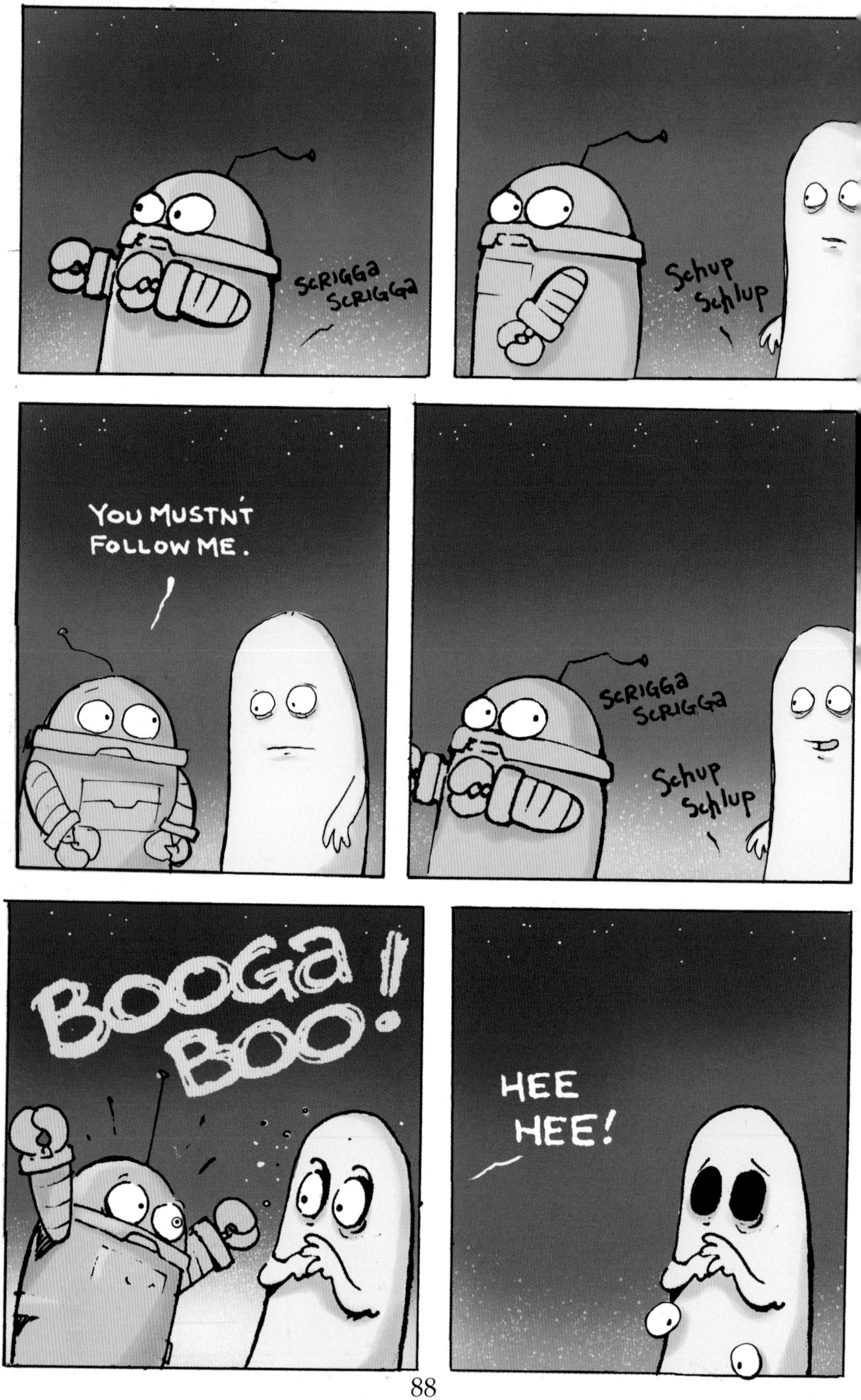
SCRIGGA
SCRIGGA
Schup
Schlup
YOU MUSTN'T FOLLOW ME.
SCRIGGA
SCRIGGA
Schup
Schlup
BOOGA! BOOGA!
BOO!
HEE HEE!

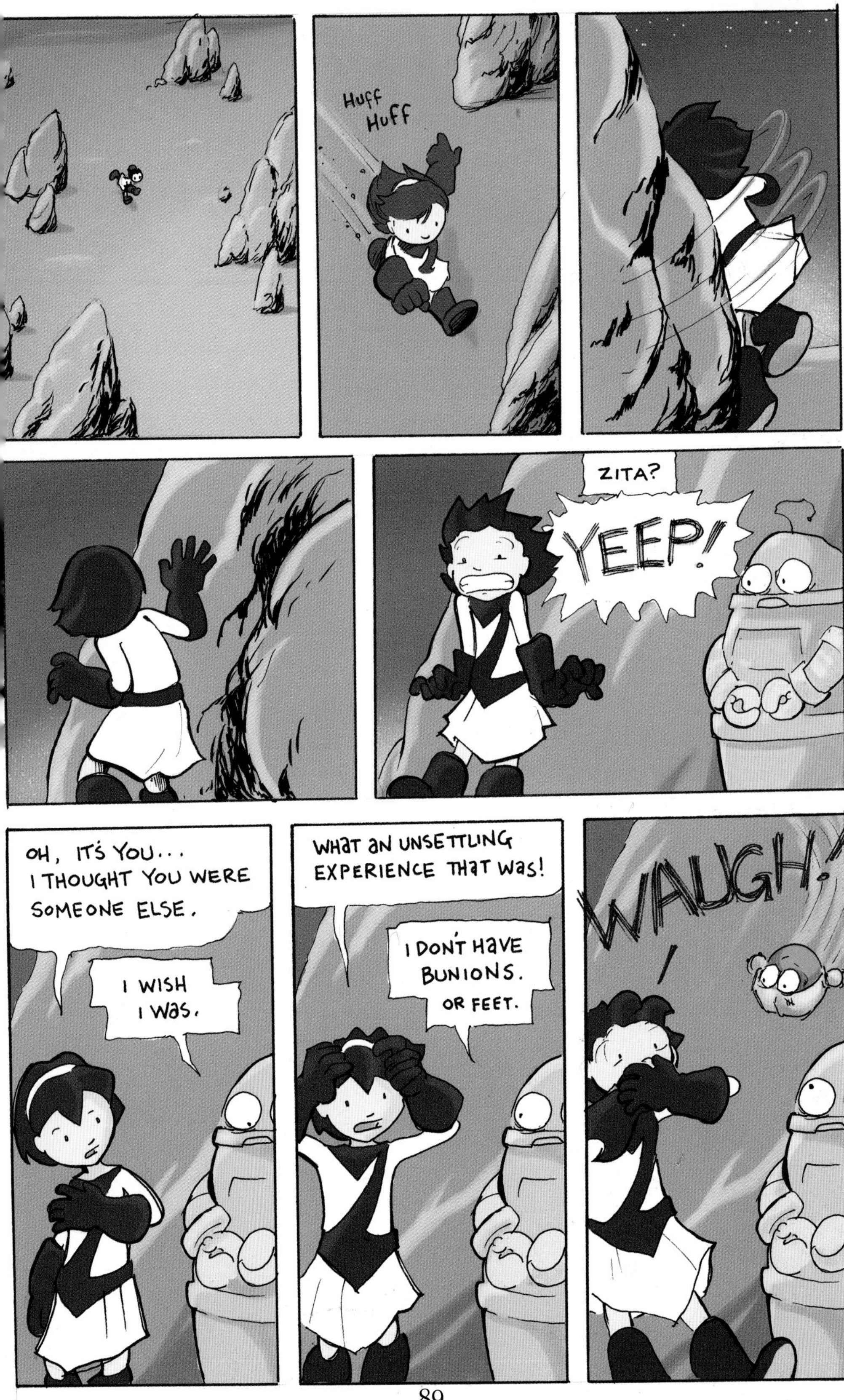
HUFF
HUFF
ZITA?
YEEP!
OH, IT'S YOU... I THOUGHT YOU WERE SOMEONE ELSE.
I WISH I WAS.
WHAT AN UNSETTLING EXPERIENCE THAT WAS!
I DON'T HAVE BUNIONS. OR FEET.
WAUGH!

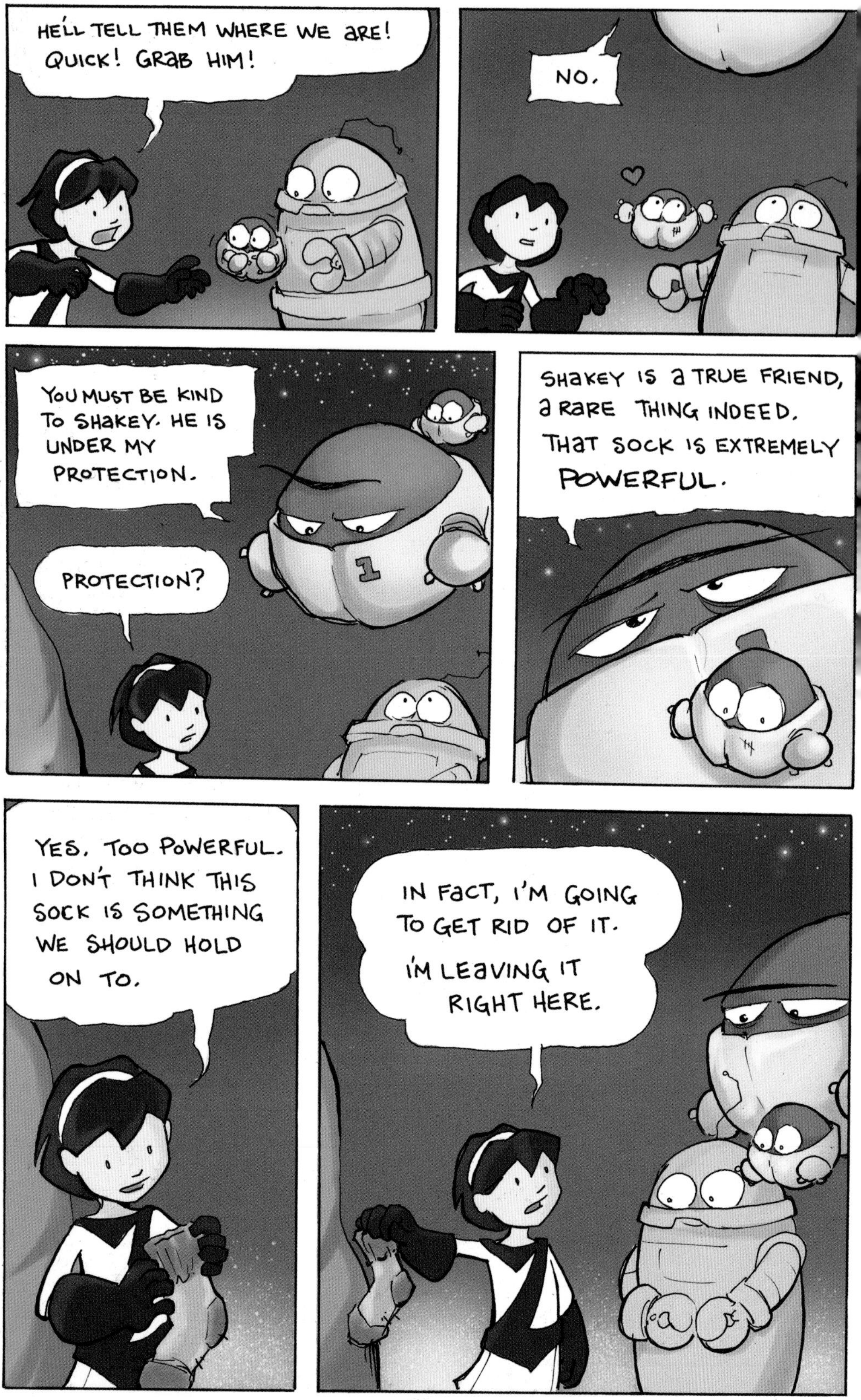
HE'LL TELL THEM WHERE WE ARE! QUICK! GRAB HIM!
NO.
YOU MUST BE KIND TO SHAKEY. HE IS UNDER MY PROTECTION.
PROTECTION?
SHAKEY IS A TRUE FRIEND, A RARE THING INDEED. THAT SOCK IS EXTREMELY POWERFUL.
YES. TOO POWERFUL. I DON'T THINK THIS SOCK IS SOMETHING WE SHOULD HOLD ON TO.
IN FACT, I'M GOING TO GET RID OF IT.
I'M LEAVING IT RIGHT HERE.

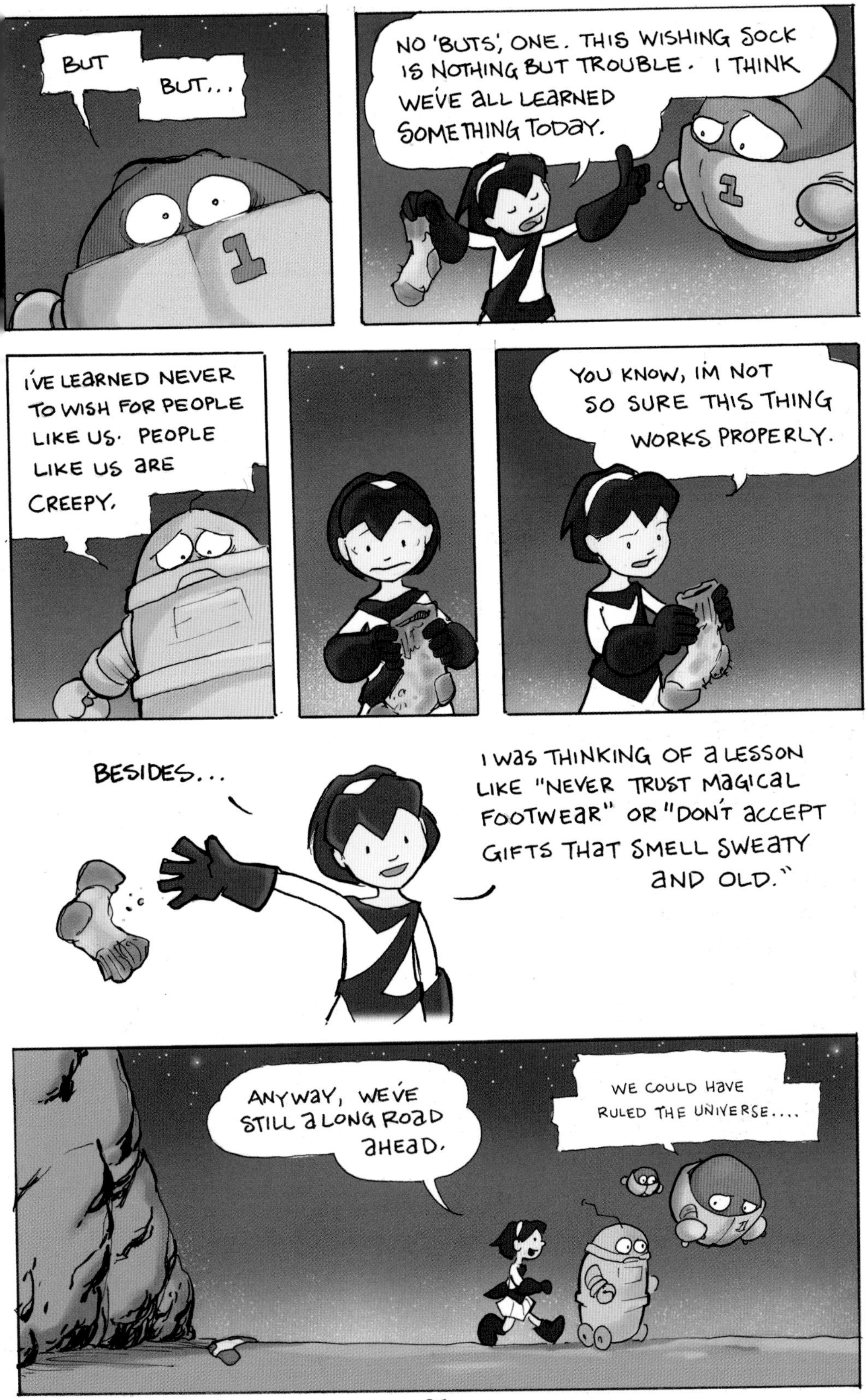
BUT
BUT...
NO 'BUTS,' ONE. THIS WISHING SOCK IS NOTHING BUT TROUBLE. I THINK WE'VE ALL LEARNED SOMETHING TODAY.
I'VE LEARNED NEVER TO WISH FOR PEOPLE LIKE US. PEOPLE LIKE US ARE CREEPY.
YOU KNOW, I'M NOT SO SURE THIS THING WORKS PROPERLY.
BESIDES...
I WAS THINKING OF A LESSON LIKE "NEVER TRUST MAGICAL FOOTWEAR" OR "DON'T ACCEPT GIFTS THAT SMELL SWEATY AND OLD."
ANYWAY, WE'VE STILL A LONG ROAD AHEAD.
WE COULD HAVE RULED THE UNIVERSE....

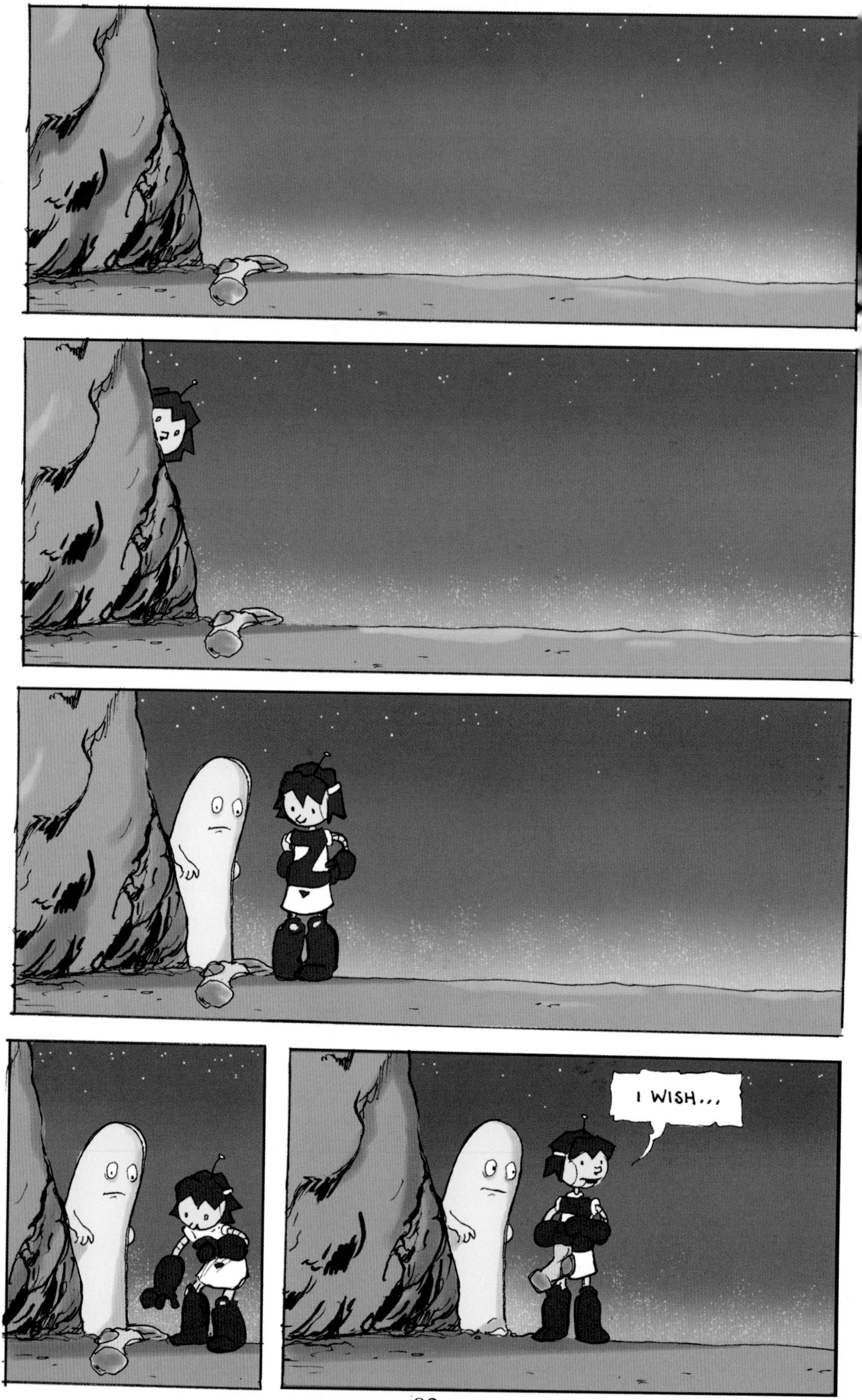
I WISH...

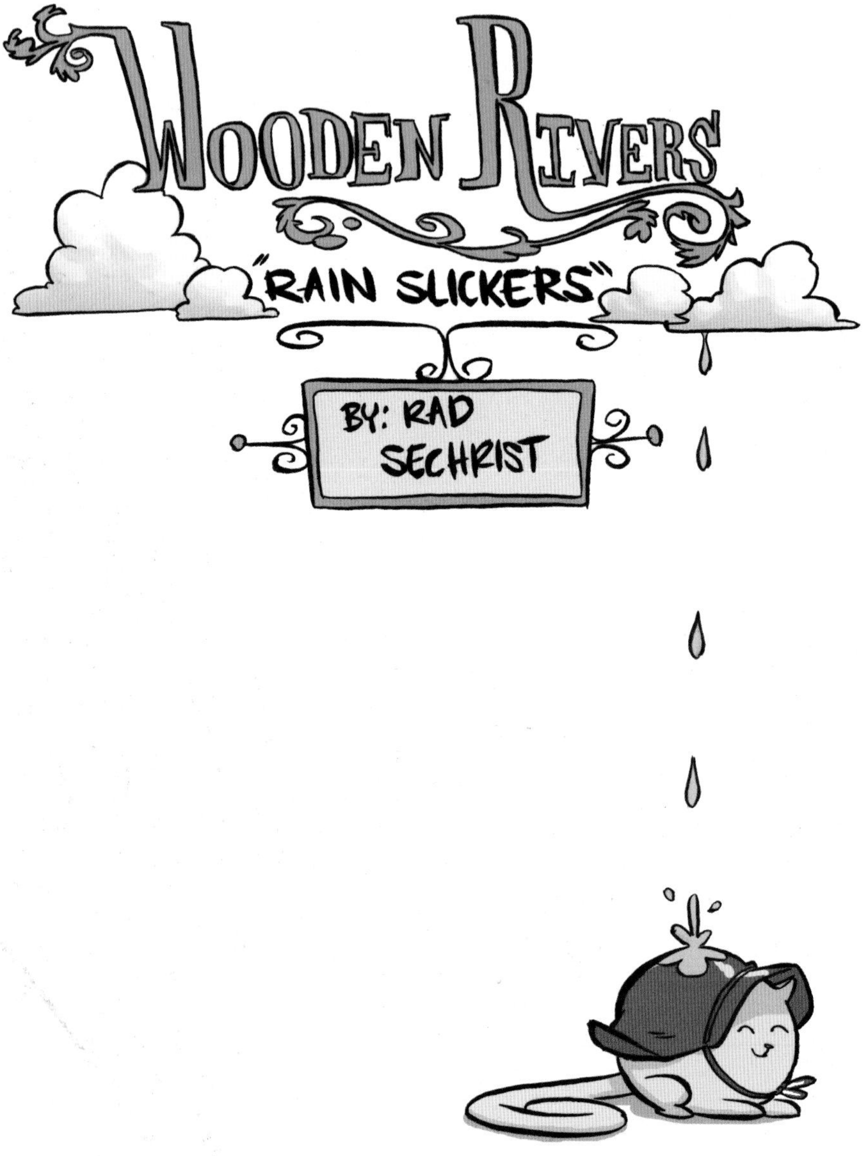
WOODEN RIVERS
"RAIN SLICKERS"
BY: RAD SECHRIST

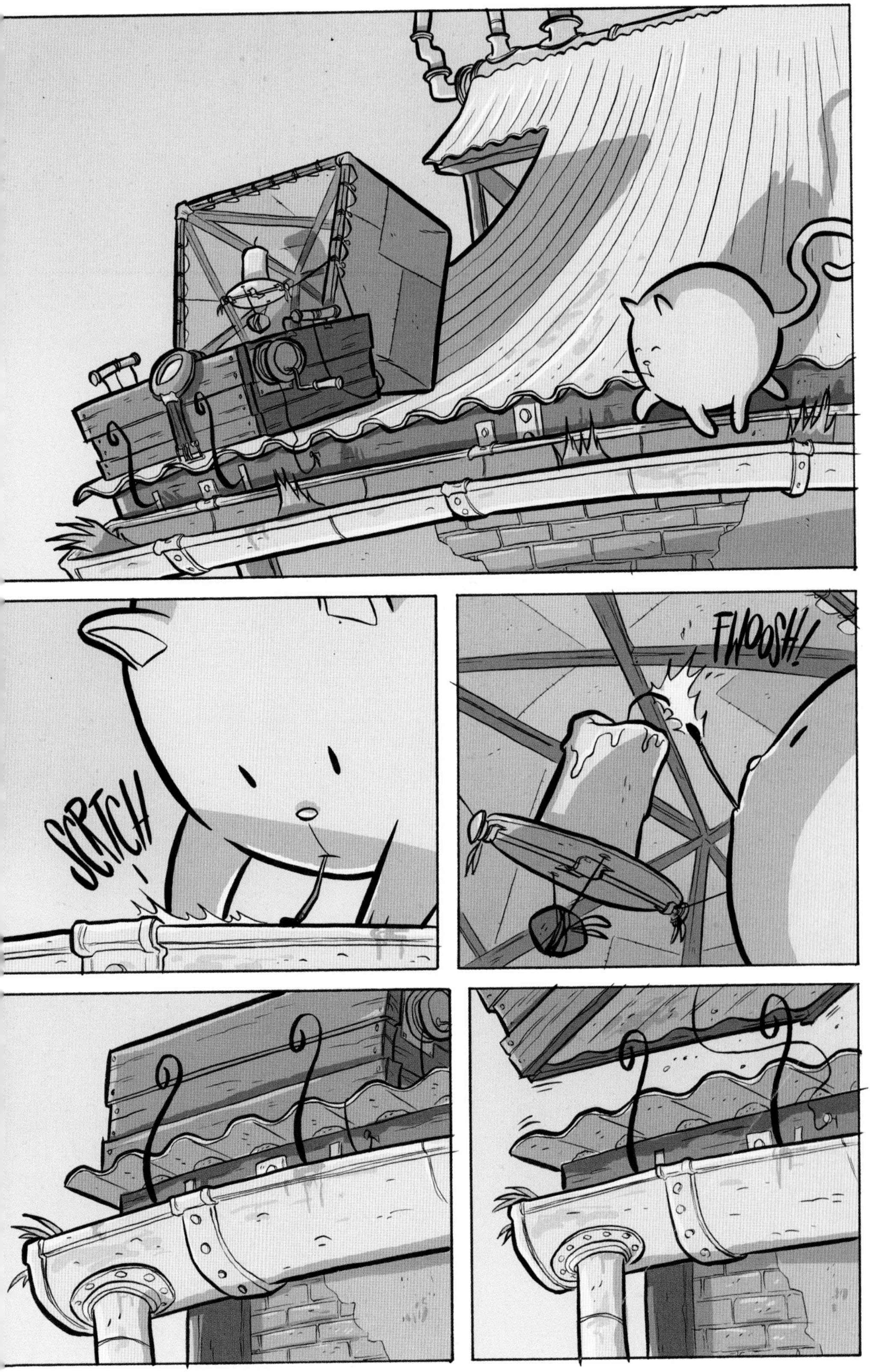
SCRTCH
FWOOSH!

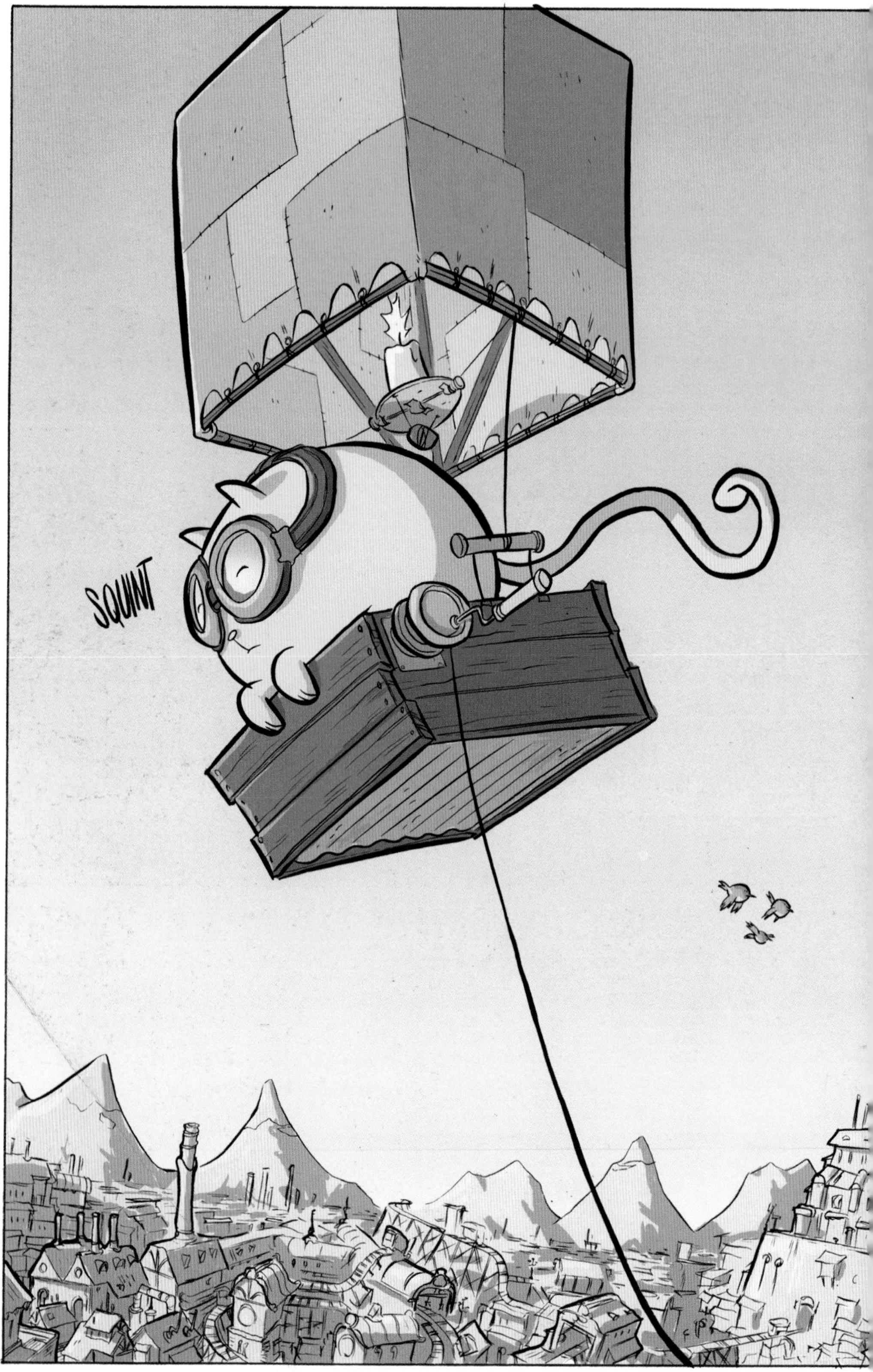
SQUINT

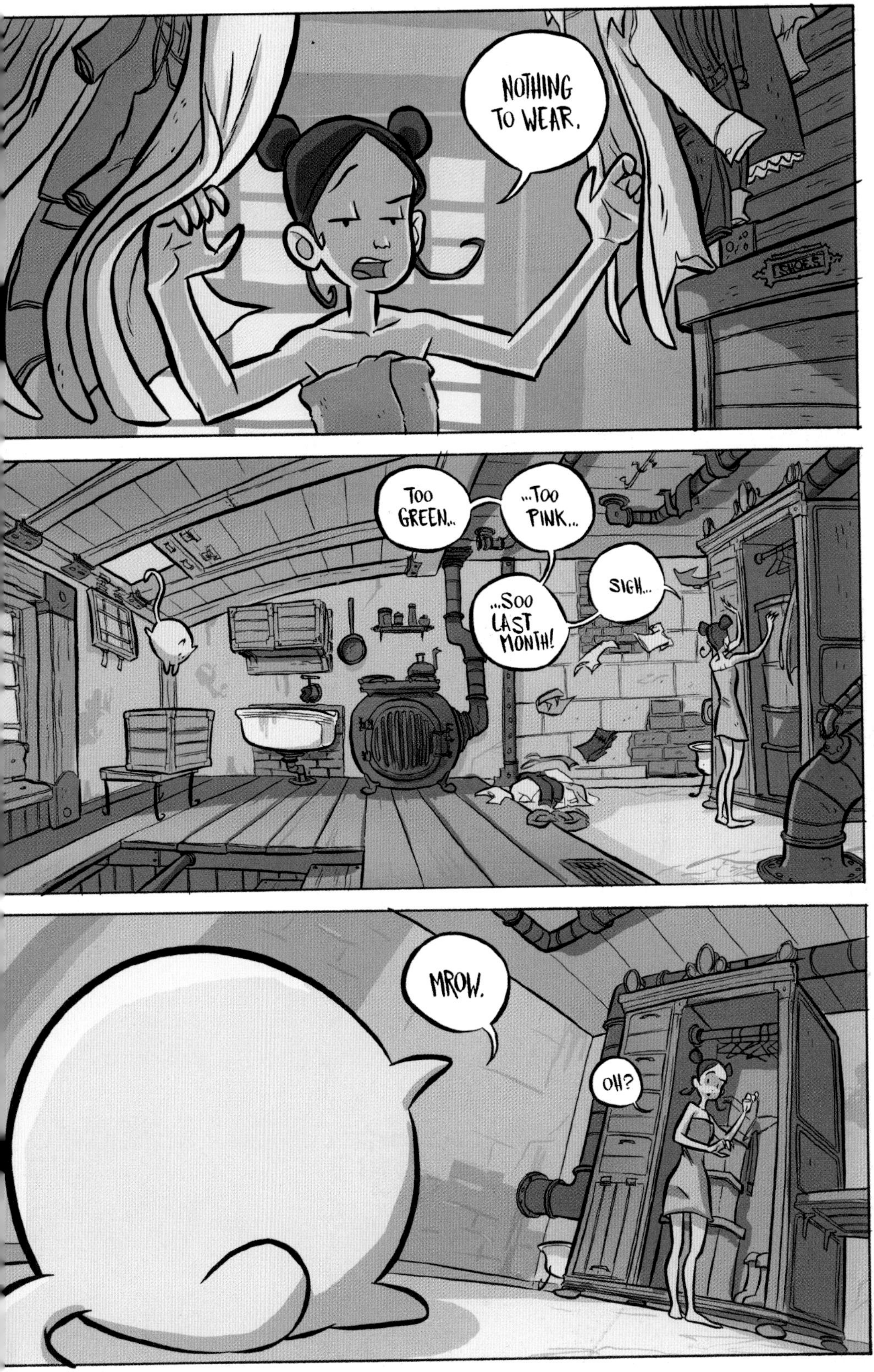
NOTHING TO WEAR.
TOO GREEN...
...TOO PINK...
...SOO LAST MONTH!
SIGH...
SHOES
MROW.
OH?

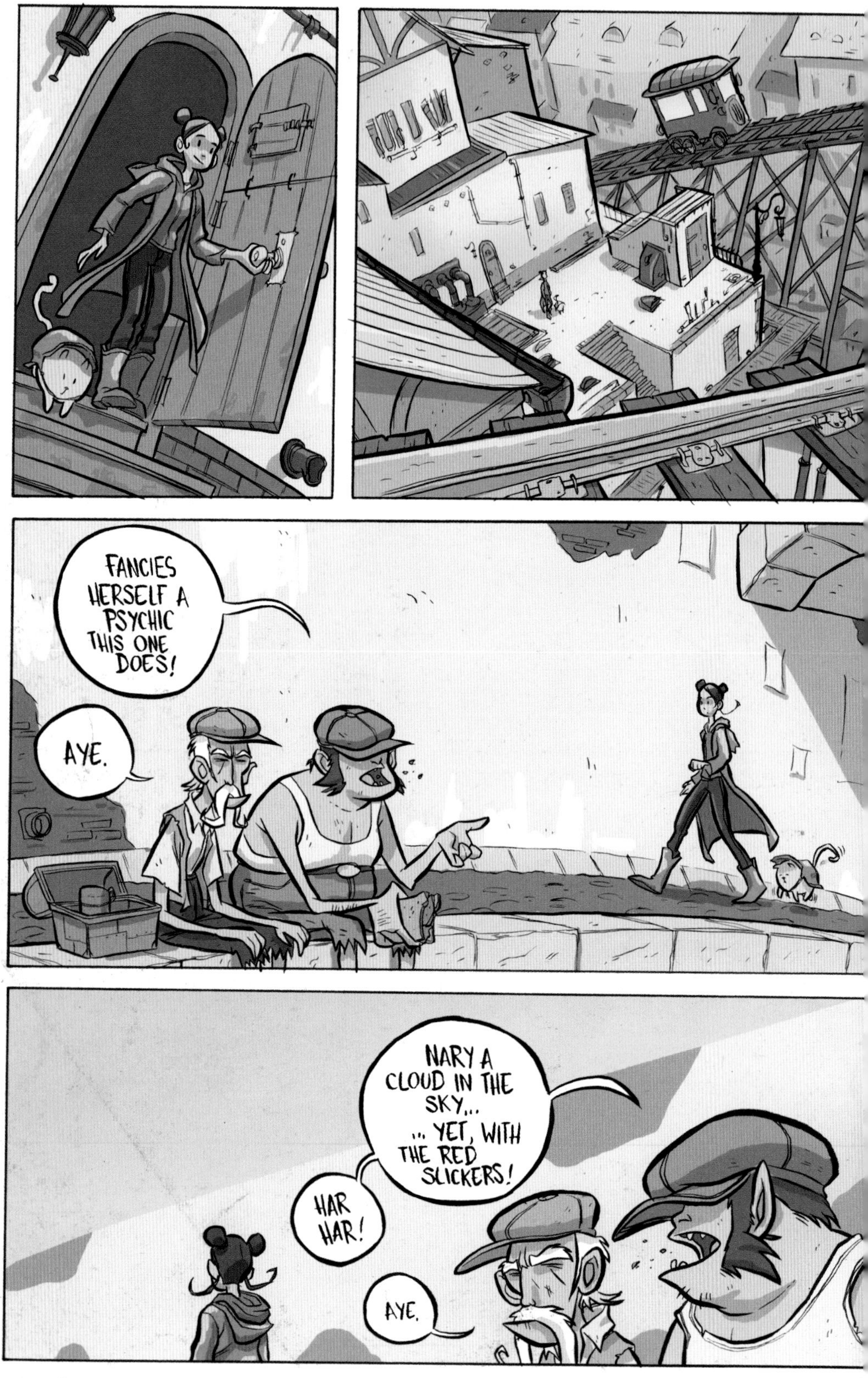
FANCIES HERSELF A PSYCHIC THIS ONE DOES!
AYE.
NARY A CLOUD IN THE SKY...
... YET, WITH THE RED SLICKERS!
HAR HAR!
AYE.

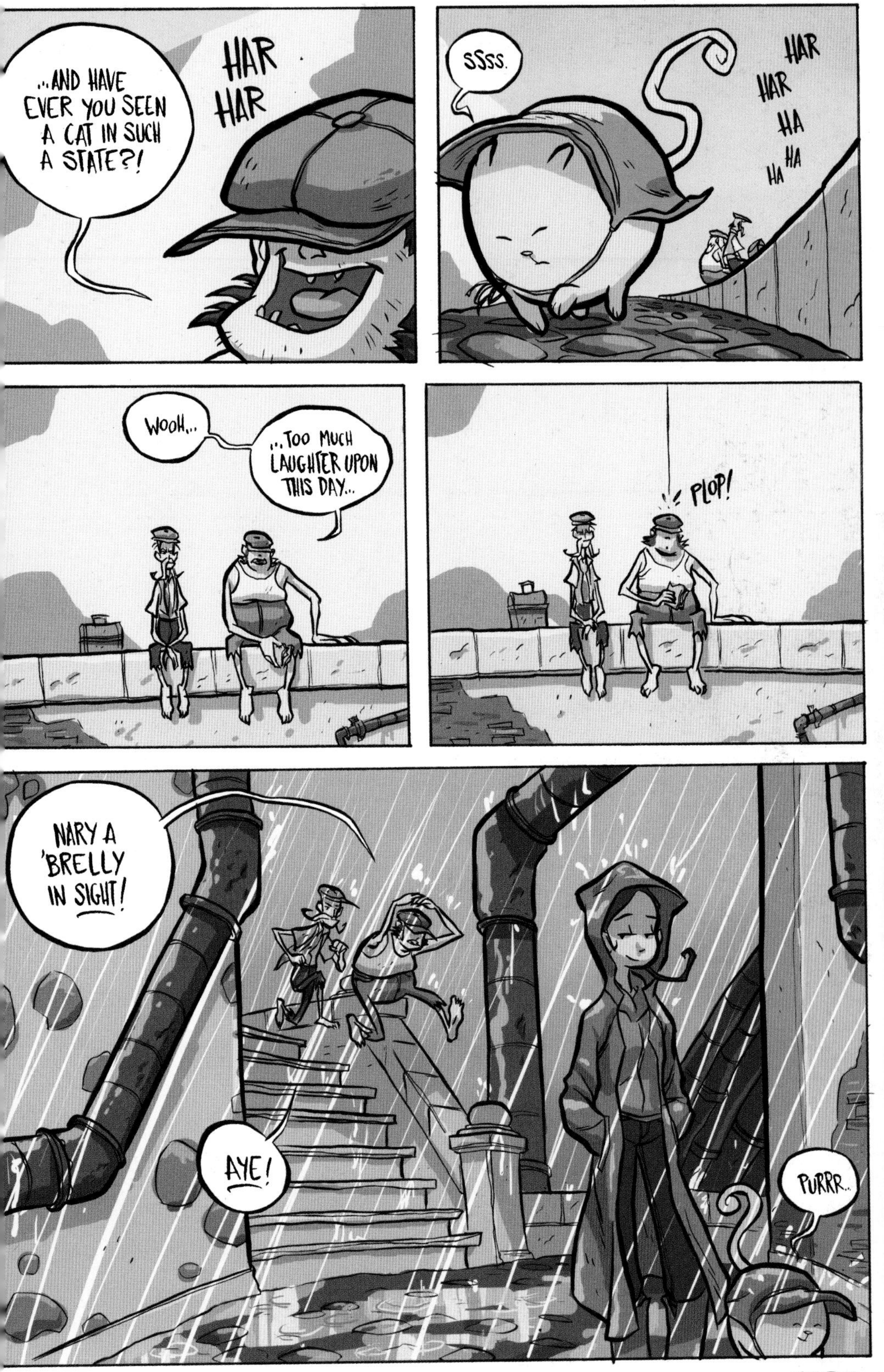
...AND HAVE EVER YOU SEEN A CAT IN SUCH A STATE?!
HAR HAR
SSSS.
HAR HAR HA HA HA
WOOH...
...TOO MUCH LAUGHTER UPON THIS DAY...
PLOP!
NARY A 'BRELLY IN SIGHT!
AYE!
PURRR..
THE END

Delivery

Story, Art, and Colors
Bannister

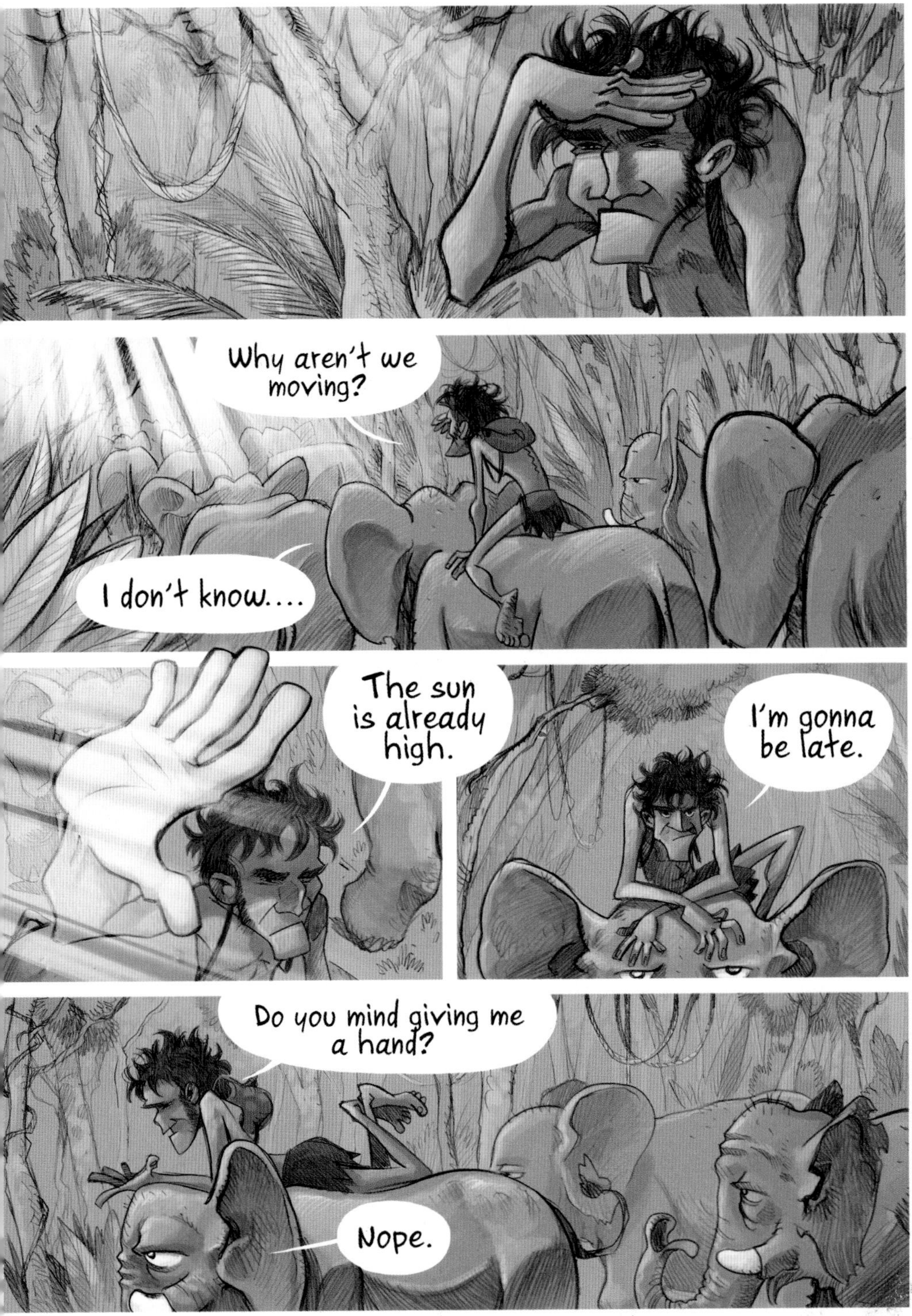

Why aren't we moving?
I don't know....
The sun is already high.
I'm gonna be late.
Do you mind giving me a hand?
Nope.

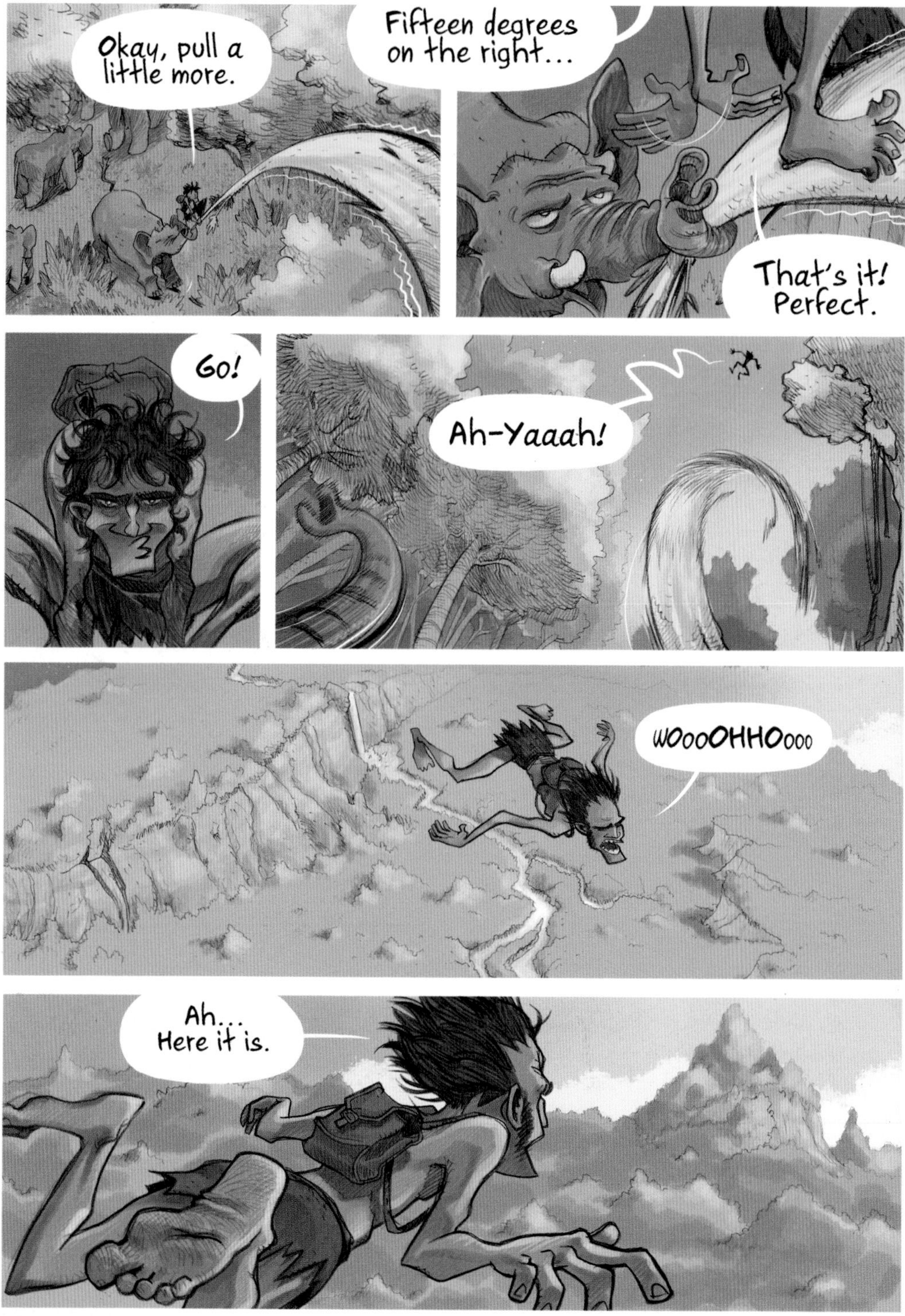
Okay, pull a little more.
Fifteen degrees on the right...
That's it! Perfect.
Go!
Ah-Yaaah!
WOooOHHOooo
Ah... Here it is.

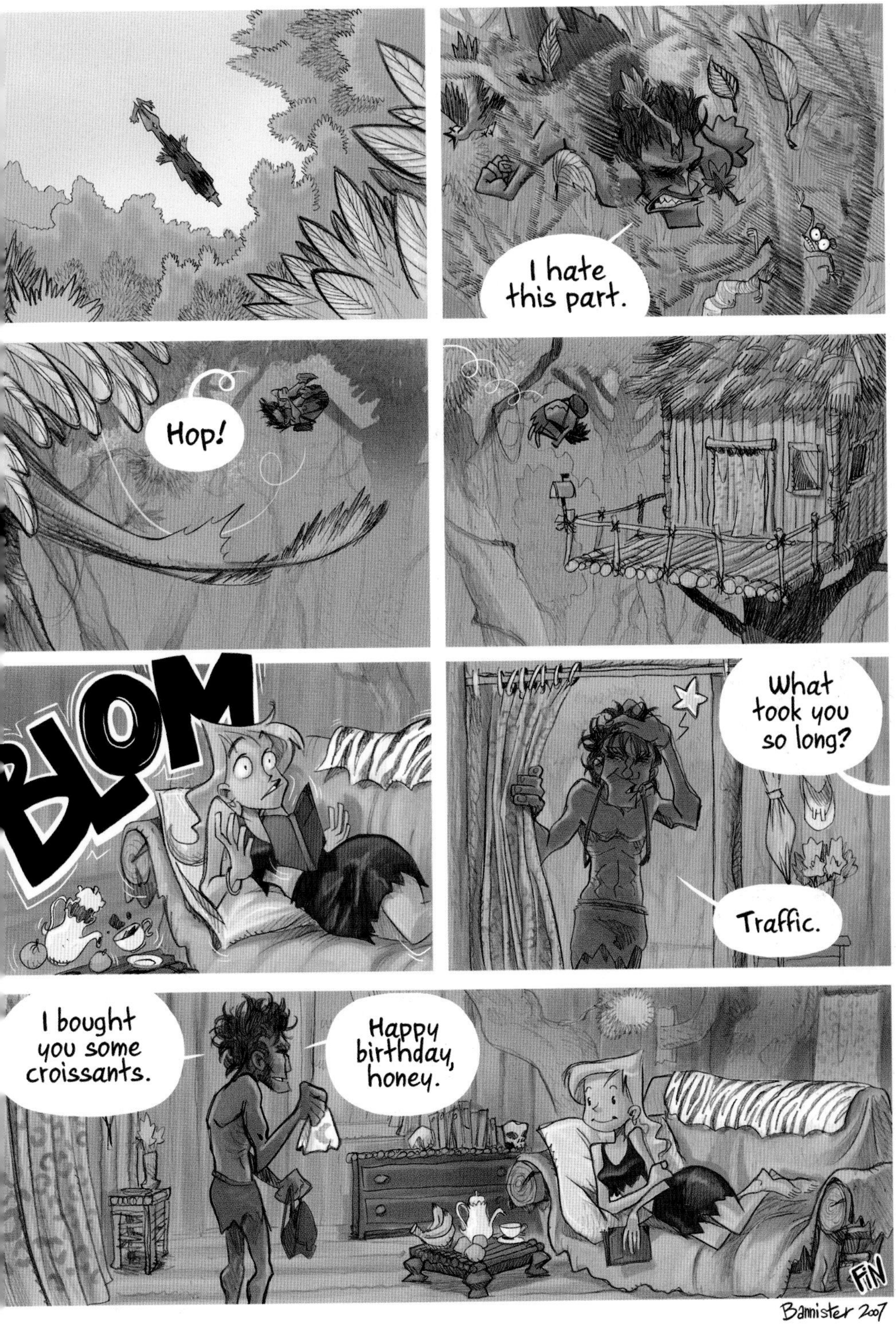
I hate this part.
Hop!
BLOM
What took you so long?
Traffic.
I bought you some croissants.
Happy birthday, honey.
FIN
Bannister 2007

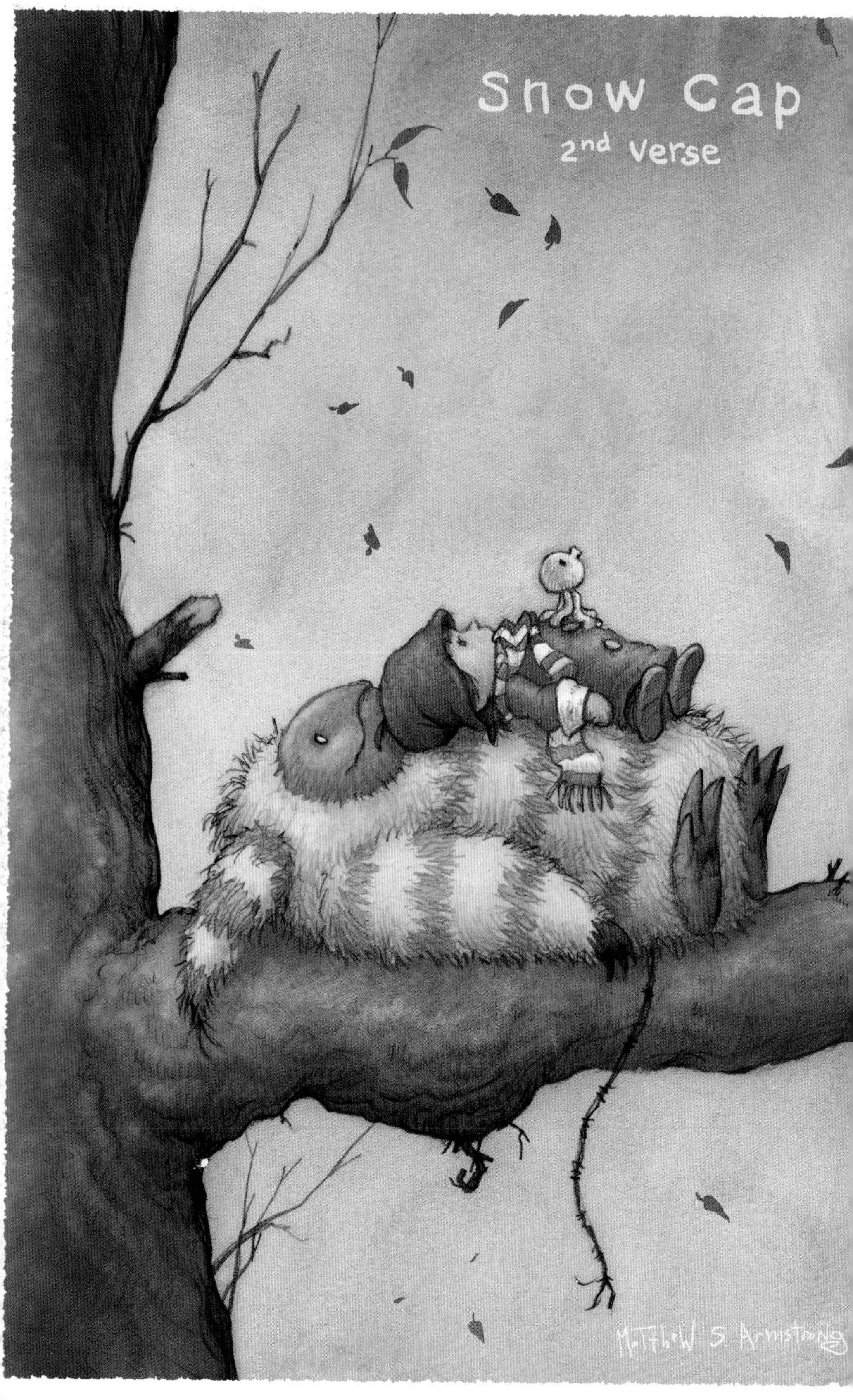
Snow Cap
2nd Verse
Matthew S. Armstrong

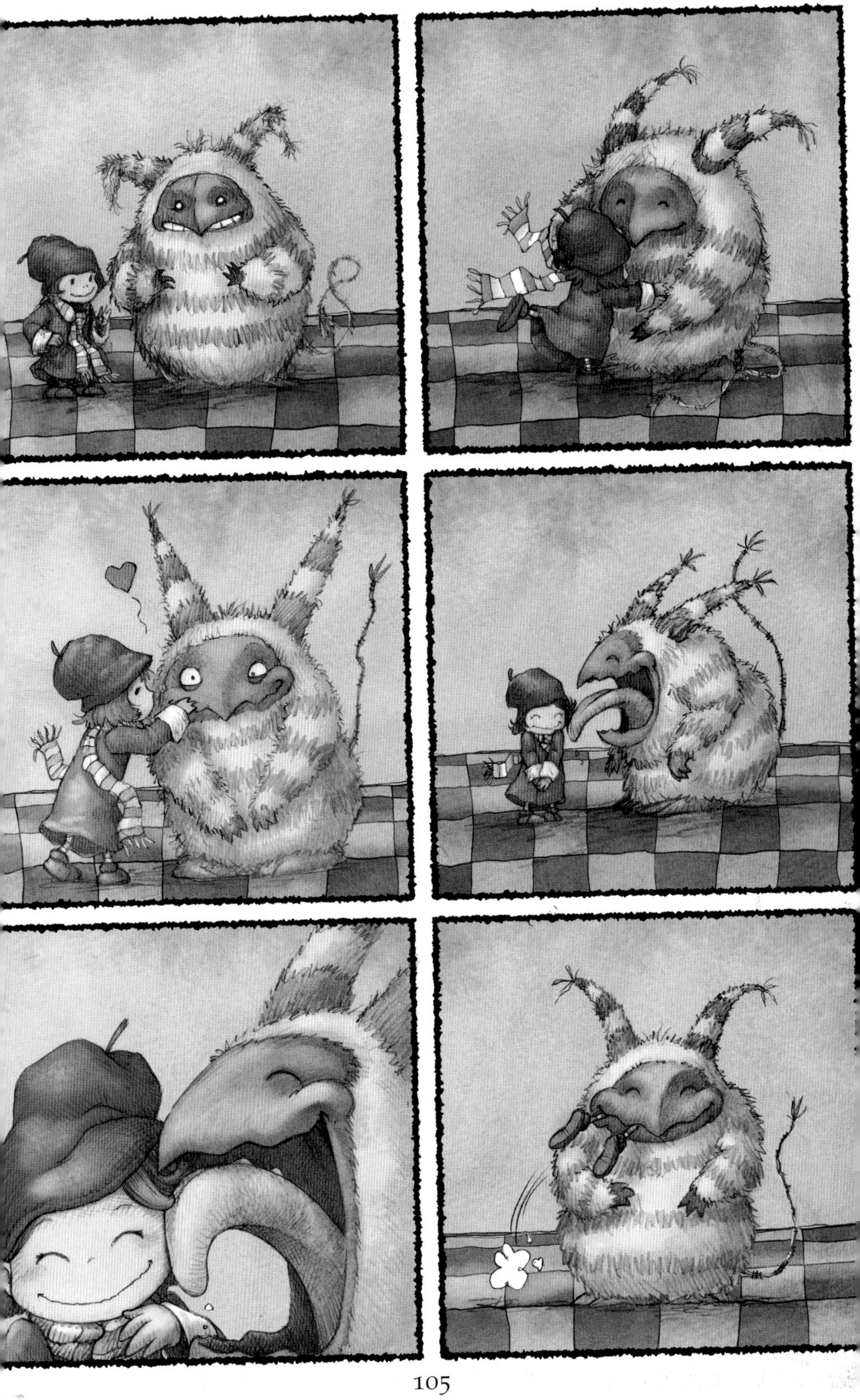

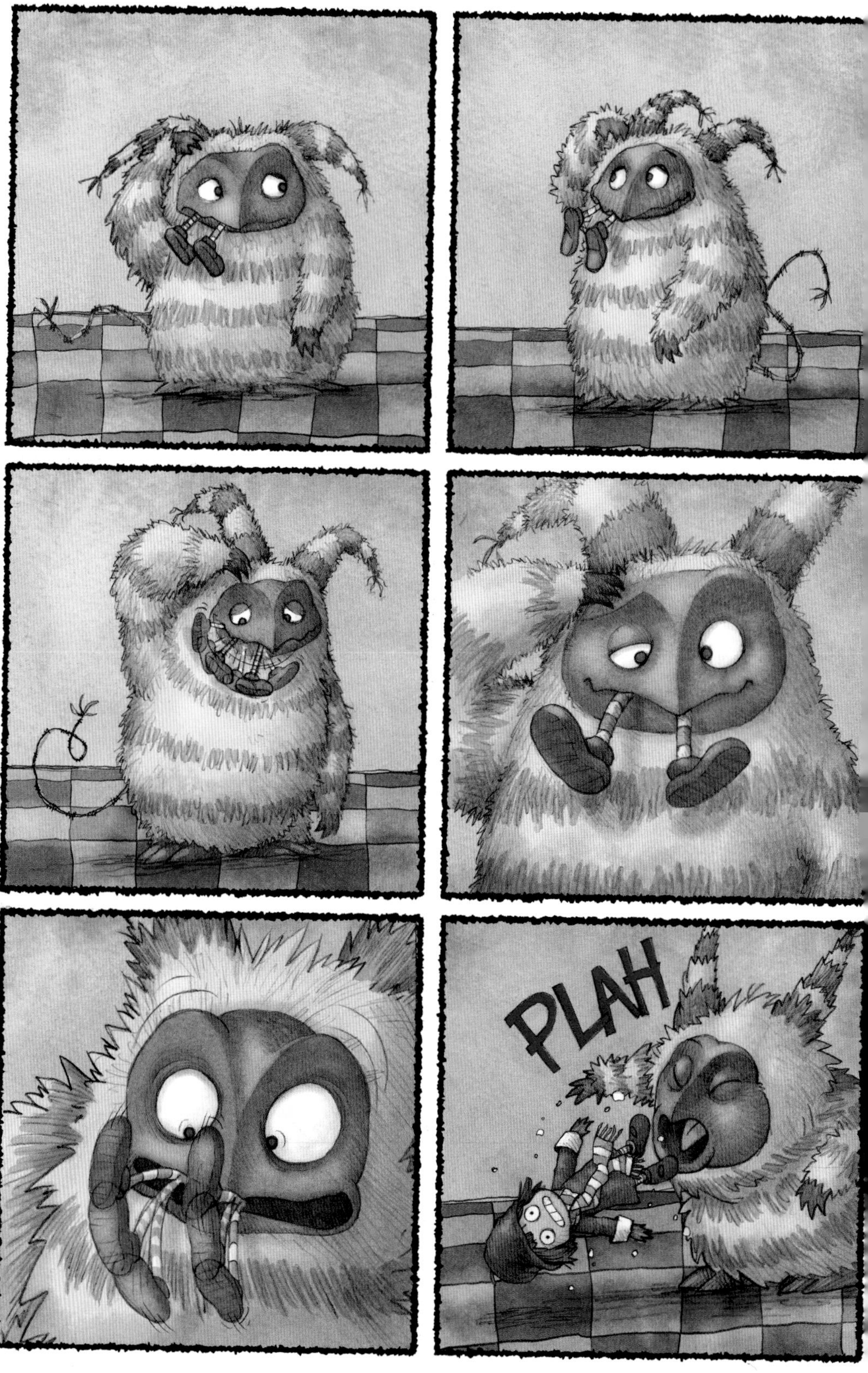
PLAH

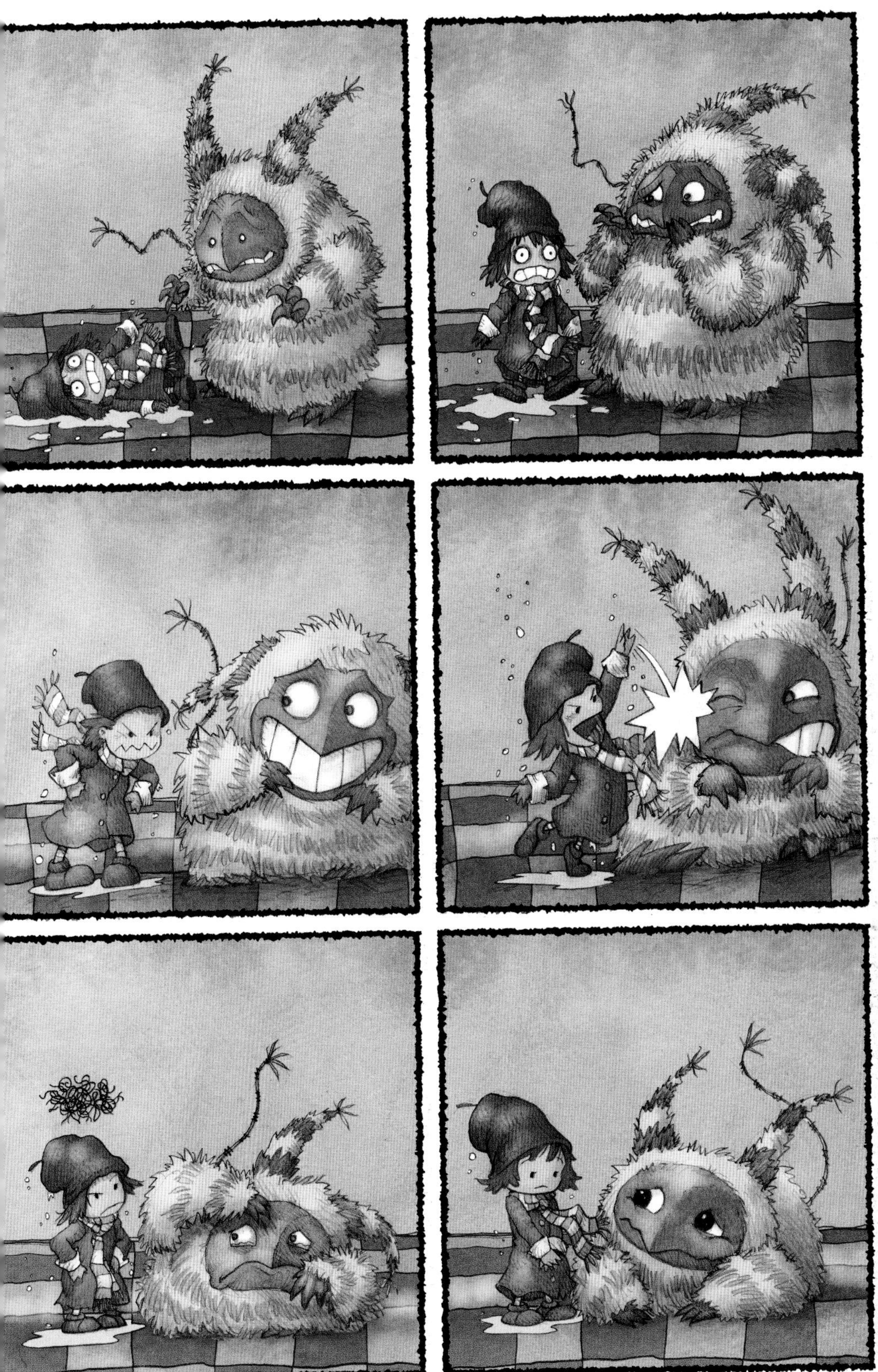

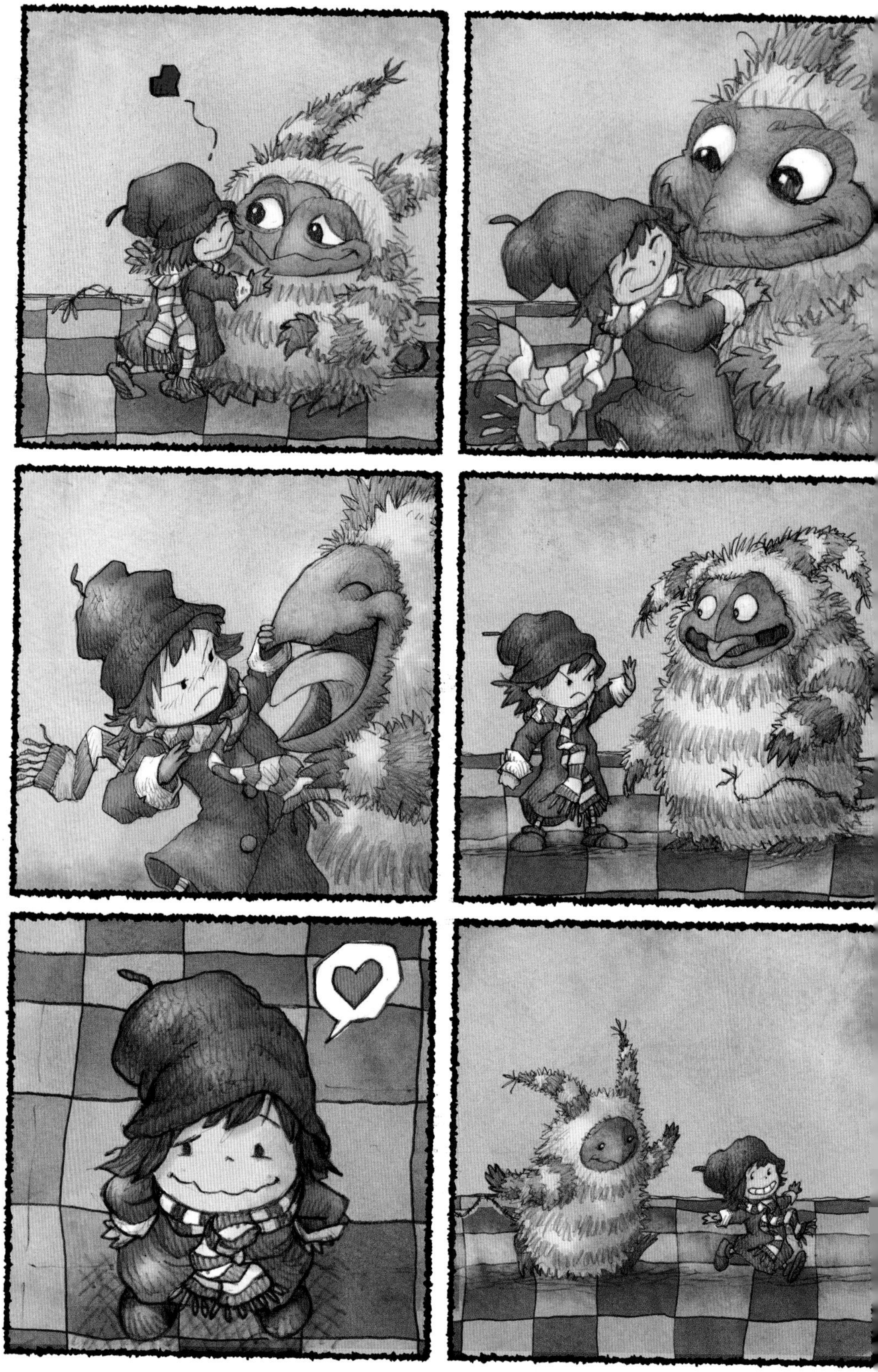

THE
END

FLIGHT EXPLORER: VOLUME ONE
CONTRIBUTORS

Matthew S. Armstrong draws and paints for video games, comics, and picture books. He writes stories, too. Some of his published works include *The Return to Narnia: The Rescue of Prince Caspian, Stuff,* and the full-color artwork for Robert Sabuda's *The Chronicles of Narnia Pop-up Book.* He is currently working on a new picture book for HarperCollins that has a lot of rhinos in it. Matthew lives with his wife and daughter in Sugar House, Utah, in a very old house by a lot of humongous old trees. His daughter reminded him not to forget to mention their little dog, too. [www.matthewart.com]

Bannister was born in 1973 in France. He currently lives near the Alps with his lovely girlfriend and no pets. His latest story, *Les Enfants d'Ailleurs,* was published in January 2007 by Dupuis Publishing. He has collaborated on many projects, both in Europe and overseas. [www.bannister.fr]

Phil Craven is from Georgia. He now lives in California. He draws storyboards at DreamWorks Animation. He eats cereal and draws some more comics. [www.bluepillow.net]

Steve Hamaker is the colorist for *Bone* and *Shazam! Monster Society of Evil* by Jeff Smith. He thanks God for his family, friends, job, and a pretty sweet life! [www.steve-hamaker.com]

Ben Hatke is a freelance artist involved in a little bit of everything. He is currently serializing a Zita the Spacegirl graphic novel online at the Secret Friend Society. His paintings and other art can also be seen online. [www.househatke.com and www.secretfriendsociety.com]

Kazu Kibuishi is the editor and art director of *Flight*. He is also the creator of Copper, Daisy Kutter, and the upcoming graphic novel series *Amulet*. He lives and works in Alhambra, California, with his wife, fellow comic artist Amy Kim Ganter. [www.boltcity.com]

Johane Matte has been working as an illustrator in both animation and video games for years. She has self-published one minicomic, *Horus*, but gets too easily distracted by other projects to continue it. But she will! Just tell her to focus, to concentrate, to—ooh, look! Kittens! [www.qosmiq.com/rufftoon/]

Jake Parker works at BlueSky Studios making movies. This marks his third contribution to the *Flight* series. His free time is spent drawing comics, shooting his paintball gun, and making paper airplanes for his kids. He lives in Connecticut with his wife and three children. [www.agent44.com]

Rad Sechrist lives in California where he works in the animation industry. In his free time he enjoys making fun little comics that he posts online. [www.radsechrist.com]

Much to his surprise and amazement, **Kean Soo** recently became a full-time cartoonist and has since resigned himself to a lifelong relationship with instant ramen. His first of two Jellaby graphic novels will be released by Hyperion Books for Children in 2008. [www.keaner.net and www.secretfriendsociety.com]